SAMPLE
DIABOLI

BRANTLEY
SAINT

PART TWO

THE ELITE KINGS CLUB: BOOK SEVEN

SANCTE DIABOLI

PART TWO

AMO JONES

Sancte Diaboli: Part Two
Copyright © 2021 by Amo Jones
Cover: Jay Aheer
Editor: My Brothers Editor
Editor: Paige Smith
Content: Petra Gleason
Line Editing/proof: Becky Fairest Reviews
Formatting: Champagne Book Design

All Rights reserved. No part of this publication may be reproduced, distributed, or transmitted in any form or by any means, including photocopying, recording, or other electronic or mechanical methods, without prior written permission of the publisher, except in the case of brief quotations embodied in reviews and certain other non-commercial uses permitted by copyright law.

This book is a work of fiction. All names, characters, locations, and incidents are products of the author's imaginations. Any resemblance to actual person's, things, living or dead, locales, or events is entirely coincidental.

To the readers who trust the process of my stories.
I'm sorry that your trust is going to be tested.
Again.

THE ELITE KINGS CLUB: BOOK SEVEN

SANCTE DIABOLI

PART TWO

CHAPTER ONE

Saint

I don't think anyone can completely explain the feeling of betrayal. The gaping hole that throbs in your chest right where your trust used to be. It can never be replaced. When someone betrays you, they figuratively tear out the trust you gave them, so viciously that there's surface damage way after it's been eviscerated. Then you start the process of trying to replenish it. It's not until you're deep into wanting, needing to trust that person again that you finally realize that where that cavernous hole now lies, they've left behind other destruction. Fissures of harm. So now anything that is being put in there simply leaks out.

Maybe I *can* explain the feeling of betrayal.

Maybe that should scare me.

Maybe it should scare them.

But what it doesn't do is change the events that happened.

That led me to where I am today. Here. Right now. After being taken away by one of the only people I have ever trusted.

There's a knock on the door. *Knock knock knock.* I should say come in. Be polite. But as I study the Band-Aid that's pressed against my throat, the dark shadows around my eyes, and the tacky straw I once called hair, I realize something.

Everything that happened last night was real.

So. Very. Real.

I was betrayed.

Badly.

Exhaling the breath I didn't realize I was holding, I place my hands onto my lap while keeping my eyes fixed on myself in the ornate mirror in front of me. "Come in."

The discreet protest of marble against heel. Quiet footsteps I don't recognize. There's a slight shift in the atmosphere, as if my simmering rage has been blanketed by a sense of calm.

"Saint." Her voice is tender, which is a complete contrast to her energy.

Interesting.

I refuse to look at her. Whoever she is, I think I recognize her voice from right before I blacked out.

A glass filled with orange juice is placed down on top of the antique vanity. I fight not to grab it at lightning speed. My mouth turns fuzzy, as if I've been sucking on cotton balls. So thirsty.

"I'm Veronica." Beads of condensation slide down the cool glass.

I shuffle in my seat.

She continues, "Welcome to my home." There's a pause. "For goodness' sake, child. Take a drink before I do it for you. It's giving me a headache, really."

I reach for the glass and stifle my sigh when the cool thick pulp slides down my parched throat. God. It tastes like it came from the Garden of Eden. Not necessarily a good thing, historically speaking.

Running my tongue over my cracked lips, I finally bring my eyes up to the figure in the mirror. "Where am I?"

She has long—impressively long—raven hair that doesn't stop until it is laying on her lap. Though with hair that long, you wouldn't expect it to have such a silky shine to it. The light, which hangs above us, reflects it like a honey glaze. Her almond-shaped eyes are enticing, yet dangerous, but the cobalt color releases a warmth over her features. A single mole is below her left eye, and on her, it only adds to her beauty. She isn't beautiful, though.

She looks dangerous.

Her slender finger taps against her pale thigh, her nails the color of Brantley's room. Pointed, sharp, dark. On her middle finger, a silver ring pierces through her nail.

Tap. Tap. Tap.

The silence isn't uncomfortable. It's as though it bathes all of the noise that runs rogue inside my head.

She wears a short leather skirt that almost looks one size too small, yet somehow only makes her curves seem more seductive, and a black leather jacket with a small bralette underneath. It is opened, revealing a sliver of the body she keeps beneath. A gold choker is clasped around her dainty neck, with a chain leading down her sternum before connecting to another that hangs around her lower belly. Thigh-high leather boots—again black. She is almost like Morticia in the flesh.

"Get a good enough look, our little Hecate?"

"Hecate?" I boldly ask, turning in my chair to finally give her my undivided attention.

"Mmmhhmmm." One perfectly arched dark brow lifts. "I take it you're familiar with Greek mythology?"

"Yes." My palms sweat. I don't want to talk about this right now. "Though I don't understand why you would nickname me after the Guardian of the Crossroads."

She studies me closely, her smug smile never leaving her face. Black painted lips, onyx eyeliner smudged around her eyes, and cheeks pinched pink. "Maybe you need to study more?"

"Why am I here?" My shoulders stiffen. I'm suddenly aware of everything surrounding me. The room, which drips opulence, the soft classical music playing in the background, an ancient clock ticking, the pungent smell of bleach.

She crosses her legs, resting the palms of her hands on top of my bed. "Well, baby steps, child. Baby steps." Her eyes fall down my body. "Your shower is through the third door to your right." Her finger points across the room, but I'm so ensnared by this strange woman that I don't look. "The one beside it is your personal closet. Use it." She pauses, her top lip curling slightly. "Though I hear your fashion style is not as you are dressed now, I beg of you to use what is there."

"Where am I?" I ask again, though I feel my patience waning. "Where is Hector?" *That traitorous bastard.*

"Ah." She stands from my bed, and I almost shrivel in the spot from how tall and dominant she is. She exudes confidence and deviance. "So many questions." She busies herself with a potted plant that's sitting on the windowsill on the other side of the room. Her fingers touch the leaves of the ZZ. "You were brought here."

"Last night?" My confusion is displayed all over my face, no doubt.

"No," she whispers, and it's as though wind sweeps through the bedroom and rolls straight down my spine. "Three days. You've been healing from the bullet that grazed you."

My hand comes up to touch the Band-Aid. "Where is Lucan?"

She winces, finally releasing the leaf and turning to face me. "He is away, for now."

"Brantley?" Saying his name out loud feels like a dagger being dragged up my throat.

"Hmmm." Her head tilts to the side, causing her hair to lengthen. "Enough questions for now." She gestures to the closet once more while walking back the way she came in. "I will meet you downstairs in eighteen minutes, Hecate." And just like that, she was gone as quickly as she arrived. I take a few deep breaths to calm my nerves.

I woke up in here not ten minutes before that knock on my door.

So why do I feel like I invited her, not only into—what I'm guessing—is my bedroom, but my mind, too.

I take a hot shower. The water pelts down over my body relentlessly, but I can't seem to find the usual solace that I would from the warmth around me. I liked showers. I liked them a lot. They gave me comfort, release, companionship. I'd sing, talk, cry to myself during them, and once I'd get out, I'd feel a sense of relief. As though all of my troubles simply washed down the drain along with my soiled water.

I sit on the floor, squeezing my eyes closed as water runs over my head and my face.

Nothing.

I need something. A single tear? An ache in my chest? The will to sing?

Nothing.

I turn the faucet off and wrap the soft towel around my body before finding my way to the closet. No light switches. As soon as I enter, the light comes on. It softens after a few seconds, as though it senses it is too bright. It isn't the lighting that is too much, it is this closet. Rows of clothes hang, with shoes lining the walls and handbags, sunglasses, and hats upon caps.

I gulp.

Fashion. I like it. It has always been a familiar addiction that I feed on regularly. Why does this closet in particular feel so empty? It isn't any bigger than the one I have at home. Maybe it is the unfamiliarity. Yes. Yes, that's it. It is unfamiliar.

I clutch the hem of my towel while reaching for something simplistic. Boyfriend jeans with gashes on the knees and thighs and a crop top that hangs comfortably off me. Now with fresh eyes, I take in the bedroom. The sheets have already been changed—probably while I was in the shower—and the music has changed now. I recognize Beethoven and Jeno Jando's "Moonlight." I played it when I was a young teen. It's Brantley's favorite.

The four-post bed is on the left side of the room, diagonally to the door, and perfect for the aesthetic of the bedroom. There's a fireplace at the foot, large windows that hide behind lavish lace curtains, a simplistic office desk, the ZZ plant—convenient since it's literally the one plant you can't kill—and a small bar fridge.

Modest, yet candidly elaborate. Everything feels strategically placed for style. What is this place?

I know that once I leave this room and go downstairs, everything is going to start changing. In the back of my mind, I know that.

But I open the door anyway, with that infamous gaping hole in my chest throbbing. The hole that I'm not interested in refilling anytime soon. I guess I don't know much about who I am. I still don't know if I died, or if my body is stuck in a hospital and I'm playing in the third realm of life. I feel like a ping-pong ball, being whacked back and forth between the human realm and this—this place of uncertainty. Maybe that's it. Maybe I'm dead and I don't know it yet.

SANCTE DIABOLI: PART TWO

You're not going to like this journey. Not one bit. I'm going to bend you, twist you, and break you until you're begging for an exit.

But that's the way it has to be.

Fog swam around my legs so thick I couldn't see my feet. It had begun to rise higher and higher, starting at my ankles to now above my knees. There was an archway made from twisted ivy that clawed its way over metal. Dead flowers wilted over crusted leaves, though I was sure they once looked beautiful.

Just not here.

Not now.

And probably not ever again.

I took the steps toward the arch, even though everything inside of me was fighting it. I knew I shouldn't follow. As a young boy, I knew it. Well, I wasn't young anymore. I had responsibilities. A need to fight. To live. To bleed. But I knew the hollow darkness that looked back at me from the other side held no promises of me ever returning, but what was the point? What did I have to lose?

Them? No. I didn't have them. I had nothing to lose.

I took the step through oblivion and found out I did have one more thing to lose.

My mind.

So, we're going to start this from the beginning. The beginning is where stories need to start, even ones as dark as mine. See, because even evil has a choice...

Chapter Two

Saint

"Y̲ou're late."

I take the final step down the glossy marble staircase, my fingers resting on the gold swirls of the rail. "By a few minutes."

Veronica's eyes narrow slightly. "Don't make it a habit." She curls her finger and turns, gesturing to follow her. "I don't like tardiness, Hecate. It's a lazy form of disrespect. If you want to piss me off, at least be theatrical about it. Draw some blood. Commit a murder. Burn down a church. But tardiness?" She turns to look at me over her shoulder while opening two adjoining doors. "Is too basic for my taste." I was right. She's Morticia.

I jump at the crashing of the doors being swung open, and before I can answer her about her rant, I pause.

Three girls sit around what is clearly a lounging area. From the cracking of an open fire to the large oversized sofa, it's about as cozy as a Hallmark movie. It's cozy, but there's still an uncomfortable ambiance that hovers around it.

Probably from Veronica.

"Welcome to The Daughters of Noctum, Saint." Veronica voices, lowering herself onto a single black chair with oversized wings that curve around her shoulders. "Your coven."

"She looks more like she belongs to Lux, not to Noctum," a girl snaps, and I find myself studying her. Brunette hair, a heart-shaped face, and bright blue eyes that almost look unreal. She is very pretty.

"Frankie, shut up. That's what you said about Ivy, and how very wrong you were about that." A girl with dark skin and green eyes stands, making her way toward me. I'm momentarily paralyzed by her beauty, and not just the obvious beauty, but there is something about her energy that feels euphorically charged and real. Every footstep closer to me is like a rhapsody of light. She wears a gold sequin short dress that hugs her perfectly curved body, but that's not the first thing that catches my eye.

It's her necklace.

Just like mine, only where ice falls down my crown, fire is around hers. My shoulders relax.

She stops a few steps in front of me. "Ahh, you've just noticed my family heirloom." Her arms wrap around my shoulders as she pulls me into her chest. "Welcome, Saint. Welcome home, girl."

She finally releases me and I fall back slightly, my eyes flying around the room to all of the other girls. They're dressed in gowns as if they'd been out to a ball.

One stands from her chair, brushing her hands down her body while making her way to me. "I'm Alessi," she says.

Alessi has copper-gold hair that's twisted into curls and falls to her small waist, bright green eyes, and flawless skin that has a natural tan to it. She points to another girl who is sitting in front of the fireplace with her ankles crossed together.

"That's Ivy, she doesn't speak and is almost always reading. And the girl who just pushed her way into your bubble is Ophelia." Alessi turns around and waves her hand toward Veronica. "And you already met the Wicked Witch of the West—*literally*."

I clear my throat, lowering myself onto the large L-shaped sofa. "What am I doing here?"

Veronica pulls a cigarette out of a gold packet, bringing it to her lips and lighting the tip. While she busies herself with her cancer stick, I take in the designs in the room.

"Am I in Rome?" I ask, distracted by the gold, white, and rose gold colors that are artfully painted on the ceiling. The floor is a bright white marble, so shiny that it could almost be a mirror. Everything bleeds opulence. From the furniture to the Neoclassical architecture.

"Yes," Veronica says, flicking the ash off into a silver tray. "But no."

Cryptic. This is going to be a long conversation. "Okay. I don't know why I'm here, but if I could talk to Hector, I'm sure I could make sense of—" I look around at the girls. "Something."

Veronica shakes her head, sucking more smoke while keeping her eyes on mine. "Hector will not return. Not at least until I say so."

"So why am I here then?" I demand, my hand coming to my neck when a shock of pain rips through my vein. "Please, just tell me what is going on."

Silence.

Ophelia sighs, falling onto the chair beside me. "Well, I'll tell her, since none of you want to be honest."

"Ophelia!" Veronica snaps. Though her voice is forceful, her smile and eyes remain on me. "Quiet."

Ophelia's mouth slams shut, the muscles in her jaw tensing. She brings her hand to mine, resting on top protectively. "She deserves to know. How can we have a sisterhood but keep one out of the truth?"

Veronica's eyes flash to her finally, narrowed and ready for war, before her cheeks relax and her shoulders shift. "Fine." She goes through another couple of puffs before finally starting. "You are still in Riverside—on the west side, commonly known as Riveredge. This home was built in the early seventeen hundreds and has housed generations of generations of witches since. Hector, your father, brought you to me for two reasons. One, he knows you are safe here, and two, this is your *home*."

"I have a home already, and it's darker than this."

Veronica studies me, her eyes falling down my body. "Hmm, so as it may seem you do, though I can reassure you—"

"—you're awfully chatty tonight." The voice that drifts in from behind me freezes me to my core. Hearing him, feeling his energy around me, the energy that once comforted me, forces me to my feet. I spin around to face him. I think in the back of my mind, I wanted him not to be here. I wanted to think that I didn't see him in that limo the night I was shot, but I was wrong. Because there he stands. All six-foot-*I can't remember* of him. Dressed in black, with his hair in the way I've come to love, and his jaw as sharp as I remember. He doesn't look at me, though. Not when I stand. Not when I make my way to him. And definitely not when my hand is flying into his face.

Slap!

My palm stings, but I don't care, because betrayal? Betrayal hurts more. He doesn't so much as move as his eyes remain on Veronica. *Anger.* Anger bubbles beneath my skin and I ball my fingers into a fist. "You—"

"—Saint, let's show you around the house and leave them to talk, yeah?" Ophelia says, hooking her arm in mine. It isn't until we're walking down the giant corridor filled with more artistic paintings and giant colossal pillars that I realize my cheeks are wet from my tears.

"It's okay, Saint." Alessi is walking on the other side of me, heels clicking against the marble. "It's going to be okay." I turn to look over my shoulder and see a blank-faced Frankie and a disinterested Ivy, but even if they think whatever of me—they are still here.

We make our way through the large foyer, breaking through the colosseum-styled pillars that line both sides of the hallway—if you can even call it that—before we reach the master stairs. White marble, more art on the ceiling, and flowing vines and plants overflowing the railing. There's one grand staircase before it splits off into two others, which lead to opposite sides of the house.

"We can show you outside tomorrow, but let's start with our wing." Ophelia gestures up the stairs, and I block out her voice when my mind drifts back downstairs to where Brantley is with Veronica.

"—so we all stay on this side, with the other for V and her—whatever you want to call her obsessions. We prefer it better this way because we like to stay close to each other."

Alessi steps up to two wide doors and slides them open, stepping into another vast space. "The spa room." Lights flicker on, exposing an octagon-style hot tub that could fit at least twenty of us, a long bar on the other side, more plants growing over furnishings, and a large projector screen that hangs behind the tub.

"It's—everything is very beautiful," I say truthfully.

Frankie scoffs, and I turn to face her just in time to catch the end of an eye roll. "I'm sorry, but are we all going to ignore the fact that we literally have a Vitiosis in this house?"

"Ignore her," Alessi chimes in, kicking off her heels and

removing the pin in her hair that's keeping her chiffon bun so tightly in place. She scrunches up the bottom of her gown, dipping her toes into the tub. "She's the only one who acts like a rich, spoiled brat out of us, but who actually isn't a rich, spoiled brat." Alessi begins removing her gown, as does Ophelia. Ivy shuffles to the bench seat, which is built into the large windowpane opposite the spa, pushing her reading glasses up the bridge of her nose.

I kick off my shoes. "He's not as scary as you think…" I say, removing my clothes to dip into the tub, leaving on my bra and undies.

"Wrong," Frankie says. "He is, just not to you."

I ignore her, sinking into the scalding hot water that feels like silk wrapping its way around my body.

"Look, and I'm just saying, okay, we all know Brantley has a taste for older women."

I freeze, despite the fact I'm neck-deep in hot bubbling water. I push my hair above my head and tie it up into a loose bun.

"So what's the bet he and Veronica are fuck buddies? It's not the first time he's been here."

"Shut up, Frankie! For fuck's sake, do you ever know when to fucking stop?" Alessi takes a cigarette out of a packet and lights the end, exhaling while submerging farther into the water before resting her head against the edge.

Warm condensation floats around all of us. I can't stop thinking about what she just said, and I know it's true. I recognize the paintings on the ceiling from Brantley's Instagram. The angel reaching for heaven.

I sigh. "I'm not here to cause trouble, Frankie. I was forced here by Brantley and my father."

"What are you to Brantley, Saint, if you don't mind me asking?" Ophelia. Sweet, beautiful Ophelia. Her chocolate skin glistens from the water, her bright green eyes pinned on me. Her hair is curly and rogue as she piles it on top of her head with loose tendrils falling down to her sharp shoulders. I love Ophelia, I decide. Which is a big statement since I barely like any of the others right now, but there's something about her that is trustworthy. As if she comforts the side of me that has always been alone.

"Well, he raised me since I was two years old. My father dropped me off at his house to his father, but Brantley took it upon himself to, I guess, take ownership of me. I never had a life outside of the manor. He hired tutors, cooks, cleaners. He gave me pets—" I try to smile through the sadness that intoxicates my soul while thinking about Medusa and Kore. "He gave me the only life I know. Then, not long ago, I was introduced into The Elite Kings, and well, it's sort of been chaos since then."

Silence. "Ah, yes, the infamous Kings," Ophelia mutters. "How could we ever forget them?" Said more in amusement than animosity. "So what about you two, have you ever?"

"She's not his age preference." Frankie snickers, pretending to look at her nails.

"Yes." I fight her, and I get great satisfaction when her lashes flick and her eyes come up to me, wide. "But not anymore. It was a mistake."

"He was a mistake?" Ophelia asks softly.

I shake my head, fighting the godforsaken tears that keep coming out. "No." I bring my eyes to hers. "I was."

It's late. My muscles protest as I slide into a pair of silk pajama booty shorts and a cotton crop. After relaxing in the spa with the rest of the girls, and ducking and hiding from Frankie's constant verbal jabs, I told them goodnight and made my way back to my bedroom. I couldn't think straight. Words and theories were running rampant inside my head.

Pulling my bedcovers down, I'm about to shut off my bedside lamp when my door opens.

I turn the light off anyway, drowning us in darkness because I don't want to look at him right now. I can't. Not now. Not if I don't want to cry again, and not if I don't want to picture him and Veronica all over each other. If his hair is messy, I'll only picture her long fingers running through it.

"I know you're angry with me."

I lie down on the bed, squeezing my eyes closed while knowing he can't see me.

The door clicks closed. "How's your neck?"

I grit my teeth. Silent. *Don't say anything.*

The mattress sinks beneath his weight. "Saint, this is the only way I can keep you safe for now."

"Safe?" I snap. Dammit. I sit up quickly, shoving the covers off my body. I don't know where he is or what he's looking at right now. "How is me getting shot at keeping me safe?"

"That wasn't supposed to happen…" Brantley growls, his tone so feral I almost don't recognize it. "That for sure was not supposed to fucking happen. You were supposed to come here until—"

"—until what? Until you wanted to continue with your secret texts to me?"

Pause. He shifts. "What texts?"

I tear the final blanket off my body, my feet about to hit the ground when his hands are on my arms, shoving me back down onto the mattress as if he knew where I was all this time.

He shakes me. "What. Fucking. Texts?" I feel his breath on my lips now, warm and familiar.

I gulp. *Stop it.*

"In the car after the accident, you told me I didn't text you back."

"I wasn't in the car." Brantley squeezes my arm, shoving me

back onto the mattress and disappearing. Light ignites his face as he tosses me my phone. "Show me the texts you're talking about."

I squeeze my phone in the palm of my hand. "You're a real asshole, Brantley."

He doesn't answer. He seems different. Distant.

I unlock my phone, the photo of Bishop and me staring back at me on my wallpaper. "Bishop. Where is he?"

"He can't come here. We've put your phone into the universe so no one can track it. You can use it from now on."

"Brantley, what's going on?"

He looks at me for the first time tonight and my heart drops into my stomach like a heavy boulder being thrown from a cliff. His jaw tight, eyes dark, and features pulled. He shakes his head. "Not right now. Show me the texts."

I open up my messages, scrolling past Tillie, Madison—I pause, looking up at him.

"Oh that? Yeah, *that* is home where she belongs now."

My lips stretch wide. "He read the letter?"

His mouth stays in a straight line. "Yeah. Then he flew straight to New Zealand and dragged her ass home. Like he should have done fucking months ago."

"Are they okay?"

"Madship?" He turns back to me. "No, but she's home and not going anywhere. Show me the texts." I continue scrolling until I reach the end of my messages. My brows pull in.

"I saved it under a question mark. Did you go through my phone?"

"I didn't go through it, because you fucking changed the passcode. Our hacker broke into it, but I didn't read your messages." He stares at me. "Should I have read them?"

I ignore him as I continue to scroll up and down in search of the messages from **?**. Even when I open my contacts, there's no number saved as the question mark.

"I don't know what's happened. Everything else is here except the messages." I toss my phone onto my bed and lean back against the headboard, pulling my knees against my chest. "You betrayed me," I whisper so softly I almost thought I didn't say it out loud.

"I did what I had to do, Dea. You can hate me all you want, but I will always do what I need to do to keep you safe."

Silence. I don't have a response right now, and I'm afraid that if I talk, I'll say something I might regret. My phone's light flicks off and we're back in darkness, where we both belong. Knowing he's beside me shouldn't comfort me the way it does because I'm still angry, but when my eyes begin to drift closed and I start shuffling down the bed, I already know. My soul forgave him already; it's my mind that won't budge.

I pull the covers up to my chin, slipping farther into the silk sheets. "I—"

"—don't talk." His voice is strained. "Just—don't. I'll be back tomorrow." He shifts off the bed and it's not until he opens the door and light sneaks in that he turns around to say, "I trust Veronica, Saint. You need to, too." Then he's gone. I don't know why, but his parting words bother me. They bother me enough to tear off my covers and run for my bedroom door. But when I pull it open, my eyes wild and my anger at peak point, he's gone.

My feet hit the conveyer belt to the beat of "Without You" by The Kid LAROI. After tossing and turning last night, I successfully managed to get two hours of sleep. I went to bed angry. I woke up angry. It's unlike me, and it's messing with my balance. I pump the speed up to twelve, turning the music up louder with the remote. My arms swing, my legs ache, and the timer on the treadmill says 145:26. The longest run I've ever done.

I'm still angry.

Squeezing my fists, I change the song. "The Bleeding"

Perfect. Angry music to match my angry mood. The treadmill stops and I tear out my AirPods, spinning around to see who turned it off.

"Girl, don't hit me!" Ophelia raises her hands. Her hair is piled up on top of her head, her toned body filling a sports bra and yoga pants. She steps onto the treadmill beside mine. "You've been running for almost three solid hours. I'm doing you a favor."

I'm still catching my breath with both hands grasped on my knees as sweat falls from my forehead and onto the black belt.

"How'd you find the gym?" she adds.

Finally catching my breath, I grab my towel and swipe the sweat off my face. "It took me a while before walking outside." The gym is right behind the pool. Built in a glass globe, giving you the feel of being in the middle of trees, while looking up at the sky.

"She built it for night gym sessions. You can see the stars some nights."

I jump off, heading for my water bottle.

"Look, I don't mean to pry, but we can all feel your energy and it's setting Frankie off more than usual."

"Setting her off?" I ask, leaning against a punching bag while tossing my towel around my neck. "How?"

Ophelia starts up her treadmill and begins a steady walk. "Well, for one, we are all sisters. Empaths on crack. The granddaughters of infamous witches that they forgot to burn, or in our case, hang. Or something like that. I read it in a quote and it's so accurate."

I stifle a laugh. My face almost cracks from the half-smile; it has been so long since I've felt like smiling. "I am in a bad mood. I agree," I say, moving back to where the treadmills are lined, taking a seat on a wooden bench that's built into the glass.

"Talk to Ophelia. Ophelia is a vault."

I sigh, resting my head against the glass as the sweat continues to drip down my sternum. I remove my tank and toss it on top of my towel. "It's Brantley. I'm not dealing well with the betrayal."

"Ah," Ophelia murmurs. She lifts her eyes to me. "Why did he do it?"

"Does that always have to matter?"

She turns the speed down on her treadmill before flicking it off. "I'm done for my exercise for this week."

I chuckle again as she sits beside me. "Look, betrayal is hard, especially if you trusted someone as fiercely as I'm guessing you did him. But sometimes, especially in the world we live in and the world I'm guessing he lives in, things aren't as simple as black and white. You have to allow some color."

"He said he did it to protect me."

"Then maybe take that for now. After you find out the whole story, then you can decide whether you're going to be angry or not. Control your emotions now, you'll have control forever."

"And I'm cranky because I miss my brother and my pets."

"Well," Ophelia nudges me with her arm, "we can keep you distracted."

I pick up my towel and throw it over my shoulder as we make our way out of the gym. Distraction could work; only, I'm still running on fumes of anger.

Round and round the mulberry bush…

I smirked from the dark corner, hidden from her in plain sight. "Ah, this time it's different, isn't it?" I stood to my full height, making my way toward her slowly. It wasn't until I was beneath the hanging single light bulb that she looked up at me, her eyes scrunched tightly.

I tapped the bulb. "Count to ten and you'll wake."

She didn't look up at me. She refused. Curled in the corner with her knees pulled to her chest.

"Are you going to start counting?" Her hair was so white, it was unreal. She had always been spectacular. Like a rogue angel begging to be violated. Slowly, she tipped her head up to look at me, her lips quivered and her eyes quickly diverted back down to the ground. "Why are you doing this to me?"

"Well," I said, moving toward her. I bent down, grazing the backs of my knuckles against her soft cheeks. "Because he simply can't kill me here."

CHAPTER THREE

Brantley

My mind feels like a blank canvas. If there was a picture to be painted on it, it'd be filled with smoke shadows and long, ugly trees that don't produce leaves. That's it. That's fucking it. My fists clench, my eyes remaining zoned in on the clock that hangs behind Bishop in his office.

Tick tock, tick tock.

"Brantley?" Bishop snaps me out of the slumber my mind is more comfortable in these days. "How was Saint last night?" Nate is beside me, Eli next to him. Since the ceremony last week, all of the other Kings have taken their respective positions, which leaves just Bishop, Nate, Eli, and me to hold shit down.

"Mad."

"That's cute." Eli chuckles. "I'd love to see her mad…"

Turning my head slowly, I glare at Eli from the other side

of Nate. "I would really be careful with that mouth. You'll need it when you go on tour."

He smirks his famous Cheshire cat grin. "Stop being jealous."

Ignoring him, I look back at Bishop. "She's *mad* mad."

"How mad?" Eli teases again, a toothpick rolling between his lips.

"She punched me in the face."

Bishop coughs back a laugh while Eli straight-up barks out his. I flip him off. "Besides that, I could snap the tension in the room that she was radiating."

"She's feeling betrayed…" Bishop murmurs, leaning back in his chair. "If she's anything like me—"

"—she's everything like you. Precisely the problem." I kick out my leg just as there's a knock on the door.

Bishop calls out, "Come in."

"Listen, I get that this is serious and I feel like a snitch for even coming in here, but Nate—" Madison growls, and I turn in my chair slightly to take in what she could possibly want. "Tillie is not doing well with not knowing what is happening with Saint."

Having little Venari back in the ballgame has been a little tense, to say the least. I mean, at least she and Bishop have both decided to pull their heads in until the twins are born, but to say she's just walked back in and it's been a happy family again would be a lie.

"Lie to her," Bishop says, brushing her off. "You're good at that."

Here we go.

Madison's back straightens, defiance flashing over her eyes. "Fuck you. How about you lie to her? Oh, I know! How about you—"

"—Kitty." Nate stands from his chair and moves toward

where she's standing, a hand on her stomach. Still can't believe there are two babies in there. She's small as fuck. "You need to go upstairs and rest."

Madison relaxes in Nate's embrace. "Please, Nate. She's not dealing well and neither am I. Saint—"

"Is fucking safe, Mads!" I glare at her, leaning forward to rest my elbows on my knees. I run my fingers through my hair, exhaling pent-up anger. "Fuck, you know, it amazes me how you all question my intentions and actions when it comes to her." I stand from my chair and walk to the only window in the room. I turn to face them, my hands in my pockets and my head resting on the wall to the side. "Actually, it's slightly insulting. So here's what's going to happen when it comes to Saint *Vitiosis*." I point to Bishop and Madison. "Both of you are going to do what you need to do, and I'm going to do what I need to do. For right now, though, she is safe."

"With Veronica, Brantley! Seriously!" It's good to have Madison home. She's back with full force.

"Yeah, Mads, with Veronica and her *coven*. A world that, as far as we know, our enemies don't know about."

Madison shakes her head but looks away from me, not wanting to say any more. Which I appreciate. She looks at Bishop. "We need to talk. Now."

Bishop's lips curl slightly. "Why the fuck for?"

"Now! Bishop."

He stands from his chair, storms to the other side of the room, and slams his office door behind him, leaving Nate, Eli, and me.

"There's too much tension. Why don't they fuck and get it over with?"

"Because," I say, kicking off the wall, "just like his little sister, Bishop doesn't take betrayal well."

"Betrayal?" Nate growls. "Are you fucking kidding me, B?

You can't seriously be taking his side on this. He is going to be a father. He needs to step the fuck up and let that shit go."

"Yeah?" I raise my brows, dropping back onto my chair while keeping my eyes locked solely on Nate. "And whose fault is it that he didn't know until last week?"

"I will stand by her, Bran. Even if he doesn't this time." Nate squeezes his eyes closed. "I should have from the start."

"No one is going to hold it against you for not doing what you should have done in the first place."

His gaze burns into mine, his jaw flexing. "Fuck you." He turns and leaves the same way Madison and Bishop did, the second door slamming in a matter of minutes.

"No cap, I've always admired you, Bran," Eli says, and if it wasn't for the seriousness in his tone, I would have ignored him. He continues, "You're the only one who keeps us all real."

"Eli?" I murmur, pulling my phone out of my pocket to open a new text. "Don't ever say 'no cap' again." He laughs, but I fade him out, opening a new text message. "What are we going to do about The Gentlemen?"

Me: What's she doing?

"We kill them all," I say, tapping my phone against my thigh as a text comes through when Bishop walks back into the room.

"See, but we assume it was The Gentlemen who did the shoot-out."

"Where the fuck is Nate?" Bishop asks, looking around the room.

I open the text.

V: She's fine. You know I will take care of her.

I do know she will. I trust very few people in this world, but

Veronica is one of them. Shutting out of the message, I shake my head at Bishop. "He's pissed. Caught up in the drama between you and Madison."

Bishop leans forward, grabbing his Glock off his desk and shoving it into the waistband of his jeans.

"We've got to handle this shit so Saint can come back."

"Why can't she?" Eli murmurs, standing before we both follow Bishop out the door.

"Because she already got fucking shot at once. I'm not letting it happen again." We reach the front door, all three of our cars parked out front of Bishop's temporary house while his home is being built.

I pull my keys out of my pocket. "Where are we going?"

Bishop smirks at me from over his shoulder, walking straight for his Maserati. "Think this trip will make you happy."

"If it doesn't involve scraping Gentlemen brain matter off of that pretty fucking grin you're wearing, I don't want in."

Bishop smirks even more. "Oh, then I've got you."

"Bishop," Madison calls out, shocking all of us.

Bishop turns to face her, his eyes traveling up and down her body slightly. They may be fighting a lot, but we've all seen the old Bishop has come back strong. No more recklessness or sadness in his eyes. Now it's wrath and anger. Bishop works best like this. The beef between him and Mads is good for us. It's what we need right now, and it's keeping him distracted enough to not go against our best interest and drag Saint out of The Coven.

I know why he hasn't. It's the same reason I haven't.

Because she's safe.

And he knows exactly why she's safe.

"I may not like you right now, but that doesn't mean I don't need you."

His mouth slams closed before finally opening. "I know, baby. Go inside."

She smiles softly before disappearing through the way she came.

"You know what? You're both so toxic they could name a fucking poison after your love."

I chuckle, sliding into the driver's seat and starting up the Bugatti.

Time. To. Fucking. Ride.

Chapter Four

Saint

Goose bumps rise on my skin as I turn the corner into the kitchen. I pause, step backward, but keep my eyes locked on the large open windows that overlook the courtyard and pool. I can't sleep. Yet again, another witching hour.

Pulling out my phone after finding a glass and pouring some cold milk, I open a new message on Bishop's name.

Me: I miss you.

Placing my phone back onto the counter, not expecting him to reply instantly, I get busy with finally looking around the house that seems to never sleep. Movement catches my eye through the window again and I freeze, my stomach recoiling anytime I find myself looking outside. The sickening sensation clings to me the same way it did at the ceremony. I'm squinting my eyes and walking closer to the window when my phone vibrating scares me back to the counter. I reach for it quickly, not bothering to see who it is, considering I know it'll be Bishop.

"Hey," I whisper breathlessly into the phone.

"God, it's good to hear your voice." At his own, my fears release, and whatever was outside doesn't matter. It can't touch me. That's how Bishop makes me feel. Safe and protected, much like Brantley, only... different.

"I didn't think you'd still be awake." I slowly drop onto one of the gold-plated barstools tucked beneath the kitchen island.

"Can't sleep much lately." He sounds tired, sleepy.

"Are you okay?" My finger circles the rim of my glass.

Long pause. He exhales. "No."

"Want to switch stories?"

He chuckles deeply, and it sets off warmth swimming in my blood. "Sure, Angel. Go ahead."

"I'm angry with Brantley."

There's shuffling in the background. "I've heard."

"And I don't know why I'm so upset with him. It's not—it's not because of the bullet grazing—" Bishop growls softly. I continue, "It's the *why*." I pause, my back straightening. "Why didn't you tell me that I was going to be taken?"

"I won't lie to you." Something about the sincerity of his tone makes me trust him further. I didn't think that was possible, since I trust him unconditionally already. "It wasn't planned until the last minute, when Eli spotted two of The Gentlemen floating around the ceremony. We couldn't make a scene because we didn't know how many more there were. Everyone we loved—with the exception of one other—was in that building. We had to continue. Play it by ear. It wasn't until Brantley told us that he knew where to take you that we came up with the plan. They're smarter now. They're different. We started a war that night by doing something, and right now, the safest place you can be is there."

"But why? Why can't I be with you all? I feel...secluded."

"Do you, though?" Bishop asks gently, sleep drowning his tone. "Do you really hate it there?"

I look around the kitchen. Everything is pristine and shiny, but the overgrowing plants that spill over all of the railings remind me of home. I sigh. "No, but I want to be with you all. My family."

"I know, but here's the thing. You have me as your brother and the Devil as your lover. What do you think is going to happen when you're threatened?"

"Okay," I whisper. "Thank you for being honest with me about the ceremony. How much longer do I need to be here?"

"Not much. I promise you I'll have you back here as soon as we've put a couple dogs down."

"Your turn. I'm finished now."

There's a long pause, and just when I think he's not going to say anything, he finally breathes out. "I don't know if I'm going to do well at this dad shit."

My brows pull in as I swipe the residue of milk off my top lip. "Are you serious?"

"Saint, look who our father is, and you don't even know half of the evil shit he has done in his lifetime—and aside from that, I can't keep my little fucking sister safe, let alone not one, but two fucking babies. *Babies*, Saint. Plural. What if they're two girls? Oh fuck, I really hope they're not two girls."

I chuckle quietly, but before I can contain it, it turns into full fits of laughter.

"Stop laughing."

"I'm sorry. Stop scowling." My giggles die out as I push my empty glass away. "Bishop, you are the most protective, loving, and dangerous man I know—aside from you know who. Every time I hear your voice, I feel safe. Untouchable. Like nothing and no one can come near me. You're going to be a great father, and if not, I'll still be here. I'll be here for you through everything and anything. Providing you and Brantley give me that freedom." My eyes roll.

His chuckle is deep. I can hear he's drifting off to sleep. "I haven't slept a full night since Madison has been back."

I begin making my way upstairs to my bedroom, closing the door quietly behind me and climbing into bed.

"Are you worried about the babies?"

"No." He yawns, and I turn off my bedside light. "I'm worried that I'm going to let her back in and she's going to walk back out when it gets tough again."

My eyes close, but my mouth keeps moving. "She won't, Bishop."

"How can you be so sure?"

"Because she made me a promise."

∽

I shoot up from my bed, my cheek throbbing from where my phone sat against it all night. Bishop must have hung up at some point. I open a message from him.

Bishop: Damn. You snore.

Saint: If I do, I got it from you.

Plugging my phone into the charger, I move around the room to get ready for the day. I'm pulling on my jeans when there's a knock on my door.

"Come in!"

"I figured since I have you here for however long I do, why not make the most of it?" Veronica leans against the doorframe, her arms crossed. She's wearing a black silk robe that falls right down to her bare feet. Her hair is half-up and half-down, her face free from any visible makeup. Her skin is pale, but it's flawless.

"Can I ask you a question?" I finish the fishtail braid in my hair and pick up my Vans.

She raises one perfectly arched brow. "I'm almost certain you're going to ask it anyway."

"True." I take a slow seat on the bed, squeezing the sheets in the palm of my hand. "How old are you?"

The corner of her mouth tips into a crooked grin. "That, my Hecate, is something I never disclose." She brings her hand out to me. "Come on. We can start the first part of our day."

I swoop up my phone and shove it into the back of my jeans, before following her down the long hallway and to the staircase. I still can't seem to figure her out. She has walls covering her emotions and exudes energy in a way I have never felt.

"So what are we doing?" I ask, following her through the main foyer and down the long corridor. Pillars line each side like the Colosseum, our footsteps echoing through the vast and empty space.

"Well, I thought I'd show you something that you might be interested in before tonight." She presses open twin doors and I freeze. The explosion of greenery rushes forward and I squeeze my hands tightly into fists. Fat, lush leaves, sprouting floral flowers, and large towering trees are placed all over the room, which I quickly figure out is a large greenhouse that seems to be attached to the main house.

"Wow." I step inside and inhale musky, sweet leaves and rich-soiled earth. Reaching toward a potted fiddle leaf tree with leaves as large as my body, I brush the palm of my hand over the damp soil. "This place is magical." The ceiling reaches as high as the main house, with every inch partially tinted windows. The air is humid and warm, without being sticky, and enough filtered light beaming in. There are sprinklers hanging from the ceiling where mist trickles out.

"It was built not long after the main house was. In the old days, my ancestors had to make do with what they had, so they created their own greenhouse-style garden deep in the forest."

"I'd love to see that one day," I say, rubbing the soil between my fingers.

Veronica stifles a smile. "You'll see it tonight for The Hunt."

I move around the area, admiring all of the plants. Elephant ears, some variegated, so beautiful that the marble of white contrasts all of the green. Monsteras of all strands and again, some variegated, and Devil's Ivy, Philodendron all growing roguishly throughout to give a natural setting. This greenhouse isn't clean. Veronica has allowed the plants to grow whatever way they want.

I love it.

"The Hunt?" I turn to face her, leaning against wooden paneling.

Her eyes flick up to mine. She grins. "The Hunt."

⁓

Tonight feels different. There is an eagerness to the air that begs to invade daylight. A sort of spell that wants to push anything light out of its path. Veronica had told me to wear white, and to be downstairs at the front door by eleven p.m. It's strange. The atmosphere feels thick. Almost as though the air doesn't allow us to breathe. I've applied makeup—heavy. Straightened my hair—flat. Now all I have to do is change. The dress Veronica chose flows off my curves and spills to the ground gracefully, but my breasts swell out the deep v-cut, more so than I would usually expose. I touch the edge of my necklace, the only piece of jewelry I wanted to wear tonight. I don't know why, but it makes me feel close to Brantley because we're so far apart right now. Emotionally and physically.

I miss him. I don't know if that makes me naïve because of what he did, but the fact is true. I miss him. But just because my heart wants him does not mean my mind is going to allow it to have him. I open my phone and send off a text to Tillie.

Me: I miss you.

She replies instantly, but I don't open it until I'm making my way downstairs, after slipping on the crystal anklets I'm wearing on both feet. Instead of shoes, she has me wearing jewels that lace and knot around my feet.

Tillie: I'm working to get you home.
Me: Don't. I'm ok.
Tillie: Not here.
Me: What do you mean?
Tillie: Look, if you needed to be put somewhere safe, it shouldn't have been there.
Me: Tillie, I'm ok. I actually like it here.
Tillie: Where is here? They're not telling me anything, and Madison and Bishop are still barely talking.

"There you are!" Ophelia calls out from down the hallway, her arms stretched wide. She's wearing a white gown similar to mine, only different. Her hair is free, hanging around her slender shoulders, and her makeup is kept to a bare minimum.

I push my phone away. "You guys are coming?"

Ivy, Frankie, and Alessi are following behind her in a trail of white.

"Of course! We can't wait for this time of year."

"This time of year?" I ask, just as Alessi opens the front door and gestures outside with a wave of her hand.

"The Hunt is when we get to meet with male witches!"

"I still don't know what that means." I step outside and pause when I see six white horses, waiting for us in a line.

They're already saddled, standing obediently, when Veronica steps to the side of me, winking over her shoulder. "Well, come on, Saint. We're going to show you what you've been missing all these years."

Veronica is wearing black. Shocker. Though the style is similar to mine, only where I have one slit carving up the side of my leg, she has two. Her black hair has been tousled in messy waves, falling down past her butt. She always looks elegant and beautiful, even when she's not trying, and it almost always seems as though she's not trying. I still can't pin her age. She gracefully swings herself onto the saddle and turns over her shoulder to look back at me. "You're not married, are you?"

My eyes widen. "What?"

Ophelia hooks her arm in mine and directs me toward the steed behind Veronica. She chuckles. "Never mind."

Ophelia points to the stirrup. "Put one foot in there and swing your other leg around."

I do as I'm told, grasping onto the leather rein as the horse shuffles under my weight. I pat its long mane.

"Good boy. Be nice to me. I've never done this before."

Once everyone is on their horse, Veronica leads us down the long driveway. Oversized candles are alight at the edges. As we trot past, shadows of trees form at the side of my eye and I have to double take to make sure they're just that—shadows. The wind is rustling, but only softly. When we're halfway down the drive, Veronica calls out to me.

"Saint, come ride with me at the front."

I kick my horse a little until it trots forward and finds its stride, just slightly back from Veronica, but close enough that we can have a conversation. "Did you know we are often drawn to animals because their energy and minds are quiet? Much like plants." She guides us off the driveway and onto an off-road path, noting the candles are now directing us through a rough yet flat clearing of the forest.

"I didn't know that, but I've always loved animals."

"Do you have any?" she asks.

I nod, even though I know she can't see me. "I do. I have two Dobermans and a pet snake, Medusa." Even thinking of them makes my heart clench. I miss the companionship that only animals can give me.

"Hmmm."

Was that a smile?

"Why am I not surprised?" She mutters the end of her sentence, but I catch it anyway.

"Veronica, what's The Hunt about?"

She sighs, looking up to the sky. It's then I realize we're on a full moon, and not just any full moon, but a blood moon.

"Every blood moon, witches join for festivities called The Hunt. It's meant for reproduction. Nothing more, and nothing less." She pauses, and even though there's already an eerie silence to the night, her silence somehow fills it. "I'm hoping things start changing for our Coven, Saint." We continue through the forest, following the candles through the trees until we come to a clearing where ivy and flowers twist and knot around an archway. We stop. The soft orange light illuminates and warms my skin.

"Once you enter this game, there's no opting out." Veronica's hand is gripped around the ivy that blankets off whatever is on the other side. "Are you ready?"

I think over her words. Witches and… would that make them warlocks? The Hunt. Deep in the back of my mind, I know that Brantley would despise me being a part of anything to do with any one of the male species, let alone male witches. But his betrayal still stings, so I can't seem to bring myself to care. He put me here. He obviously trusts Veronica, for reasons I still don't know, so he will have no one else to blame but himself.

I bring my eyes to Veronica. Wolf gray against dark brown. "I'm in."

Tick.
Tock.
I craned my head, taking a seat beside her in the corner. "Are you ever going to stand?"

"Why do you keep doing this to me?"

"Now, now..." *I silenced her with a finger pressed against her soft lips. I licked my own. She was so delicious. I'd always seen the obsession.* "Don't kill my dream too soon. It has only been two visits."

"Two?" *She narrowed her eyes at me, and I had to admit, she had balls. No doubt they came from her caretaker.* "You've been doing this for months, only in different ways."

"Ah." *A smirk curved my lips.* "I guess I have. Tell me something..." *I turned to her fully.* "Are he and I the same?"

She clenched her jaw. "No."

"Oh, don't be so kind to him."

"I'm not," *she purred, tilting her head back to rest on the concrete wall, unaffected by the way moss was growing between the cracks.* "He's so much worse."

A deep chuckle erupted from my gut as I stood to my full height and started walking backward. "You say that like I'm not sent from Hades himself." *I tapped on the single light bulb.* Tick. Tock. Tick. Tock.

"Maybe." *She smiled, and it tilted me off-balance at how confident she was, even in the eye of an enemy.* "But what does that tell you about him, if not even you scare me?"

She was brave, I'd give her that, but if she wanted to play games, all right then. We'd play.

I punched the light bulb, and everything went black.

CHAPTER FIVE

Brantley

It was dark. I didn't know what I wanted or needed to do, but I always somehow found myself in front of Saint's bedroom. As if my soul ached for her while my flesh bled through my pain. This time was different, though. I finished a job like always, but this one. Was. Different. This one would impact her in years to come, and I knew that. I knew that if at any time I could free her from the cage I'd built around her, this… this would come back to haunt her. Fucking Lucan.

I opened her door, not caring fuck all if she heard. I never came home much anymore, but I needed to see her. To check on her. Ending another life always made me want to see her still living hers. As if I needed reassurance that God hadn't started punishing me because he knew the first place to start.

Nothing good would ever come to me, and the only good I had in my life I had to fucking force to keep. I was a piece of shit.

That was a given. But as she breathed the same air we did, smiled whenever she saw me, and walked along the haunted floors of the Vitiosis Manor, I knew. I fucking knew it was all going to be worth it. She was going to be worth it.

The door slammed against her wall and the bottle of rum I had clutched in my hand dropped to the floor as I clenched the doorframe with the same hand. She shuffled in her bed before her body shifted up and her soft little voice sang out, "Brantley? What are you doing? It's—God, it's four a.m." Not a hint of fear in her tone. She had never been afraid of me. Not when I'd come home with blood on my clothes and a haunted kind of darkness in my eyes. Not ever. She was never afraid. That scared me most about her.

"I need to ask you a question, but I need you to answer me honestly."

"O-okay?" she answered, but I knew the stutter wasn't from nerves. It was from sleep.

"Have you been sleepwalking more often lately?"

She shook her head as I stumbled farther into her bedroom. Kore and Hades were fast asleep in their beds in the corner, not a single flinch at my being in her space.

"I don't really know," she said softly. "I don't know if I've been doing it and then walking myself back to my bed."

At this point, I was directly beside her bed, the poison of rum strong on the tip of my tongue. I dropped down onto her mattress, right beside her. It was dark, with the only crack of light spilling in from the hallway. "You need to tell me if you know."

"Why?"

She didn't get to finish her sentence because my fingers were wrapped around her chin and my mouth was an inch away from hers. "Promise me you will tell me."

"Yes, Brantley." Her hand was on my cheek, and my eyes

squeezed shut when she lowered it onto her lap and looked down to it. "Is that blood?"

The question I know we are all wondering is who, if anyone, is haunting her now. That's the one fucking thing I can't get out of my head. Our lead on The Gentlemen has gone cold. We chased it all the way to an old warehouse near the Canadian border, finding it had been completely emptied.

"We'll find them." The second I pulled the trigger that ended Elijah Garcia, I knew it was going to start a war. One I wasn't sure we knew how to win. It's hard to win a war when the opposing team goes ghost. "Maybe bring her home. I don't know, Brantley. Something about this makes me feel uncomfortable. They're too quiet." I understand what he's saying. The Gentlemen have always operated this way, which is what make them such a viable threat to The Kings. We are loud, forceful with our power, and precise, but The Gentlemen are pure stealth.

"Are we going to ignore the elephant in the room, meaning Hector?" Eli asks from behind us. I snicker, running my fingers through my hair while making my way out of the shed.

"Oh, I'll take care of Hector." We have a plan, and I'm not so sure he's following it.

"Brantley!" Bishop snaps, and I knew it was coming. I pause. "I know you're angry with him, as am I, but he thought he was doing the right thing for her."

I spin around. "He thought he was doing the right thing for her?" I mimic, and an ugly laugh escapes me. "When the fuck will any of you get it that I'm the only person who will always know how to keep her safe?"

Bishop's jaw tightens. "You need to accept that other people are a part of her life now. *I* am a part of her life now."

I ignore him, not wanting to go into more detail about Hector. If it were up to me, we would have put a bullet in him a long time ago. People have died for a lot less than what Hector Hayes has done.

∽

It doesn't take long before I'm back in the heart of New York, arriving at the penthouse where Hector is staying. Scarlet isn't with him; she's away on set for a new film.

I kick open the door and find him staring out over the city, dressed in a suit with his hands buried in his pockets. It's as if he was waiting for me to enter. "Do you know who my first kill was, son?"

I shut the door behind me, strolling farther into the sitting room. "I don't know, but if I had to take a guess, I would say it'd be someone you stabbed in the back. Someone who trusted you."

Hector finally turns to face me. "No." He relaxes into a leather sofa. Brown and distressed, as if it has been sat on millions of times before today. His eyes narrow on me, though his smile is tense. "Not quite. He was young. A boy, really, but then so was I."

I close my eyes, shaking my head. It doesn't disturb me. It should, but when you've been assassinating people for the better half of your life, you become void of feeling any sympathy about death. Except one. "You were going to allow me to think she was dead."

"Ah, that's what this visit is about." He leans forward, unbuttoning his jacket to reach forward for his glass of whiskey. He sits back, his eyes on me. "Yes, I was. And given the chance, I would do it again."

"She's mad at me."

"Hmmm, why ever would she be mad at you?" His eyebrow cocks, and I have to fight everything inside of me not to reach forward and tear his throat out of his body.

"She said she saw me in the limo."

He doesn't flinch, simply swallowing the amber-tinted liquid in a fast-enough gulp that has my thirst quenched. "Hmmm, I do recall her saying your name in the car."

"Why?" I snap, my upper lip curling. "And just so we understand each other." I lean forward to rest my elbows on my thighs. "I'm not in the mood to play games. Not when it comes to her, not ever."

"Brantley." Hector places his now empty glass onto the coffee table in front of him while keeping his eyes trained on me. "What makes you think I know what she saw? I was simply as shocked as the next person."

"Which was?" I ask, my patience wearing so fucking thin I'm pretty sure I could floss my teeth with it. "Who was in the car with you?"

"Just myself. I was planning to take her to Perdita to keep her safe."

"*We* had a plan, and that was to allow Veronica to take her, and besides that, you *hate* Perdita."

He challenges me. "I wanted her safe more."

I exhale a deep breath. It was a conversation we both knew we had to have.

Blood slid down my arms in a rain of horror. Screams and gunshots rang out, but all I wanted to see was Saint. She was shot. Even though I knew instantly it was a flesh wound, I was well aware she was slowly slipping into shock. I moved across the room, kicking the body of the hooded boy on the floor and making my way back to where she lay when I last saw her.

It was empty. I found Bishop behind me, his eyes wild and filled with rage. He swung between me and the empty spot on the ground then back to me, before turning to the exit and pointing. "Go! I will handle this!"

I did. I ran to the exit and out into the alley where Eli had the Bugatti idling on the spot. He pushed open the passenger door and I threw myself inside. "Go!" Eli zipped out onto the road and flew through the lines of cars. We were all good drivers, but Eli was better than all of us. "Did you see where he took her?"

"I'm taking wild guesses right now, but I don't know. Something tells me out of town, so we'll go that way." My anger bubbled beneath my skin, but my rage? Oh, my rage was like gunpowder, waiting to ignite.

"Find that car, Eli. Fuck."

"We will, bro. We'll get her back."

"Are you thinking about that night?" Hector interrupts my thoughts, and I instantly snap up to him.

"Oh, you mean the night I killed you?"

He laughs, flicking the ash off his newly lit Cuban cigar. "Hmmm, I have felt more like a ghost since that night." His index finger and thumb rub together. "Am I dead?"

The corner of my mouth tilts up, flashing a smug grin. "I don't know, Papa Hayes, what did I say would happen if you fucked with my girl?"

"There!" Eli floored it forward and I shot back into my seat. Everything but that black city car blurred out of focus. As we neared closer and closer on the highway, my pulse quickened. Beads of sweat slid down the bridge of my nose, and that rage was slowly being tipped onto the burning fire of my anger. "How are we going to stop it?"

"Hit him," I said, teeth clenched while reaching for my gat.

"Bro, Saint is in there."

"Fuck!" I slammed my fist into the dash of the car. "Drive beside it. He'll see he's been found and will pull over."

"Then what?" Eli asked, doing as I said and dropping it into third gear to shift up to the side of the car.

"Then I kill him."

I ignore the ringing of my phone as I stand off with one of the most powerful men I have ever known, ever will know.

"Are you going to answer that?" Hector asks with genuine intrigue. A clock ticks down the hallway, the sun setting in the sky. Orange hues bounce off building tops, falling behind the Brooklyn Bridge.

I ignore the call. This conversation needs to happen and he knows it.

"Have you told Bishop what my plans were?" Hector asks, unbuttoning the top of his shirt. "I'm guessing no since he hasn't got a gun pointed at my head."

It took one minute for the town car to pull off onto the shoulder of the highway. I flew out, ignoring cars zooming past me and headed straight for the back door. Hector was already climbing out of the other side, but this side was locked. Motherfucker.

"Son..."

I strolled straight to him, clenching my fist before it was flying into his face.

"Don't fucking son me!" Blood sprayed everywhere. Hector stood back up, fixing his suit while swiping the blood from his lip.
"Where is she?"

"She's going somewhere safe."

"Hector, I swear to God, I am not one to fuck with right now!" Rain began to pelt down on my face. It did nothing to put out the fire inside of me.

"Brantley—" A voice. Familiar. Burned. Hot.

I turned toward it. "I will take her." Long black hair, bleak eyes, and enough swagger to put every model to shame.

Veronica.

I winced, narrowing my eyes back on Hector. "What the fuck are you playing at?"

Hector blinked at Veronica in shock. And before he thought I could catch it, he corrected himself. "That's right. I wasn't changing the plan. Veronica was here all along."

I tilted my head to where Veronica stood outside the driver's side door. "I will be there in the morning to check."

Veronica nodded. "I will wait."

Hector slid back into the car and I watched as it drove away. "We good?" Eli asked as I slipped back into the passenger seat.

"Yeah," I murmured. "We good."

"You and I both know that you didn't plan on Veronica being in the driver's seat of your car." It's true and he knows it. The question is, does he think I know she was there all along, maybe arranging the hostile takeover of his plans?

"Hmmm," Hector murmurs. My phone blares off again and I swipe it unlocked, bringing it to my ear. "What?" My blood turns cold, and I find myself floating to my feet. I squeeze my phone, my teeth clenched together.

"What is it?" Hector asks, but I'm already almost at the door before I can answer. I turn around at the last minute. "The reason why I haven't told Bishop is because I want to be the one who puts the bullet between your eyes if I find out you have any ill intent toward her, not him—and believe me when I say, he will."

CHAPTER SIX

Saint

There are four bonfires set up in a circle with wooden chairs spread out around them. Vines and flowers intertwine with each other while candles light a pathway to a small river. I look up to the sky, where fireflies buzz around in circles like little beads of light. Smiling, I bring my mulled wine to my lips and take a long sip. It's the first time I've felt relaxed since waking here. Music spills around the place, as Ivy and Ophelia laugh and dance against each other near the flames.

Veronica drops down beside me with a rolled cigarette in her mouth that smells oddly like a sweetened version of a cigar. It's weed. I know because of The Kings. "Are you having a good time?" she asks, offering me the long white trunk.

I shake my head, declining her offer. "I am actually." I inhale the night air deeply and close my eyes, relishing in the heat of the flames caressing my frigid skin. "Can I ask you something?"

Veronica glances up at me from behind her lashes. "You're going to ask anyway…"

"What do these mean, and why did Brantley force me to wear it once I became public knowledge?" My fingertips graze the diamond on my necklace. It was a question that I've wanted to ask since seeing Ophelia's.

"Ah, so he demanded you wear it but didn't explain why?"

I look out to the crowd of people dancing, obviously high or drunk or otherwise. The Hunt hasn't started, but I recognize all of the new men who are already here. No new witches, from what I can tell. They are all young, around my age, maybe younger, and all athletically built. There are five of them. Though they sit in one place, they all watch the girls closely.

"That necklace," she takes a shot of alcohol and places the empty glass on the grass, "is recognized by anyone who may want to hurt you. Brantley made you wear it because while you wear that very expensive emblem, you, my dear, are entirely untouchable by the magic of your ancestors. Brantley has always been a skeptic, but he wasn't going to gamble on you."

My fingers brush over it again. I think I knew deep down that was why Brantley made me wear it, but it doesn't explain how he came about it.

"So it's a witch thing?" I ask, allowing the shot of alcohol to slide down my throat before a passing waiter wearing a shiny plastic doll mask stops beside us, offering more drinks and appetizers.

Veronica laughs. "A witch thing, indeed."

"So he's always known?" I reach for another shot of vodka before the waiter disappears. "He knew I was a witch all along, because he gave me this necklace when I was a child."

Veronica exhales, her eyes falling to the now full shot glass in my hand. "Be careful with those drinks. They're not mortal strength, and that is something you might need to talk with him about."

Jealousy stirs in my belly and I know I'm being ridiculous, but I get the feeling Brantley has had another girl he has cared about too all along: Veronica. How far does this bond go? Are they sleeping together? Is that why he has photos on his Instagram of her house? Is that why he always sleeps with older women because he wants to see Veronica in them? Veronica doesn't seem like the type of woman who wants to settle down. Is that why he has never had a girlfriend? Because he can't have her?

I stand from my chair, just as a siren blares. It sounds all too familiar to the one on *The Purge*. Chills break out over my skin, and I turn to see where the sound is coming from, desperate to get my mind away from the road it is heading toward. I can't be jealous. If it's true and he does have a *whatever* with Veronica, then what does that make me?

A little sister?

My throat contracts to keep my food down. My mind is dizzy. *That drink was a little strong.*

"The Hunt is about to commence," Ophelia calls, standing on a pile of burning embers and branches. "Who will be catching me tonight?" Her body moves around the witch men, her finger grazing their taut bare chests. Abs upon abs, though their faces are hidden behind the same plastic doll-like mask the waiter sports.

Alessi steps forward, stripping out of her dress. "Catch me if you can, bitches..." Then she dashes off into the thick forest with my sister witches following closely behind her.

"Wow!" I gasp, amazed by how quickly they moved through the clearing.

The warlocks all stand still, as if waiting for their call to chase.

Everything feels eerie, as if people are watching me from all angles. Twigs snap beneath the soles of my feet, my vision blurring as I step closer and closer to all five of them. They're in a half circle, but all standing still. I don't realize I'm holding my breath until I release an exhale, bringing my finger up to the chest of one of them. Abs tight, skin slicked in oil. None of them bear any tattoos, all naked, exposed. My palm comes to his left pec, my eyes closing.

Everyone is quiet. I don't know why they haven't run off for my fellow witch sisters, but something in the back of my mind says I don't care. My eyes open, and I'm staring up at the mask that hovers over me. His eyes. I can't see them clearly with the light, but I feel them.

I reach up to the edge of his mask, testing to see if he will allow me to touch him.

"Saint… honey, that's not allowed—" His hand comes up to silence Veronica.

"I—" My fingertips touch the plastic of his mask, peeling it off slowly. Just as I'm about to drop it onto the grass, a loud roar of a motorbike cuts through the clearing, and I turn to look over my shoulder in shock.

"Saint! Get on the fucking bike!" a familiar voice barks while swinging his leg off.

"Brantley?" My eyes pop open, and suddenly whatever I drank earlier isn't potent enough to keep me drunk. Not in his presence.

He ignores me and goes straight for Veronica. "Give me one good reason why I shouldn't kill all these fuckers right here and right now."

"Ah." Veronica looks between Brantley and me before she folds her arms in front of herself. The muscles in her face relax, and a flash of understanding brushes over her features. "Go hunt. You've spent enough time being fascinated by our little Hecate." They must all scurry off because dust kicks up around my feet.

"Our?" Brantley takes another three steps up to Veronica. "V, she is not *ours*, she is mine. What the fuck is this shit? You sending her out on a fucking hunt?"

My mouth opens and closes. I want to say something. Anything to help Veronica, but I can't get the words out.

"Actually, no, she wasn't. She was observing, and Brantley, I didn't realize it was like that for you and her."

He spins to glare at me, pointing toward the idling dirt bike. "Get on the fucking bike!"

"I don't know how!" I make my way toward the both of them. Maybe if I stand in front of Veronica, he won't tear her head off.

"I trusted you…" Brantley's eyes narrow.

"And you can trust me, Brantley. She wasn't going out on The Hunt, even if I didn't know about the two of you. She simply—" Veronica's eyes flick to me, "is too good."

Once I'm standing between them, my hand is on Brantley's chest. He's wearing a thick dark hoodie, but I swear I can feel his heartbeat beneath the palm of my hand. My cheeks flush. "Brantley, you're being unreasonable."

He pauses and slowly cocks his head down to look at me. Actually not look. To study me. "Oh yeah?" His hand wraps around my wrist, yanking me farther into his chest. "How fucking so?"

"Well." I peel off his fingers with my other hand, but it's no use since his grip is like steel. "For starters, I'm not yours anymore."

He growls, just as the corner of his lip curls in a snarl. He leans down to my height, close enough for our noses to touch.

"On. The. Fucking. Bike." His other hand is on the back of my neck, squeezing. "Now." He shoves me away.

I turn to face V. "I'm so sorry."

She offers a small smile of sympathy, but her eyes have new worry lines indented around the edges when she goes back to Brantley. "Please don't take her away yet."

"You fucked up." He grabs me by the hand and begins dragging me toward his bike. "And you're really fucking lucky I don't peel the skin off that piece of shit she touched."

"Ever the romantic, Brantley."

"You would know…" he snaps, shoving the helmet into my chest.

"How would she know?" I ask, though I wish I'd said it louder, maybe with some bite. How can he threaten the life of some innocent boy just because I touched him, yet he and Veronica clearly have history?

"Do tell her…" Veronica says from the side of me.

Brantley turns over his shoulder, flipping her off before swinging his leg over the bike. I see the back seat where I'm supposed to sit. Even the pegs where my feet go. But I don't want to leave.

"Brantley…"

He turns around, his eyes hooded and his jaw tight. I shouldn't be testing him right now. "You really want to do this right here?" His fingers find mine and he yanks me into his leg. His fingers are around my chin as he tilts my head down to him. "Never pegged you as the jealous type, Dea." A crooked smirk is on his mouth.

I pull away from him defiantly. "You wanted me here, but since I touched someone, you now want to take me away?"

"No—" He turns partially to face me. "I was coming here to take you home anyway" —his traitorous eyes fall on Veronica— "because everything is sorted with The Gentlemen."

My mouth closes, but goose bumps break out over my skin. How can everything be resolved with The Gentlemen so quickly?

"Then when I found you with your hand on his chest, yeah, I almost went ripper. But I didn't. You should be thankful. That's progress for me."

I cross my arms. Heat radiates from the side of my face, as if someone is watching our exchange. My eyes flick to the side where The Hunt began. Darkness through the trees, so thick I can't imagine how they would be able to see.

"Saint, honey, you might want to take the monster home before the rest of the crew gets back."

I hook my leg over the bike, wrapping my arms around his torso. "But we're staying here. We can leave tomorrow."

He revs the bike loudly before we zip forward onto the man-made pathway.

We pull into the long driveway, where I see Brantley's Bugatti parked on the curb outside the front steps. He turns off the bike and helps me off the back while I pull off the helmet.

"Saint..." he says, but it's too late.

I'm walking to the front door, not interested in continuing any conversation with him. For the first time ever, I don't know what I'm feeling. Jealousy? Anger? Betrayal? Do all of them somewhat feel the same?

I'm still climbing the oversized steps when his hand comes to my arm, spinning me around. "What the fuck is your problem?"

"I don't have one." I wince, unable to look him in the eye. "I don't have a problem."

With his fingers beneath my chin, he tilts my head up to his. "Have you forgotten that I can read you like an open book?"

"How! How do you do that? And more so, can you stop?"

His grip on my arm tightens. "Because every fucking chapter you have is written for me." His fingers spread from my chin and onto my cheeks. He clenches gently while tugging me closer to him. "And I ain't stopping."

I pause, my eyelashes fanning out over my cheeks. "Why are you doing this?"

He licks his bottom lip and nudges his head to the side. "I'd rather do this in the morning. I'm fucking tired."

We make our way upstairs and into my bedroom. He closes the door and heads into the bathroom while I slip out of my dress and into the shirt he dumped onto the floor when he removed it. I wipe off my makeup and brush my hair as he moves to one side of my bed, running his hand through his thick hair.

"How did you take care of The Gentlemen so easily?" I place my brush on the dresser and make my way to my side of the bed. I slip beneath the sheets and watch as every muscle in his back tenses and moves.

He exhales. "I don't want to talk about that."

I yawn loudly, shuffling deeper into the sheets. My soul feels as though it's wrapped in a gentle peace I haven't felt in a long while. "Why was I in so much danger?"

The mattress sinks as he shuffles on top of the covers. "Because I was their main enemy. His son and I had a beef so fucking thick you couldn't cut through it."

I turn over to face him, though the lights are out and I can't see. "I don't understand why there was such a panic to get me to safety."

My heart skips a beat when I feel the cushion of his thumb against my bottom lip.

"Because they're smart." He pauses and my stomach rolls. "Way fucking smarter than I am."

My breathing halts as my blood turns to lava.

"You done being jealous?"

The sensual way the words leave his mouth has a direct line to my core. All this time I have been here, I've felt a void inside my chest. I thought that void was from betrayal, but I was wrong. That emptiness was from not having Brantley here with me. Close. Not knowing where he was or what he had done, or why he had done it.

"I am," I whisper, and right as my lips part, his thumb dips inside my mouth.

"Come here."

"I—"

He flicks the blanket off my body, grabs me by the hips and rolls me on top of him.

I press on his chest to keep myself upright as his hands glide up beneath his shirt. I lean down until my nose touches his. "I missed you."

Silence. Nothing but silence. I push off him to sit back up, but he leans forward and catches my mouth with his. My tongue slips between his lips greedily as he directs me over and down his girth. Every stroke has my heart rate pulsing until sweat beads at my temples. He pulls out slowly, sucking my tongue farther into his mouth as I guide my hips down over his thick length. He hooks his thumbs into my panties and tears them off, flicking them to the other side of the room.

"I'm angry," he growls, biting on my jaw.

"Well, same," I say, guiding my hips over him as I slide down his length.

He hisses, and the sound is so animalistic I almost pass out. "Fuck."

I place my hand on the front of his throat as I ride him slowly, allowing him to slide out just enough before slamming back down onto him so hard his balls hit my ass. He squeezes my hip bones, directing me over him faster. I have control for all of five seconds before he flips me onto my back and drives into me. He leans down and flicks his tongue over my collarbone. I moan softly as he leaves a trail of pain down the edge, the tip of his canines biting into my flesh. My back arches off the bed, my core convulsing as he grinds into me with forceful strokes.

"Don't ever touch another man again, Saint." He squeezes my wrist with his hand, forcing it above my head. He shoves it farther into the mattress. "Answer me."

My eyes flutter closed. "I won't." He slips out of me and I groan in frustration, until he trails bite marks down my sternum, past my belly, and across my inner thigh.

Positioning my leg over his shoulder, his tongue flicks over me and ignites a fire so hot I don't think I'll be able to last long. My hands are buried in his hair, tugging every time he sucks my clit into his mouth. My muscles tense all at once before releasing, my legs jerking as I come down. He licks his way back up my body and slowly drives back inside of me. His pace is slower this time, but still the same depth. His lips come to mine and he kisses me gently, his tongue overlapping mine. Our bodies slap together as sweat drips off his forehead and falls onto mine. He brings his hand up to rest his thumb on the cushion of my lip, and I sweep my tongue over it. His eyes darken as he picks up the pace, falling back into our deep tangle of kisses. Kissing Brantley is like kissing the angel of death. He takes my breath the same way. My legs wrap around his back, my arm hooking around his neck.

"I—" I choke on my words when my orgasm obliterates all sense to talk. My eyes roll so far to the back of my head that white dots flicker like strobe lights. He collapses on me after finishing but doesn't move. Neither of us moves, our breathing heavy and in sync. Slowly, he peels his sticky body off mine and rolls to the side, onto his back.

"I fucking lost my shit seeing you touch him."

"I know," I whisper gently, turning over to face him while dragging the sheet with me. "But it wasn't what you're thinking."

"Yeah?" he snaps bitterly. "Well, it sure as fuck looked like it."

"Brantley, you're being ridiculous."

"No." His head tilts sideways to face me. I can't see him because it's dark, but I can see the edges of his jaw and the slight glistening of his skin. "I'm not. I've watched Bishop and Nate go through having to tolerate their girl having a side-piece. I'm not playing that game. You get Bishop and that's it."

"You *were* the side-piece…"

Silence. His arm wraps around my waist and he pulls me on top of him forcefully. "Shut up and fuck me."

I don't bother searching for Brantley this morning. I figure he's not telling me the whole story, but I'm also hoping that if there's something I *need* to know, he would tell me. I'm pouring granola into my bowl, still wearing his shirt, when Ophelia whistles from the entryway.

"Well, shit." She chuckles. I turn around to face her as she's opening the fridge. "You look thoroughly fucked, girlfriend."

I take a spoonful. "How was The Hunt last night?"

Ophelia sighs, pouring a tall glass of milk and resting the glass against her cheek. "I hope it went well, but I guess only time will tell."

I pause my chewing, tilting my head. "What does that mean?"

Ophelia opens her mouth, but it's not her voice that comes through, it's Frankie's, bouncing into the kitchen while tugging off her headphones. Judging by the sweat and clothes, I'd say she has just come back from a run.

"Morning!" Frankie smiles sweetly at us both, and I look to Ophelia in question. Frankie is never nice, and definitely not to me.

I don't answer.

Ivy and Alessi are walking in together next, both already dressed for the day, which only leaves me and Ophelia in our sleeping clothes.

Alessi looks me up and down. "I know you didn't join in on The Hunt last night, so I'm guessing I missed something."

I place my bowl on the counter, my cheeks flushed red.

"Do I smell the way you all do? Is that it?" The smell of sweat, earth, and something spicy filled my nostrils the second Ophelia made her appearance this morning.

"Yes, but with blood..." Frankie says, an eyebrow quirked at me. "Hey, no judgment here."

I empty my bowl and rinse it, placing it inside the dishwasher. A coven of witches who are all synced together. I guess I'm still partially new, so I'm not getting as good of a read on them as they are on me.

"Well, speak for yourself..." Frankie mutters, rubbing her forehead with the back of her hand.

"What? You didn't?" Ophelia asks, her eyes swinging around to all of them. Obviously, I'm missing something.

"Nope," Frankie exhales, falling onto one of the barstools with a glass of water gripped in her hand. "I don't know. Maybe we're just not the right match, no matter how often he always finds me."

"Impossible," Veronica interrupts, standing at the threshold of where the kitchen meets the main foyer. Her words are for Frankie, but her eyes are on me. "You're both perfect for each other. Give Samael time." She uncrosses her arms and tightens the belt of her robe. "He just needs time."

I try to ignore her as she moves around the kitchen.

"Saint, nice shirt."

I run my tongue over my bottom lip, chewing on it softly.

"I can't say I'm surprised, but I didn't exactly peg it either. My apologies."

This is the time I should ask her about their relationship and what it is about. After Frankie saying that Brantley usually goes for older women, I want to know about Veronica and what she is to him. It's only fair since he seems to fly off the handle by me simply touching another man. I could ask Brantley, but I don't want to give him the chance to lie to me. It would hurt too much and make me overthink about *why* he's lying to me. Mostly, I'm just wanting to get a read on Veronica herself, but she's not easy to read. I've never had this problem; usually people are much easier to analyze, but Veronica has emotional shields strong enough to withstand an apocalypse.

She chuckles slightly, raising her mug to her lips. Something stirs inside of me that knows that chuckle was aimed at me. Not for me. *At me.* I turn to face her. I snap.

"What are you to Brantley?"

Everyone falls quiet. Even Ophelia has nothing to say.

Veronica takes a long sip of her hot coffee, closing her eyes before opening them onto mine and placing her mug on the counter. "I think that's something you should ask Brantley."

"Ask Brantley what?" He walks into the kitchen shirtless but with his running shorts on, oblivious to the way every single one of the women in this room is gawking at him. Or maybe he does know and he just doesn't care.

I squeeze my hands into fists at my sides, annoyed at myself for showing any kind of emotion toward their—whatever it is. Veronica's eyebrows are raised as if she's waiting for me to repeat myself. I'm not going to give her the satisfaction, so I head back up to my bedroom. Jealousy burns inside my gut a lot worse than it did yesterday, and I'm sure it has everything to do with the fact we, once again, had sex last night. I knew if I stayed in there any longer, I was going to either embarrass myself further, or worse, expose myself. Back in my bedroom, I find all of my clothes packed up in suitcases at the end of the bed. I sort through the closest one and find some bike shorts and an oversized Nirvana shirt, pairing them with white socks and sneakers. I leave my hair out in natural waves, shoving Brantley's shirt into the bag I took clothes out of. I should go back down and face him. He's going to find me anyway and ask what I was talking about. At least now I don't feel so vulnerable wearing nothing but a shirt.

The hallway is long, marbled, and clean. This house feels more like a museum than it does a home. Furnishings are oversized, the doors, staircase, and even the artwork the same. Yet among the pristine walls and silverware, I feel at home here. Much like I do back at the manor. I reach twin doors at the end, both handles dipped in gold to match the artistic paintings all over the ceiling and walls. My hand is on one, while the other is at my side. Should I knock? I should knock.

I push the doors open and freeze. Brantley is leaning against Veronica's desk while she sits back looking up at him from her chair. From this angle, she looks snug between his legs. My stomach drops, and I'm almost certain all that granola I just ate is about to projectile out.

"Brantley…" I say, my fingers wrapping around the gold handle so tight I feel as though I might tear it right off the hinges. I might just kill the Devil. What an unexpected turn of events that would be.

He looks over his shoulder at me, unfazed. My eyes water, but I keep the tears down. Pain is begging to be felt, but it will have to wait. Anger is more important right now.

"Don't ever touch me again." I spin around and run out the way I came. So much for anger. My anger just dissolved into more pain and now I need my phone. Need Bishop. *Need to be alone.* What the hell am I doing here? I should be with him. My family. I know he'll come to me right away; he always will.

"Saint!" I hear my name, but I can't see. I can't focus. Water has blurred my eyes, and all of the pretty art pieces I admired on the way down here are nothing but that—watercolor. Hands are around my wrist and I'm being tugged backward. "You're fucking pissing me off."

I pause when my face hits his chest, and I'm looking up at him through the tears.

"Fuck," he whispers, his fingers on my cheek, swiping them away. "Fuck." His arm is around my waist, his hands on my upper thigh as he picks me up from the ground.

"Don't fucking touch me!" My heart is as bruised as the scars he leaves on my skin, yet my legs find themselves around his waist anyway. In this moment, I hate myself. I hate that I'm not strong enough to fight the way he makes me feel. I hate that as much as I feel sick to my stomach by what I just saw, I still need him to wrap me in his arms and tell me he's mine.

He tugs on my hair to hold my head in place, his lips touching the shell of my ear. "As much as I love hearing such filthy words come out of that innocent little mouth, you're not about to walk out thinking I'm fucking someone else." He places me back onto the ground and closes the doors behind us. I realize we're back in Veronica's office, if that's what you would even call it, and she's still on her chair, legs crossed and a cigarette between her fingers.

"I don't want to be here, or in the middle of whatever this is." I turn to face Brantley. "You once asked me if it was something I could want." I take another step. His eyes cross slightly when I come too close. "Maybe being with other people like so many are in the EKC world." My fingers are at his chin, squeezing before he can answer. "The answer is no. I would have been happy with just you. Just you. But that's the thing, isn't it? It's not about what the women in the EKC want, it's about the men."

"Saint?" He grabs my hand and squeezes, intertwining our fingers together while pulling me into his chest. He spins me around to face Veronica while his other hand is pressed against my lower belly, shoving me closer toward him until my back is hard against him. Veronica smirks, bringing the end of her cigarette to her lips. "Veronica is my mother."

"I like it here," I said as she gazed into the bedroom. This time she stood in the center, right beneath the light bulb. I wanted to push her, see how far she would go, but I had to remind myself why I was here.

"Who are you?" she asked. Such a simple question, yet simple was not something I was familiar with.

"I thought that was obvious?" I chuckled, circling the small room with a scrape of my nail. "Do you know what this room is?"

She followed me closely. Good. She was catching on.

"No. Though if I had to guess, I would say I'm dreaming."

"Tsk, tsk…" I wiggled my finger. "Such a basic answer."

Her eyes closed. "What do you want from me?"

"I want to play a game." I clapped my hands and the walls melted away, placing us in a dark forest filled with fireflies and trees so tall they almost looked mystical. She began to panic. Good. She should. That meant she was smart, smarter than I initially gave her credit for. "I'll ask you a question, and if you answer incorrectly, I'll bring back one of the memories from your childhood —"

She started to interrupt, but my hand went up, stopping her.

"—I must say, I've seen most of them and they're not pleasant."

"You're not Brantley…" Saint whispered so softly, I almost didn't hear it above the wind whisking through the leaves.

I stepped closer to her until my face was all that was in her view. "Are you sure about that? How well do you really know him?"

Her eyes crawled up to me, her shoulders back in defiance. God, she was hot. She had this innocence about her that was so fucking sexy and untouchable. Or maybe that was because she literally is untouchable. Well, at least she was. I knew if I wanted to have her, I could. But the thing about me, I liked to play games.

So the real question she needed to answer was if she was sure I wasn't Brantley?

Chapter Seven

Brantley

Seeing Saint cry was like a cold dagger being dragged over my heart, but not to pierce it, just enough to warn me that it could. I didn't fucking like it. At all. Never in my years have I given a shred of a fuck about anyone crying until just now. As the tears on her cheeks dried, my anger only intensified. I wanted to tell her about Veronica, but V being V, she couldn't part with the lifelong secret that she was, in fact, still alive. Little did she know, The Kings knew. Hector and his generation may have kept secrets from each other, but we all agreed that wouldn't be how we ran things once it was ours. I told Bishop as soon as we started initiation, but we all kept it from Hector's generation. Bishop started keeping secrets from his dad the second he started threatening Madison.

I shove my way through the back doors and find Saint sitting beside the pool, her legs hanging in the water. After finding out about Veronica, she didn't say a word. She simply turned and left the room. Typical Saint.

"I really miss Hades and Kore." Her voice is soft.

"We'll go home." I kneel down beside her. "Saint, look at me." She doesn't, her eyes glued on the water. I glide the cushion of my thumb over her chin, tilting her head toward me. "I wanted to tell you, but it's complicated."

She shuffles, turning her body toward mine, while her eyes immediately summon me. "Do you remember when you gave me this necklace?"

She hadn't left her room today. I was already feeling agitated, so I probably shouldn't have been around her, but I needed to be. I made my way through the back garden, ducking beneath the vines and floral roses. It smelled like honey and leaves. It smelled like Saint. She turned to look over her shoulder, dirt smudged on her cheek. "Oh. I thought I could sense you." She placed the metal watering can onto one of the garden railings. "Is everything okay?"

I fisted the diamond necklace in my hand before holding it out to her. Her wide eyes fell on it, her mouth agape. "Brantley—did you steal that?"

I rolled my eyes. "I don't need you to wear it yet, but when it's time to, I need you to understand the importance of what this necklace means."

She searched my face, tugging her bottom lip into her mouth before zeroing in on the necklace again.

"So you don't want me to wear it right now?"

I shook my head. "No, but you need to take care of it now."

Her brows pulled in as she slowly reached for the gold Cuban chain and diamond crown. Anytime our skin touched, there was always a flood of warmth that followed, but like always, I swallowed it like a shot of whiskey. I may be a billionaire outlaw, but what she was capable of making me feel was something I would never be able to afford. My pockets were deep, but not deep enough for love. Not ever. Not even with her. So what I offered would always have to be enough for her.

She took the million-dollar necklace into the palm of her hand. The heavy gold was a contrast to her dirt-covered hands. The lozenge-styled icicles fell off the crown sharp and precise between her fingers. "I'll look after it. What does it do?"

I smiled tensely at her. "One day I'll tell you."

"That necklace is from this part of your life."

"—Brantley, can I talk to you for a second?" Veronica interrupts from the patio.

"Go make sure you've got all your shit. I'll handle this." I grit my teeth, standing and making my way toward where V stands, her eyes never leaving mine.

"Hmm, I'm interested to see how you plan to allow this to carry on with her."

I pass Veronica and enter the main living area, falling onto the sofa.

Veronica places a cigarette in her mouth and lights the tip. "You do know that this can't last?"

"This isn't anything. She's my responsibility." Even as the words leave my mouth, I feel like a fucking liar. The famous words I've always used as a shield to hide the truth.

Veronica flicks off the ash of her smoke into the crystal ashtray. "She belongs here, Brantley. You know it, I know it—hell, even her sisters know it," she mumbles, crossing her legs. "Even if Frankie doesn't like her, she still understands that Saint belongs here."

"Saint." I bare my teeth. My anger is hanging dangerously close to the edge. "Belongs everywhere I am, not this coven or you. I appreciate you taking her under your wing while I needed to handle business on my side, but she's coming home tonight."

Veronica looks at me, eyes slit and lips in a straight line. She may be my mother, but everything between her and me has always been strictly business. She left when I was a kid, faked her death, and got in contact with me when I was old enough. There's zero love between us. Everyone assumed I got my coldness from Lucan, but that's because they'd never met my mother.

She sighs, leaning forward to rest her elbows on her knees. "Brantley, I think she has broken our curse."

Chapter Eight

Saint

He disappears back into the house with Veronica not far behind him. His mother. How? How is that even possible? She looks barely old enough. I pause. *How old was she when she had Brantley?* Then again, it is Lucan. I can't be all that surprised.

My phone dings and I open the text. It's a group chat with Madison and Tillie. I can't believe I'm going to call them my normalcy, but they are.

Madison: When are you allowed out of that coven? I need to vent.

Tillie: You could vent to me, but you don't want to.

Madison: No, it's because you're crazy right now. Saaaiiiint?

I begin typing out a text to them, my mouth stretching wide with a smile. I missed them.

Me: I think we're coming back today. Some weird shit happens here.

Madison: Trust me. We know weird.

Tillie: We need you to balance our pregnancy hormones.

I shuffle backward out of the pool, taking a seat on one of the sun chairs.

Me: Mad, how are you and Bishop?

The text bubbles flash. Then disappear. Then reappear. Then stop.

Tillie: Let's just say we're all scared.

Madison: I think he needs you.

I pause, my heart racing. I hate that I've been here when I should be there for Bishop. Obviously, the news of him becoming a father would have been big for him. My shoulders feel heavy as the sudden urgency of fleeing surges through my veins. I make my way back into the house, bumping into Ophelia.

"You're leaving today?" She pouts her bottom lip. "I've more than warmed to Ophelia while being here. I can safely say that she is someone I will miss completely.

"I am, but we're not far from Riverside, so we will see each other often." I pull my phone out and hand it to her. "And in the meantime, text."

Ophelia's bright green eyes falter as a ghost of a smile briefly spreads on her lips. "If only that was true." She takes my phone and punches in her details, handing it back to me. "Please keep in touch."

I tilt my head. "Are you okay?"

"I'll be fine." She moves toward the pantry, taking out a bag of Cheetos and falling onto one of the barstools. Clawed steel curves up her back, molding her into the chair. The chairs are eccentric and gothic. After she's chewed one, she sighs. "Okay, fine, maybe not. Frankie is acting crazy because she can't seem to attain the attention of Samael."

"Samael?" I lean against the kitchen counter. A breeze swims through the air, twirling around the nape of my neck and igniting goose bumps down my spine. "Was he one of the warlocks?"

"Yup." She pops the P before downing another fat Cheeto. "He's a little particular with who he chooses. We've always known that. I personally cannot stand him and will never actively seek him out during a hunt."

"But Frankie does?" I ask, an eyebrow quirked.

Ophelia locks eyes with me. "Every single time." She shuffles off her chair. "I hope you come back, Saint, or at the very least, don't be a stranger."

⁓

Driving down the manor's dark, gloomy driveway brings back a surge of memories from the last time I was here, preparing for Bishop's ceremony.

"For the record, this was Bailey's idea. Did I mention she has moved in?" Brantley pushes the driver's side door open. Cars line the circular driveway, and when I say cars, I mean *cars*. It's easy to notice all of The Kings' cars because they're styled the same. Blacked out and palatial. Nate's Lambo, Bishop's Maserati, Eli's Porsche.

I slide out, stretching my arms above my head. "Hey, what did Veronica want before we left?"

Brantley keeps his eyes on mine, not even a flinch. "Nothing."

My eye twitches, but I take his hand anyway. Regardless of how annoyed I am that he just lied to me. I'm, once again, angry with myself at how easy it is for my body to cling to him.

"She threw a party?" We make our way up the front steps. The familiar lion head stares back at me from the handles. I don't know what I feel for Brantley anymore. The attachment and bond are obvious, but anything else… I'm not sure. I wonder if there's too much spilled deceit between us for me to push forward. I'm confused, my mind is one big scribble that I can't erase or redraw.

"She did." He pushes the doors open and I step through to a spray of confetti thrown in my face and music vibrating the walls.

"Surprise!" Bailey and Tillie jump out from behind a wall that separates the kitchen and living rooms, a smile on both their faces.

I shake my head, laughing. "You really shouldn't have…" *I mean, they really shouldn't have.*

Tillie waves me off, flicking her shorter hair to one side of her shoulder. "Ah, yes, yes, I did." She pulls me into her arms. "This asshole is never taking you away again."

"Let the favorite sibling through…" Bishop's voice hits me like a sip of hot chocolate on a cold winter's night. I duck to the side of Tillie to see him barreling toward me. Before I can shake my head and back away, he's flipping me over his shoulder and I'm staring at everything upside down. "Missed you."

"I missed you, too! But can you put me back down so we can hug and make everything less awkward?" The pattern of the wooden floor tells me he's taking me into the living room, and then out to the back patio, where more laughing and music are coming from.

He finally places me onto solid ground and I fling my arms around his neck, pulling him down to my height. "I missed you, too." His arms are clasped around me, stubborn like their owner. I step backward slightly, but note he still doesn't release my body. "You look good."

Bishop laughs, bringing a tumbler to his lips and taking a long sip of the amber liquid swirling inside of it. "Mmmm, that's entirely you, little sis." He pulls me under his arm, pressing a soft kiss on my head. "Bailey planned all of this, but I put my foot down on the guest list. Only people here are ones I would trust with you."

I look around the place. "Bishop, there's like ten people."

He swallows the rest of his drink. "Precisely." Kicking out a lawn chair, he points down to it while taking the other, unzipping his hoodie.

I turn over my shoulder, but my breath catches when my eyes land on Brantley, watching us from inside with a bottle of whiskey being raised to his lips. His eyes say the words I know he isn't capable of speaking. Not because I know he doesn't feel them, but because he thinks he doesn't deserve to.

"He'll be fine," Bishop interrupts, bringing my attention back to him. A shiver glides over my spine when I exhale. I'm currently surrounded by my favorite garden. Well, it's a close call between this one and the one at The Daughters of Noctum. This one is sentimental, though, because I grew it.

"I don't know." I lean back in my chair until my head is leaning against the edge and all I'm left looking at are the stars in the sky. "Hell & Back" by Machine Gun Kelly and Kid Ink plays loudly, yet somehow not loud enough. "He's worse than before."

His silence fills the space between us. Bishop picks up a bottle of alcohol and pours some into his cup, handing it to me and resting the bottle on the top of his knee. "I need to ask you a question."

I bring my eyes to his, resting the glass against my lips before swallowing a generous sip. I hiss down the burn, nodding. "Go ahead."

I focus on his Nike Jordans.

"If he can't offer you anything more than what he already has, will it be enough?"

I think over his words. I want to say no. I know in my gut that being with Brantley will be no easy feat, so that in itself makes me want to say no. No, having a cold, distant partner in life isn't going to be enough.

"Yes." I swallow around the boulder that swells in my throat.

Bringing my eyes up from his shoes, I repeat, "One hundred times over, yes."

Bishop leans forward, his finger grazing my neck where *Vitiosis* is tattooed. "And that is exactly why he needs you." Bishop leans back, just as I hear chatter coming toward us from behind. "Don't give up on him." His eyes go over my shoulder, and when I turn to see who he's looking at, Madison is coming toward me, smiling.

I shoot up from my chair and pull her into a hug when she's close enough, sighing. "How are you?"

"Good. Pregnant, but good."

I step back, tucking my hair behind my ear and pointing at both her and Tillie's bellies. "This is too cute." I pull out my phone and snap a photo. "How far apart are the two of you?"

"We're due in the same month." Madison rests her hands on top of her swollen stomach. "Sorry it took so long for me to get out here. I had to yell at Brantley for a bit." I reach aimlessly behind me for the bottle when Bishop's fingers come to mine to take the glass from me and refill it.

"Yes, well…" My throat is swollen with emotion.

Bishop pulls me in and kisses the top of my head again. "Speaking of, I've got to talk with him." He leaves and I find myself watching his back as he disappears through the open doors. My heart aches, but my soul feels as though it has one hundred knots through it.

Both Tillie and Madison take either side of me and hook their arms into mine. "Let's go somewhere quiet where you can drink that and no one can hear us talk." I clutch the bottle in my hand and allow them to direct me through the garden until the music dissipates and we're standing directly in front of the cemetery archway. It's a quiet night, but the air feels restless.

"I'm all for creepy shit, but this place really scares me." Tillie tilts her head up. "I mean, who the fuck has their own cemetery?

Do people even check the graves to make sure every death is legal? I swear Brantley could write a book on how to get away with murder."

I stifle a laugh, dragging them both through the high-wire gates. "That would give away all of his secrets."

Madison snickers. "They're all such top-notch men."

I'm dodging the aged concrete headstones until I find myself in front of the one that is unmarked.

"Well, that probably wouldn't be such a smart move." Tillie gestures to the stone. "An unmarked grave is just begging to be discovered."

Their joking dies out in the distance, that same eerie wind whipping me across the face. "Every time I'd have a vision, Brantley would find me right here. In this spot."

Silence.

I run the palm of my hand over the cement. "Never thought much about that until now."

"Well, can you not?" Tillie shivers. "Honestly, this is—can you imagine the Vitiosis family as fucking ghosts? I mean, as humans, they're creepy enough."

I fall down onto the grass, leaning against the headstone. They both glare down at me.

Madison is the first to slowly lower herself, opposite me, while holding the bottom of her stomach. "I'm not bold enough to sit on an unmarked grave, but I'll sit here."

Tillie remains on her feet.

I bring the bottle to my lips and swirl some back. It's not until the burning leaves my throat and drops to my belly that I open my mouth. "I'm seeing Brantley in my visions."

They both pause, but I don't move my attention away from the dark, starry night.

"What do you mean, you're seeing him?" Madison asks,

stretching her legs out in front of her. "As in he's—wait, what do you mean?"

I clear my throat. "I don't know what it means right now, but he is very real." I look up at Tillie, who's already watching me with worried eyes. "It's sort of like Ava Garcia, only this time, instead of Ava showing me what's happening with me, watching and experiencing it through her eyes, I'm seeing it from his point of view, only he's showing me, me."

They're both gawking, though Madison looks more confused than concerned.

"Have you told Brantley?" Tillie asks, finally resting against a larger tombstone beside Madison.

"No." The cool rim of the bottle sits on my bottom lip as I tilt my head back and take another sip. "I don't want to add another load onto his already heavy shoulders. He'll blame himself, push me away, and then we'll be back at square one." I'd learned the hard way how Brantley copes with most things, and it's self-destruction.

"Well, okay. We will help you," Madison murmurs. "And anyway, I need to be distracted since Bishop is finding it difficult to hold more than one conversation with me a day."

"You'll both be fine, Madison."

Her eyes swing to me. "How can you be so sure?"

I shrug. "Because he loves you, and Bishop doesn't give up on the people he loves."

"But he did, though…" Madison whispers, and I almost think I missed what she said.

"No, he didn't." I shake my head, bringing my eyes back up to the sky. "He never once gave up on you. He was waiting for you."

Tillie sighs. "Well, this is depressing. Can we go inside now?"

I chuckle as Madison stands, swiping the dirt off the back

of her pants. They're both a force to be reckoned with. You can see it anywhere they appear. They're like yin and yang. "You guys go up. I'll be in soon."

"Saint, you're my sister and I love you, but the creepy shit you're into definitely doesn't come from mine or Bishop's side."

I smile up at her. "Well aware of where it comes from, Tillie. I'll see you guys soon." They both leave, and once they've left, I pull out my phone and scroll through my contacts again, searching for that **?**. "How are you not here?" I whisper to myself, desperate to find anything. Even to be able to contact him again, maybe ask why he's showing in my dreams or visions.

"Still trying to find your secret pen pal?" Brantley steps out of the shadows. A hoodie is over his head, shading the curves of his face. He pauses when he catches the stone I'm sitting against.

"Do you know whose this is?" I had to ask.

He lowers himself down and takes the exact spot where Madison was just sitting. "I don't. Been there for as long as I can remember. Why?"

I turn, bringing my palm to the moss growing between the cracks. "Just asking." I swing back around. He seems closer now, a breath away.

He pulls a leg up to his chest, and my throat turns dry. The silence is peaceful, my heart heavy since he's here now. Minutes pass. More minutes. I can feel the tension slowly begin to enter, but I pray I'm wrong. When he opens his mouth, I know I'm out of luck.

"I can't have you."

The words are like a verbal punch to the gut. I can feel my intestines swallow his fist whole. My throat turns to fuzz as I attempt to find the right answer.

"Even if I say I'd be happy to just have you like this?" I sound weak, but what is it to be human if you can't show your vulnerabilities?

One leg is stretched out, the other bent in with his arm hanging off it. "Especially then."

"Brant—" I whisper, shuffling up.

He cuts his name off. "Don't, Saint."

"Don't—what?" My cheeks heat and my chest flutters from nerves.

"Touch me like you know it's my undoing every time you do it."

"You can undo, Brantley." I shuffle farther, and I swear a hiss escapes his mouth. I don't care. I continue until my hands are secured on both his knees. "I know how to put you back together again."

"But you don't!" He whacks my hands off him.

"Stop pushing away from me." The tears that threaten taste dangerously close to finality. I move closer, my hands now on both his cheeks, and before he can remove them, I spread my legs over his lap until I'm straddling him. I tilt his face up to mine. The moon glowing in the sky offers all of his sharp features on a silver platter. "Tell me you don't want me and I'll get off you right now and never touch you again—"

He grabs me by the back of my neck and shoves my face down to his, his mouth a whisper away. He grazes the swell of his lips against mine. "Don't say the words." He can't stand for me to say the words, but expects me to do it? Frustrating male.

"Then kiss me, because I'm not kissing you first."

He tilts forward slightly, just enough for our lips to brush against each other, and then he kisses me. Soft, warm, familiar. I open my mouth for him, his tongue licking mine. I wrap my arms around his neck and grind myself over his crotch. He groans so low that it rocks my core from the inside and has me almost spilling over my control. This is easy for us. Our bodies are familiar, our souls connected, but his mind? His mind is what I need to conquer. He slides his hands beneath my shirt and up my bare back, unclasping my strapless bra. I toss my shirt over my head before reaching for the edge of his hoodie. Nothing is in a panic, everything almost painfully slow, but somehow perfectly paced. He tosses his hoodie to the side, his hand on my breast. The corner of his mouth tugs in a half-smile as his thumb glides over my swollen nipple.

"Still need to get these pierced."

"We do," I half-moan, my hips still thrusting against him.

"Come here." He leans forward and sucks a nipple into his mouth, tugging it between his teeth hard enough to make me wince in pain. His other hand travels from my belly, up my sternum, until it's resting against the front of my throat with his long fingers spreading over the side of my jaw. "What if you find out that what I can give you isn't enough anymore?" His hair is wild, his eyes hooded. He runs his tongue over his bottom lip. "What then? Because if you think I'm going to let you walk away from me, Saint, then you're about to get a front row view of why people fear me. This, right now..." He pauses, flicking my nipple with his index finger. "Is your getaway. But if you choose to stay here with me, then it's done. It's sealed. You can't change your mind when you find out I'm a heartless piece of shit."

I think over his words and try to reason with myself as to why this wouldn't be a good idea, but even as scenarios fail to come to my mind, I know my answer. I know because I could never see my life without him in it. Brantley didn't use bricks to build the wall he has to keep people out; he used the flesh of all his victims, in hopes it will scare people enough to never come near him.

I lean down and shake his grip off my throat. "Even if I didn't want it. Even if I fought against it. The fact could never be changed..." I place a gentle kiss on his lips. "I'm yours." I attempt to lean back, but he catches my bottom lip between his teeth, those glorious canines sinking into the sides. Reaching for his jeans, I move them down while never breaking our kiss. He flicks the button off my jeans, and I push them down while his hand rests on his length. My mouth waters.

He looks up at me from beneath his thick lashes, a devious smirk on his face. "What? You wanna suck my dick in a cemetery?"

Before he can stop me, I lean down and flick my tongue over the piercing on his tip.

He reaches the backs of my thighs, flipping me onto my back as his heavy body rests between my legs. His breathing is steady as my legs tighten around his waist. He slowly sinks inside of me, and when my eyes roll to the back of my head, he leans down and licks me from my lips to my temple. It feels animalistic and wild, but more than anything; it feels like ownership. He squeezes my throat while riding my body, sucking and kissing the curve of my jaw while tracing his sharp canines over the bone. If I didn't know better, I'd say he was carving his name into my cheek. His tongue laps up what blood slips through, until his mouth is back on mine. He drives inside of me, our bodies slapping together with every thrust until he flips me over and directs me on top of him, yanking me back down to his lips. Every second that passes feels like hellfire rippling through my blood. I roll my body against his to the same rhythm until I feel my muscles tighten and my vision blur. He hooks his arm around my lower back, holding me in place as he drives his hips up to mine. Sweat slides between our bodies, my hair sticking to my cheeks when his lips graze the shell of my ear and he groans through a tight, "Fuck."

My stomach coils together like live electrical wire slapping over a road, desperate to find anything to destroy. He slows his pace but guides my body over his with rough precision. Every single thrust I feel his piercings graze against all of my sensitive areas. "I'm—" A rush of energy pours out of me as my muscles twitch and my thighs tremble. My orgasm erupts inside of me and I swear I pass out.

He sinks his teeth into my neck as his cock jerks, filling me to the brim. I collapse onto his chest as we both catch our breath, his giant body like my own personal bed. He reaches for something to the side before draping his hoodie on top of my body like a blanket.

I run the tip of my finger over his skull tattoo. Seconds pass before I ask, "What did Veronica want to talk to you about before we left?"

His arms are on the outer side of the hoodie, protective and strong. "You broke a generation curse that was placed on that coven."

I pause my tracing. "What did it entail?" I ask, the music from the main house somehow sounding louder than it did moments ago. Yelawolf's "You and Me." The tune is hypnotic and trance-like, and the lyrics embed themselves into the marrow of my bone. When he doesn't answer, I lean up and brush my long hair to the side, resting my face on my hand. "Tell me."

His eyes stay on mine for a moment too long before he says his next words. "The history of The Coven is fucked up. It was basically said a long time ago, that they were to never breed or have sex with someone who doesn't practice or is born into witchcraft—" He rolls his eyes. "Veronica fucked up when she got with my dad, so she 'sparked' a curse on The Daughters of Noctum. Or some shit like that. For the record, I don't believe any of this shit. I think it's all in their head, but Veronica? Veronica is obsessed with this life. She lives and breathes the belief system. Lives by the code, as she would say." He sighs, and I almost choke on my breath. "So this curse basically makes their coven barren until it's broken. No one knows how the curse was going to break, but Veronica seems to think you played a part in it."

"How? I mean, we obviously use the term *witches* lightly, right? Magic doesn't exist."

Brantley's chest vibrates. "There are new-age witches who practice a sort of witchcraft that they call *magik*, but legends have said that the ones who are chosen, which mean who basically have gifts, acquire some of the originally styled magic. It's what makes you special, Saint."

I don't know if I would call them gifts. Mine is feeling more like a curse.

"I don't know why Veronica is so set on the fact that it is now broken, but she's saying it has to do with you since it happened while you were present during The Hunt."

"So one of them is pregnant? How can she know straight away?"

Brantley shrugs. "Veronica has always known weird shit. Even when I was a kid, she would tell me stories of sorts about my past and Lucan's. She just swore me to never tell him that she was still alive. She was afraid he would want her back, and as much as she loved Lucan, she said she couldn't be in his life and live as a witch. She wanted to make right what she fucked up." His thumb is beneath my chin, gaining my attention. "You have to understand that the relationship I have with Veronica is not like a typical mother-son relationship."

"I gathered as much," I say, pushing off his chest and allowing him to slide out from me. He protests slightly. "I just got the feeling she wasn't telling me something, and that she didn't want me to leave." I pick up my clothes and shuffle them on, keeping Brantley's hoodie before tossing him his clothes.

"Oh, she didn't want you going anywhere." He changes quickly, leaving his jeans unbuttoned. "But since right now everything in the Kings' world is smooth while Bishop gets into the swing of everything, you needed to be back where you belong, and witch or no witch—" He's directly in front of me now, his fingers buried in my hair. "You belong with me. With all of us."

I could fight the smile that's demanding to be seen on my mouth, but I want him to know how happy that makes me. "I know."

We make our way back to the main house. It's quieter now, with everyone gone except Abel. I started in this world alone and spent all of my time with myself and my dogs, so being told I now have three half-siblings, it's a lot to swallow all at once. I've spent so much time with Bishop, and even with Tillie, but none with Abel.

"Hi."

He looks me over, his face a lot similar to Bishop's, only not as sharp. "Hey." His eyes move up and down my body.

"I'm very familiar with this conversation now since I have had to do it two times over." He pauses with empty bottles in one hand and trash bags in the other.

"Yeah, I figured you'd talk when you're ready, and besides, Brantley keeps the locks on you tight."

Brantley walks past him and pats his head like one would a cute puppy before disappearing upstairs.

I gather up a couple of empty Grey Goose bottles. "Who drank this much?"

"Bailey. She packs them away pretty fast." Abel dumps everything into the trash.

"Where is she?" I ask, shaking my head to stifle a laugh. I can't imagine tiny little Bailey drinking that much alcohol.

"I put her to bed." Abel turns to face me. "It's fucked-up how Hector literally had his dick in everything, and Scarlet still stays with him."

I nod as we make our way into the main house. I don't know where Brantley disappeared to, but being back here, being home, already has my soul at ease. For once, I feel like things are finally fine-tuning.

"I guess that's between her and him." I stop at the bottom of the stairs, desperate for a shower since I know my hair contains particles from the cemetery. "I'll see you in the morning?"

He smiles up at me. "Sure."

As I make my way up to my bedroom, I can't fight the feeling of Abel. He's a good kid, but there's a sadness in his soul that I'm not sure anyone can fix.

Closing my bedroom door, I breathe out a sigh of relief, finally having peace and quiet. Both Kore and Hades jump off my bed and I let out a small squeal, dropping to my knees to be slobbered in dog saliva.

"Oh, I missed you both, too." I laugh as they jump and dive over me.

The door opens from behind me and I pause, turning to look over my shoulder. Brantley's standing dressed in black. Dark jeans, hoodie, leather jacket, and military-style boots. He shakes his head though a small smile hints on the corner of his mouth. "I've got to head out, but I'll be back in a couple days."

I pause, standing to my height. "Where?"

He doesn't answer, but his eyes say the words his mouth does not. I swallow past the swell in my throat. "I haven't decided if I want you to know the full extent of what I do."

"It doesn't matter," I whisper, blinking. "It won't matter to me."

He allows the silence to spill between us before taking a step in and closer to me. "You say that you could handle me. This, what I do for The Kings and what I will most likely be doing until it's passed down to" —his mouth snaps closed— "until it no longer needs to be done, but it's not going anywhere."

I reach for his fingers and he tenses, but I feel him relax

slightly before our fingers intertwine. "I want to know what you do. I want to know everything."

"Saint…" he warns. "This is real shit."

I bring my eyes up to his, hooking my hand around the back of his neck. "When I said I would be happy with you, I meant all of the parts you aren't happy with, too." I squeeze his neck when he doesn't answer. "You don't have to live with your demons alone."

He chuckles softly, wrapping his arm around my waist to pull me closer. "I don't have demons, Dea. I *am* my demons." Chills break down over the arch of my spine. He leans down until his lips trace the shell of my ear. "Does that scare you?"

My eyes close when my blood turns warm. I shake my head.

He nibbles on my earlobe. "I'll have to see about changing that." He steps backward, rubbing the back of Hades' ear before reaching inside his pocket and tossing a small black rectangle device at me. "Your Tesla."

I squeeze the glossy black device. "Freedom?"

He snorts. "Hardly. Install the Tesla app on your phone so you don't need to use that and risk the chance of losing it. I'll see you when I get back." He turns and leaves, throwing his hoodie over his head.

A sadness throbs deep in my belly. How long has he been living this life, and just how much damage has it done to an already dark soul?

She stood at the end of the hospital bed, watching as nurses and doctors rushed around, frantic to take control of the situation.

"You need to push!" the nurse said. My fingers tingled with anticipation. I knew what was coming. Oh, but I knew what was coming. My heart raced, as did Saint's. I could feel it. Taste it as it drummed against her chest.

I stepped up beside her. "Why did you bring me here?"

I laughed so loudly that I almost thought I would interrupt what was happening in front of us. "Did you know that anything you see in your visions can't be fabricated, they can only be displayed? It's why it's called a gift. The gift of truth."

"Yes," she hissed. "I knew that, but why are you showing me this?"

"I'm not controlling this one, child."

"What do you mean?" she asked around the screams of the woman lying on the hospital bed.

"I mean, this vision is not from me, I'm merely here for observation."

I kept my eyes on the woman, my knuckles white. Saint wasn't afraid of me. I got that. It was hard to scare a girl who was raised in the belly of the beast. Nothing would frighten her. I knew that. But I also knew that nothing would separate the pet from the monster. Nothing. Not ever. I didn't even want to try; I don't think anyone did.

Until now. I couldn't say I was surprised with the extent of the effort.

"It was you who texted me, wasn't it?" *she said and the words left her mouth in a type of revelation as if she knew all along, or at the very least had an inkling. That had nothing to do with what was unraveling right now, but I answered anyway.*

I turned to face her, eyebrows raised in defiance. "It was."

"So the texts, they never existed?"

I smiled, swiping the tip of my thumb across my bottom lip. "Who says I don't exist?"

Her eyes snapped to mine, and all of the softness that she was known for vanished. Flames blazed in her eyes when her shoulders straightened. "Why?"

I folded my arms in front of myself and we both turned to watch as Veronica's face turned bright purple.

"Yes! Push! Again! Again!" the doctor yelled, anticipation driving his tone.

I decided I'd rather watch Saint's confusion, or what I was hoping was disbelief. "Why am I here watching this?"

"I wish I could help."

Pause.

"Congratulations, Mrs. Vitiosis, your baby is a girl."

CHAPTER NINE

Saint

I wake up with a scream so loud it burns the hairs on my throat. I reach for my bedside lamp with both Kore and Hades at the end of my bed, staring at me with worried eyes. "I'm okay." I scratch them both behind their ears. "I'm okay." I think over the vision I had. Whoever it is, is clearly very manipulative and skilled with what he does. I know it's not Brantley now. At first, while I was at The Coven, I assumed it was. I should have known better—but he sure did. He knew not to allow me to get too close because I would feel that it wasn't. Smart. Which makes me wonder what he's playing at now with Veronica birthing a girl. Brantley having a sister? Highly unlikely.

My door swings open and Bailey is standing at the threshold with her eye mask pulled to the top of her head, her eyes frantic and wild. She sighs, her shoulders sagging in relief when she sees me awake and cuddling the dogs. "Fucking hell, Saint! I about had a damn heart attack." She walks slowly into the room, keeping the door open. "Brantley would literally kill me if anything happened to you." She lowers herself onto my bed, massaging her temples. "I think I'm still drunk."

I look at the time displayed on my bedside clock. Five a.m. "You probably are."

"I'm seriously never drinking again." She turns to face me. "Are you okay? Was it one of your nightmares again?"

"Brantley told you about that?"

She shrugs. "Before he left, he may have briefly mentioned it."

That's when it hits me.

I shuffle backward, tucking my legs beneath my butt. "Do you know who your parents are?"

Bailey tenses, her eyes shining up to mine. "If we have a conversation about my parents, I will need to have another drink just to make me feel better."

"That bad?" I pull the covers to my chin. I haven't really spent time with Bailey or know a lot about her, but from what I've noticed with how so many love her, she's pretty special. She handles Brantley just fine, too, which is saying something. "How are you related to Brantley?"

"We're second cousins. My dad and his dad are first cousins. My dad wasn't a second-generation King, obviously, but he was a little like Spyder." Her mouth opens and then closes. "Can I ask you a question?"

"Sure." I nod.

"Abel is… hard. He had a rough start to life and didn't come into this world until very late. After losing his mom, his only family, he has struggled to find his way. I'm trying to be a good person, good girlfriend to him, but it's hard. So my question is, how do you do it with Brantley?"

I think over her words. I figured Abel had a much different

life from any of the others, but that's not because anyone told me, it's because I felt it. The heaviness in his soul. It's different, though. Brantley is fire and ice, all in one. Brantley burns on the inside but is a corpse on the outside. Abel, I can't figure out yet. Maybe if I spend more time at The Coven, I will know how to better read the emotions I'm feeling from someone.

"Brantley and Abel are very different, but I guess it just feels natural. We've only just started sleeping together and being like… this, yet it feels like we've been together since the day I walked into this house. I wish I could help you with Abel. If he needs someone to talk to, I could try?"

Bailey's eyes soften around the edges. "That would be nice. Thank you." She stands and makes her way to the door. "Don't scare me like that again. I saw my life flash before my very eyes." She's giggling when she shuts the door and I slide farther into my sheets. Bailey is not what you would expect from a Vitiosis. Not at all.

Chapter Ten

Brantley

One bullet. Nine yards. It was clean, neat, and will never be traced back. The names that roll onto the list are there for a reason, but even if they weren't, I would still do it. This is what I was manufactured for. It's what I've been training for since I first learned of TEKC. I don't flinch when the bullet explodes against their forehead. I move on, go about the rest of my life.

I push the door closed in Bishop's office in the city and head straight for the liquor cabinet.

He turns in his chair. "The Gentlemen. You told Saint that they were handled?"

I take the first swig of whiskey before pouring more. "I did."

Bishop pauses. I can practically feel his anger pulsing off his body. Possessive motherfucker. Anyone would think he's the one with Saint. Or whatever the fuck we are right now. "You've claimed her."

Another pour. Another sip. Another burn that slides down my throat to match the one I can't seem to put out inside of my head anytime she's near. "I don't need to."

"Stop being stubborn."

Finally, I turn to face him, just as he leans back in his leather chair. His eyes bore into mine.

"If you're risking her life by bringing her back too early, then we're going to have a problem."

I squeeze the glass cabinet behind me. "I've stopped trusting Veronica."

He freezes. A range of emotions pass over his face. From shock to disbelief to anger. "Why? I thought she was the one person we could trust from the outside. You told me when we were kids that we could trust her whenever the time came. What changed?"

"And we could," I say, taking the steps to the window seat behind his desk.

His eyes follow my movements eagerly, waiting for me to spill. I clench my jaw.

"But that was right up until the point where she made it very fucking apparent that Saint is far too valuable to her." I shoot back the rest of my whiskey. "I want to know why."

He tilts his head. "You know why. She broke the curse and that's why. She's obsessed with righting her wrongs within The Coven, regaining the respect she lost from all their elders."

I shake my head, rolling my lips between my teeth. "That's what I thought initially, but now something feels off. Until I figure her shit out, Saint is not to go near her."

Bishop spreads his legs wide, and I scowl at him. "Don't fucking man spread me."

"What?" He smirks, closing them again.

I shake my head, flipping him off. "Madison not servicing that dick she so viciously claimed?"

He lets out a pained groan. "She's fucking killing me, like usual."

"Doesn't matter." I shake my head, thinking about pouring that third finger. "You're both in it for the long haul."

Bishop rubs his hands over his chin. "I'm going to fuck up this dad shit."

I roll my eyes. "You're running a secret elitist cult that has been passed down from generation to generation. Raising kids will be the easiest thing you do." I lean back against the glass, my eyes heavy and mind lost. I need to know why Veronica wanted Saint so badly, and I'm not for a fucking second buying her curse shit.

"What if they're twin girls?" he yells, raising his hands. "I'm fucked."

"No, if they're girls, they'll be the most protected little brats in the entire fucking world. Chill."

"I don't know, man. Tillie is a natural. Madison, not so much. And she and I are still not on good terms. We barely tolerate each other in the same room."

"But you love her."

Instant. "Yes."

"And she loves you. So you're both fucked." I sigh, resting my elbows on my knees. "Which is why I need to figure this shit out with Saint."

"Would it be so fucking bad to have her?"

I bore my eyes into his, tensing my fist around my empty glass. I need that third. "Yes. It would. I can't give her the feelings she is going to want from me, B." I point to my chest. "Dead as fuck inside, remember?"

He reaches for the pack of cigarettes on his desk, banging

it against his chest before placing one in his mouth and lighting it. He inhales the toxic smoke.

"Saint will kill you for smoking that shit one day."

He blows out. "I've cut back to five a day just to make her happy." His knee jiggles. "There's movement still going on in Riveredge that we need to fix." Riveredge is the official name of the west side of Riverside. "The Gentlemen want your head and I don't think they're going to settle until they have it. There's also the pressing issue of who it is that is feeding them information. There's someone else working against us in this and we need to find out who, and I don't mean someone in our Kings' world."

The door opens behind him, but neither of us bother to see who it is. Only a King would walk into this office without knocking.

"Bishop, we have the scan today to see what the genders are."

His eyes straight up dilate in front of me. I snicker, leaning back. And Madison. Madison would walk into this office without knocking. He looks over his shoulder. "That's not until three p.m."

She squeezes the door handle. "I know. I'm going over to see Saint, so can you pick me up from there?" My lips roll between my teeth to stifle a laugh.

"Yes, Kitty. I will pick you up from there. Is that fucking all?"

I sigh, leaning back and attempting to block them out.

She smiles sweetly. "That's all." Before she gets to slam the door in his face, Nate and Eli walk in. They both take a seat on one of the many chairs scattered in the room.

"Tillie is at your house," Nate says, nudging his head at me.

"Figured."

"Did we all pick the worst fucking girls to settle with? They're all different, but none of them are compliant. They all wanna fight, and aside from that, why the fuck do they all get along so painfully well? I'm telling you all now, we're fucked.

They're like a tiny gang, and the only one we don't have control over. Fuck." Bishop squashes his cigarette in his ashtray.

"Oh, did you finally claim Saint?" Eli asks with a bold smirk.

"I don't fucking need to. When is your little brain going to get that?"

Eli winks at me. "Maybe when I see it. Live, preferably."

Bishop shakes his head, squeezing his eyes with his index finger and thumb. "There's something we need to talk about. It involves" —his eyes go to Eli— "you."

Eli's smirk falters. "What?"

Just as Bishop opens his mouth, his office phone blares off and he answers, "What?"

"Are you all there?" Hector says, but his voice sounds different. Strained and exhausted. "There's something I need to tell you all."

CHAPTER ELEVEN

Saint

I REMEMBER WATCHING *Coyote Ugly* AND THINKING HOW IT must feel to have a group of friends you could trust. Like always, I'd try to relate with the characters I'd be watching, since it's about as close as I would get to feeling it, but it was always a fleeting moment. So I started reading, which gave me more in-depth feelings of what it felt like to live a life that isn't yours to live. Tillie and Madison haven't been in my life for long, but to imagine my life without them in it would cripple me.

We're dressed up and I don't know why. Denim washed Levi's with a slit right below my left ass cheek, a black drop-top, and a Gucci belt is secured around my waist. I'm wearing black heels with thin straps crisscrossing over the top of my foot that I hadn't been able to find an occasion to wear them for, and my hair and makeup are probably the best they have ever looked.

"Daddy Bran Bran left the Tesla." Tillie wiggles the "key" to both Madison and me, just as Bailey walks into the room dressed and ready. "We are getting into so much trouble tonight."

Madison finishes her lipstick, popping her mouth open. "We're having a boy and girl." She hasn't said much since Bishop dropped her back off after her scan. She almost seems more tense than usual, which I'm beginning to realize that when she's tense, that means Bishop is going to get grief.

"Madison!" My heart swells. "Congratulations!" It takes me a second to realize her shoulders are tight and her brows are knotted together in distress. "Wait, what's wrong?"

She flicks her perfectly manicured fingernails. "I'm so happy, Saint. So happy." There's a long pause, and I'm almost afraid of what she's going to follow up with. "But I don't know how to fix us."

Tillie and Bailey move in closer and I lean against my dresser to face where she's sitting on the stool.

"I would usually say give him time, but I don't think you should." I squeeze the wood of my vanity, stained a pure white. "In the weeks I have been around my gloriously unique brother, I have found one thing that is constant, and that is he likes honesty, despite the fact he's so good at keeping secrets. I think you need to bare it all with him. I've seen him when you weren't here, Madison." I bore my eyes into hers. "It broke me in one thousand different places to see him the way he was."

Tillie clears her throat. "Are you saying that she should maul him?"

Bailey snickers, blowing out a catcall.

"I am." I shrug. "Maul. Him." I smile down at her. "Make him realize what he's been missing for so long."

"Fine." Madison brushes back her hair. "But for right now, we're getting you into trouble. Which, by the way," she turns and narrows her eyes at Tillie, "why are we playing with Brantley like this?"

"Simple!" Tillie says matter-of-factly. "He shouldn't have fucking allowed her to be taken away."

I push off the vanity and we all make our way out of my bedroom and down the gloomy hallway. Heels click against the ancient wood floors when we hit the foyer.

Bailey pauses, grabbing my arm. "Wait! We need some pre-drinks." She dips into the kitchen and I laugh, shaking my head.

"Bays! Hurry up! I'm scared right now that he's going to come home, take one look at Saint, and ruin our night!" Tillie calls out loudly, fixing her hair in the large Victorian-style antique mirror that hangs on the wall.

"Too late!" Brantley slams the front door closed just as Bailey is rounding the corner, the cheesy smile she had on her face sliding off like makeup on a rainy day. She lowers the two bottles of vodka as we all jump in place, turning to face a furious—no, *livid,* looking Brantley. "Where in the fuck do you think you're all going? Hmmm?"

Bishop and Nate step through the front door and pause, their eyes flying around the group of us.

Bishop's eyes turn to slits on Madison before going back to Nate. "See? The fuck did I just say?"

Nate's brows are raised at Tillie, but he doesn't do anything to hide the tiny smirk on the corner of his mouth. "And where the fuck do you think you're going pregnant that doesn't involve riding on my dick?"

"And, we're caught," Madison whispers.

Brantley's dark eyes hit me and I swear I feel the reverberations throughout my bones. He doesn't need to say anything, because I already know he's pissed.

"We were going to the movies…" Bailey lies effortlessly, attempting to save us.

"Yeah?" Brantley's eyes remain painfully focused on me, but

he's still talking to Bailey. "You're a shit liar, Bailey. I suggest you work on that so you don't disgrace our family name."

Bailey flicks off the cap with her finger and raises the bottle to her lips. "Oh well, my bitches. I tried."

Brantley points to the back patio. "Outside. Now."

"Wait—shit!" Tillie calls out just as I turn around, but it's too late. I forgot all about the massive slit in my jeans beneath my ass cheek.

Hands are at the back of my neck. "Out-fucking-side." He shoves me forward and I turn to look over my shoulder to see him pointing at Tillie. "You better beat her ass tonight, Nate, or I swear to God…"

Tillie blows Brantley a kiss. "Then don't try to take her away from her family again!"

I hit the back doors and the cool air whips me across the face. "What's your problem?" I turn to face him, but it's too late. His hand is already on my mouth.

"Shut the fuck up and listen to me, because I've been real patient with you so far, but that ends now."

My breathing hitches, my chest swelling against his when he smashes me against the wall. His other hand dips into the slit in my jeans and he squeezes the fat on my ass. And there is a decent amount of fat on my ass.

"You cannot walk around like this without me near you. If someone touches you while I'm not there." He leans down and forces my body closer to his. "How the fuck am I supposed to kill him?" He closes his eyes and I almost think he's counting in his head. "Give me a fucking minute to calm down."

I stay in this position, his hand over my mouth and his other tight on my ass. Slowly, I feel the tension release and his thumb work circles over the curve. "

"There are people who want to hurt me, Saint, and the only way they can do that is through you. Do you understand?"

I nod.

"Good." He releases my mouth, moving his arm around my neck to pull me in farther. I need to crank my head to look up to his full height.

"Is that it?" I brave. "That's all the trouble I'm in?"

He laughs. "Oh, for now." His dimples sink into either side of his face. "This will be finished in bed later, but for right now—" His mouth is on my earlobe as he nibbles on the thin skin. He whispers breathless words into my ear and I smirk, bringing my arm up to hook around his back. *I win.*

"Yo, we've got a problem." Nate opens the door wide. He looks at Brantley. "Your mom is here."

"What?" Brantley tugs me under his arm and moves us farther inside, his footsteps far too wide for me to catch up fast enough.

There, standing at the threshold of the front door, in all her dark-haired beauty is Veronica—I don't even know her last name.

"Well," she says, looking around at us all. "I'm glad you're all here because I've got something to say." I squeeze into Brantley, staggering closer to his protection. My hand ducks beneath his hoodie until my palm is pressed flat against his abs. I relax.

"What the fuck do you want?" Brantley moves me behind his body slightly, ever my crazed monster. "You really need to call before making appearances." The room is still, the silence almost unbearable. My heart rate quickens and a bead of sweat falls down my temple. *I never sweat.*

"Mmmm, no, actually, I don't." Her almond eyes slowly swing to me. "Saint, I need you to come back to The Coven."

I freeze.

Brantley takes one step closer to Veronica. "No, she's not."

Everything suddenly moves in slow motion. Her eyes swing to Brantley, the corner of her mouth tilting up in a harsh curve, flashing her obscenely straight teeth. Veneers. They have to be. But then Brantley's is the same—why am I so distracted!

"Actually, yes she is, and you're going to let her go, Brantley…" Her words are like blades running down the apex of my spine.

"I will kill you, your entire coven, and anyone else who tries to take her from me, Veronica, and you fucking know it."

"Mhhm, you're right, son, I do know it." The smile has not once left her lips, and as each passing second goes by, I find myself more and more anxious. "Which is why I'm going to disclose to you something you were to never find out." She tucks her lips between her teeth, as if she's anticipating to finally say something she's been holding on to for years.

Bishop growls, "Spit it the fuck out, Veronica. I'm sick of the theatrics."

She raises her coffin-shaped nail. "Saint is my daughter." Her eyes go to Brantley. "Your half sister."

My hand slips out from beneath his hoodie, but Brantley's grip on me remains. "You're lying."

"Am I?"

Bishop steps forward. "I've heard enough. What the fuck are you talking about and you better have some proof to back up these claims. No one comes onto our territory and tries to drop a fucking bomb like that."

I go to pull away from Brantley again, but his grip on me tightens. I can almost hear him inside my head. *Don't you fucking dare fall for her shit.*

"Oh, I do…" She presents a manila folder to Bishop, but Brantley snatches it out of her hands.

I take this moment to step well away from Brantley. My mind is closing in around me and everyone that is here no longer exists.

"Hey!" Madison and Tillie are suddenly on either side of me. "It's going to be fine."

"We can do another test, or you can call them, if you like." Her eyes come to me. "But something tells me you won't need to."

Instantly, I feel all eyes on me.

I begin stepping backward, but my knees buckle and I fall to the ground. Tears pour from my cheeks as pain I never thought existed erupts inside my chest. *No. No. No.* "She's not lying."

"What?" Brantley snaps at me. "What the fuck do you mean 'she's not lying.'"

"I saw it, Brantley!" I glare up at him. "In my vision. I didn't tell you this, but I've been seeing you almost every night that I close my eyes. Those texts I told you I was receiving? It was from—whoever that is coming to me. I don't know, I can't explain it. But I had a vision of her giving birth to a girl. *A girl.*"

Tillie stands to her full height, her hands balling into fists on her sides. "Nate, a word?"

They both disappear down a long hallway and Madison grabs me under my arm, pulling me back to my feet.

"It's going to be okay, Saint."

I place my hand on top of hers, unable to look at Brantley. "She's right. My visions can't be manipulated truth, we all know that."

Brantley says nothing.

Bishop freezes.

I straighten my shoulders. "I will leave with you."

"What the fuck! Fuck! No!" Bishop yells, but his words are cut off when Brantley launches forward, his hand around Veronica's throat.

He squeezes. "I'm going to rip your fucking heart out so you know exactly how I feel right now. Whether it's tomorrow. Two days from now. Months. I hope you remember this exact moment, and I hope it haunts you until I come for you—and make no mistake, Mother, I will come for you." He shoves her away. My lips tremble as he pushes past me. Not another glance. Not a smidge of acknowledgment. Just pure, undiluted coldness. As if I'm no longer his Dea.

Which I'm not.

Veronica curves her finger at me. I can't fight the tears anymore as they slide down both cheeks. My heart crumbles. My throat tightens as air struggles to come in. I want to seek out Brantley. *I need him.* But I can't. I can't. Because everything was a lie. The reason why we feel so close and why I am so co-dependent on him is because he is my half brother.

My hand flies up to my mouth to stop the bile that's crawling up my throat, threatening to spill all over the floor. Dashing down the hallway and into the guest bathroom, I kick open the toilet bowl and watch as everything I have eaten in the last twenty-four hours exits. I hit the lever, turn back around, and close the toilet, resting on top. My fingers shake as I swipe the tears from my eyes.

"Saint…" Madison is at the door. She enters and closes it tightly before kneeling in front of me. "We will figure this out. I promise." She rests her hand on my thigh, taking my shaking fingers into the palm of her hand. I trust Madison with my life. She's one of the strongest women I have the pleasure of knowing, but will it still be the same now? I no longer belong here. At that thought, my lip trembles and another wave of pain washes over me.

"He's my half brother, Madison."

She winces and all of the life that lived inside of me empties. "I slept with my half brother."

She blows out a steady breath of air. "You didn't know it at the time. You and Brantley are not to blame for this. This is on Veronica and fucking Hector. I swear that man needs to be put to sleep once and for all."

Even though I hear the words she's saying, I don't want to take them in. I can't see past the fact of what I have done.

"You don't have to go with her, Saint. If you don't want to live here, you can move in with Bishop and me. You know he will do anything for you."

I squeeze her hand with mine. "She won't stop. She's done this for a reason, and I need to know what that reason is."

Madison tilts her head. "You're going there to find out?"

I tuck my hair behind my ear and tug on the roll of toilet paper to wipe my face. "Yes. And then when I find out why I'm getting visions of her and who this man is I keep seeing—" I pause, closing my mouth. Scorching flames blister over my throat and I can't find the words to say. My heart is literally broken. I rest my palm over my chest and feel the slowing pitter-patter of beats in my chest. It feels abnormal.

I can't say the words to her.

"Then you will come with Bishop and me?"

I smile, even though it physically pains me to do so. "Yes, then I will."

We both stand and make our way back out to the main entrance area of the house. Deep inside my head, I hoped I'd walk out to a bloodbath, but then I would never get the answers I need.

Bishop's eyes run over me quickly before he turns back to Veronica. "You can't take her."

I wipe the tears from my cheeks before looking up at Veronica. "It's fine, Bishop. I'll—I'll be fine." I pull both Tillie and Madison, and then finally Bailey into a hug. "Where's Abel?"

"I don't know," Bailey says absently, squeezing her eyes closed before opening them. "It's why I wanted to go out tonight to distract me from the fact I haven't heard from him."

Everything she says is white noise to me. Maybe I'm being selfish, or maybe it's my defense mechanism kicking in, but I can't hear anything or see anyone past the fact Brantley is my *half brother*.

 I finally bring my hands to Bishop, whose eyes are pained and hard on me. He shakes his head, his jaw clenched and his cheeks tight. He's angry. I know that. They all are.

 I run my thumbs over his cheeks, keeping eye contact. *I'll be fine.*

 He relaxes slightly.

 "All right, I don't have all night and we have work to do." Veronica gestures to a black Range Rover. "Come on, Hecate. Let's get you home."

CHAPTER TWELVE

Brantley

I had two options before I walked into The Palace. One, I could kill Hector on the spot and talk later, or two, I could wait. Study his answers, move around the words he says to find the truth in his lies. He's good at that. Lying. Bishop is filling Hector in on what happened, though he doesn't need to. Hector is no longer holding the gavel, but Bishop being Bishop, he wants to keep his father close.

Me? Not so much.

"There's something I didn't tell you…" I say to Bishop, my finger working my upper lip to hide the smirk on my face. If I don't think about her, about everything that just happened, it doesn't exist. She never existed.

Bishop's eyes narrow on me, pausing mid-sentence with Hector. Hector shuffles in his seat. "You shouldn't."

I glare at Hector. "Oh, no… I should. You see, I wanted to

be the one to destroy you if you had done anything to put Saint in harm's way, but I realized something. You were counting on that. Because if there's one thing you cannot stand, that's Bishop being angry with you."

"What the fuck are you both talking about?" Bishop hisses, and Nate moves around the other side of Hector. Nate is like a shark when it comes to murder. He can smell it. Sense it. Revel in it. *Feast in it*. He's exactly as his last name is translated. *Evil*.

"When I chased him out of the ceremony, he had taken Saint out. Away."

Bishop leans in closer.

"Veronica stepped out of the passenger seat of the town car he had her in, but I'm guessing Hector was shocked to see her. I'm thinking he had another plan for her." I kick my leg out in front of me. "Am I right?"

Hector's face falls. Over the years, time has been good to the old king. He looks painfully similar to Bishop, only older. Side-shaved head, tattoos over his neck and some on his face, built strong and tough. When we were kids, there was nothing scarier than being stared at by Hector Hayes. The problem with fear is, if you show any weakness, it does just that. Weakens.

"I knew she was there, Brantley. What I didn't expect to see was you. We had all planned it, that Veronica was going to take her. Why would I try to do anything else?"

My eyes narrow. I've been spending all of my days trying to figure out why he seemed shocked and where he could have been possibly taking Saint when all along, I could have played right into his hand.

My fists clench to my sides.

Bishop interrupts, "Why? Why were you taking her to Veronica when we had already planned her to take Saint? Did you know she was your other lover's baby mama? Seriously, Dad—" Bishop glares at him. "I've had about enough finding out about all these fucking love children." Their bickering dies out, and everything inside my head seems to tick left to right like collision balls. The corners of my vision begin to darken.

"Bishop," I say smoothly, but the indents of crescent moons into my palms claim anything but. "He has four seconds to explain his redemption before I kill him." I bring my eyes to his. "And you know I will."

Three.

Two.

"I had planned it with Veronica before the ceremony. She and I had an understanding."

"So before you told us the plan, you had already set it up? So you knew there would be Gentlemen there that night?"

"Son." Hector looks to Bishop. "The Gentlemen aren't our only enemies right now. And to answer your question, yes, because I knew you would go along with it to protect her." Hector's eyes come to mine.

My lip curls into a half-smile. His eyes travel down my chest and to the button of my jeans. I tap at the black button clipped there.

Hector stares up at me, exposing a glimpse of the man everyone fears. He nods.

Chapter Thirteen

S*aint*

Since arriving last night, I've thought a lot about the past few hours. Even now as I stare back at myself in the mirror, holding a compact in my hand, my mind can't seem to wrap around the revelations Veronica spilled out. Upon her saying those words, I think I lost a bit of myself. Of who I had become.

I swipe the makeup sponge over my cheek, knowing I should be dabbing, but struggling to find even a smudge of energy to care. The smooth pasty white covers my skin perfectly, but I don't think it's going to be enough to hide the dark circles sunken beneath my eyes. I let out a sigh, placing the compact back onto my vanity and turning in my seat. Unable to speak, or to so much as undress out of my pajamas, I find myself looking around the bedroom I once found comfort in. Annoyingly so, I continue to find comfort in. The plants offer the oxygen that

I can't seem to breathe in. Every time I think of last night, my stomach cramps and my toes curl. The pain is too much for me to face. I feel bruised, battered, and worn down to my very bones.

There's a knock on my door. I swallow past the heavy swell in my throat, but refuse to answer. It opens anyway.

"Hey, girl…" Ophelia whispers quietly. "Can I come in?"

I nod. I like Ophelia's company. I always have.

The door closes behind her and she patters deeper into my room until she's seated on my bed. "How are you holding up?"

I turn in my chair. She's wearing yoga pants and an oversized cardigan, almost matching my style. "Not really." My lashes fan out over my cheeks. "But I'm glad to see you again."

She waves me off, rolling her eyes. "Pshhh. You're stuck with me—" She leans forward. "Forever. But I just want to check on you. These halls are a little more full these days." Her eyes glass over. "So stick near me, okay?"

I don't bother to ask her what she means, only nod and allow her to guide me downstairs.

⁓

She wasn't lying when she said the halls were busier. I pause at the threshold of where the kitchen meets the foyer, shuffling in my step. "Ah…"

"Saint," Veronica purrs from the head of the dining table. It might just be the largest dining table I have ever seen. With the simplicity of timber legs but the elegance of a marble top, it fits the decor of this mansion well. "Take a seat here." She kicks out the chair beside her and pats a perfectly manicured hand over said elegance.

My feet refuse to move because my eyes are stuck on the man beside her. His shoulders are broad. They may match the same broadness as Brantley, but what they lack is the confidence and power that he carries on his. His eyes are blue. The kind of blue you can almost call basic because it's the common color you always find. He reminds me of a football player. Maybe young. Maybe my age. His face is strong and thick—if that even makes sense—and his skin is covered in tattoos.

Veronica obviously catches me staring. "Saint, this is Samael. Samael, Saint, though I'm sure he recognizes you, I'm sure you do not him."

I finally bring my eyes to hers, confused. "What?"

She slides a perfect round grape between the swell of her lips. "Samael was at The Hunt." That's when recognition washes over me and I finally make my way to the chair, pulling it out and taking a seat.

I haven't finished spooning toasted granola into my bowl when I catch him watching me. He studies me closely. A little too closely. It's as though he has read the cheat sheet of my soul. "Nice to see you again, Samael." I pluck exactly three grapes from the bundle and scatter them onto my granola before spooning a dollop of yogurt on top. The clinking of my spoon hitting the ceramic edges of my bowl somehow sounds loud.

"Mor—" He's about to answer me when he's interrupted. I don't bother to turn around. I already know the scowl that will be displayed across Frankie's face. She never makes an effort to hide it.

"Did I miss something?"

I run the tip of my tongue over the soft inner skin of my lip before sinking my teeth in.

"Good to see you again, Saint." Samael shocks me, and instantly I don't care about Frankie's obvious and tiresome hostility.

I spoon-feed myself—stress does not suppress my appetite—if anything, it incites it. There are two other men beside him. Both on the leaner side and neither very attractive. Though the way Alessi is giggling as one of them is leaned into her ear would prove she would say otherwise.

"You still hungry?" he asks, his voice toneless. Bland, yet I want to talk with him. Maybe it'll be easy to.

"You can tell?" I joke, though my face remains frozen. I know exactly what I look like right now. Like a dead zombie that has shed too many tears for her cheeks to handle.

He leans forward and I hold my breath. He slides my plate to the side and places his in front of me. It's filled with—

"What is this?"

Samael leans back in his chair, an easy smile on his mouth. "It's a pancake."

"Hmmm," I murmur, picking up my fork and poking at the surface. It wiggles like jelly after every nudge. "Seems a little bit too thick to be a pancake?"

"It's a Japanese pancake. Try it." He crosses his large arms in front of himself as I poke at it again. Maple syrup has already been poured over the melted butter pat on the top. I sink my knife into it and cut a tiny triangle, bringing it to my mouth. It dissolves in a cloud-like texture, leaving a sweet and subtle savory taste behind.

A small moan slips from me as my shoulders sag and my cheeks heat. "Oh my God." I cut another piece. Eat. Moan. My neck heats. Another. Eat. Moan. I feel the color washing back over my face. Food. Food mends a broken heart. "This is the best thing I have ever tasted." I swipe the residue of syrup off my lips and lean back in my chair.

Veronica giggles. "Good. You're both getting on. That's very good." She brings her mug to her lips and blows into it. "Very good. Saint, why don't you take Sam for a walk through the garden? I'm sure he would love that."

Sam's eyes flick to Veronica. "Ah, you don't have to—"

"It's fine," I say, standing from my chair. "I owe you after that."

Sam looks between Veronica and me before finally standing and coming to stand next to me.

"Don't say a word, Frankie." Veronica smiles up at us both sweetly. "If you still want your teeth."

Frankie stomps around the table and takes the spot where Sam was, dumping her plate onto it. She listens to Veronica, though. She doesn't say another word.

Chapter Fourteen

Saint

"So, this garden?" Sam says, his fingertip grazing the sharp edge of a stray leaf from a Devil's Ivy. "Is there something special about it?"

I wrap my arms around myself to stop the cold from creeping in. "I don't know. You tell me, you're the professional man witch…"

He raises an eyebrow at me while taking a seat on the bench that's in the center of the rounded greenhouse. "I get the feeling you don't want to be here."

"Hmmm." I sit beside him, aware how close our fingers came to touching. "It's not that I don't want to. I love The Coven. It gives me a sense of self that's away from my usual life—but…"

He hangs onto my words as I try to find the next ones.

"I guess you could say I found out some information recently that flipped my world upside down and now I'm trying to live with it." He doesn't answer. I appreciate that. I'm not talking for answers. I'm not looking for anything.

He crosses his leg over his knee, turning inward toward me. He's dressed in a suit. I have to stop the comparisons that whiz through my brain. The complete opposite to Brantley. Might be good to talk with someone who shares no resemblance to my deepest and dirtiest nightmare. "You want to talk about it?"

"Nope." I keep my eyes locked on the peace lily in front of me. How ironic. "Tell me why Frankie is obsessed with you." I say, suddenly desperate to focus on anything but Brantley.

Sam laughs, his head tilting back. "Ah, Frankie. She and I have known each other for a little while. I guess she doesn't like being told no."

"So you and her?"

He stares at me. "There is no you and her." I find his words trustworthy, but then maybe that's what he wants me to think.

"Oh, there you two are!" Veronica sashays through the entrance with a train of black satin not far behind. "I got an interesting invite from The Kings." I pause. I've ignored all of Bishop and Madison's texts, even Tillie's. The truth is, the only reason why I was so quick to jump into the car with Veronica is because I thought the memories might choke me. All of them remind me of the life I knew in one way or another. I can't stomach them right now. I hope they will understand.

"What?" I whisper, though I'm not sure they heard.

Veronica picks up a rose gold watering can and begins showering the greenery. "The reopening of the high school and the college. They would like us to be there, along with my friends."

"Why?" Sam asks dubiously.

"Well, the invite extended to all of the… families that reside in Riverside, and on the outskirts, too. I guess we are only part of that." She places the can back down and turns to look at me. "It's not for another two weeks, Saint. Until then, we can focus on you learning your craft a bit more and you can spend time with Sam and your sisters." Veronica leans down, her fingers on my knee and her eyes pointedly on mine. "And when you show up to that ball, my dear," the edge of her nail glides down my cheek, "we're going to make them wish they never lied to you." She pushes off me and pats my head. "We're having a feast tonight. Wear your best attire." She disappears the way she came, like a tornado sweeping through an innocent village and taking any and all prisoners. As time goes on, I've found my level of trust and admiration for Veronica fluctuate. There's an invisible vise sealed around my heart that will never let her in. I know it will never give it up.

Samael stands. "I've got to hit the gym. I'll see you later?"

I smile up at him, though it doesn't go unnoticed how heavy the edges of my mouth are. As if I have to force it. "Sure." Once he has gone, I close my eyes and count to ten. I know I should check my phone. I should let him know I'm safe.

I unlock my phone and stare down at the blank screen. White. Nothing but the black clock numbers stare back at me. I swipe it unlocked and open a new message to Bishop.

Me: I'm ok. I need time.

Once I hit send, I place my phone onto the seat and move toward the cuttings of plants that are sitting in glass vases. Some I don't recognize. Actually, all I don't. Pink and whites ripple through the leaves of one, while another is completely black. Even darker than the black raven plant. I tap my fingers against the counter. My thumbs drum to a beat, grazing against the imposed carvings in the wood.

I tilt my head and move the plants and vases away, desperate to see what the images are or what they make up. Patterns connecting together are carved into the wood. I don't know what I'm supposed to fill my time with during the day here, so I make my way back up to my bedroom, ignoring the laughter and chatter coming from the lounge and lock my door as soon as I'm safe inside. A sigh of relief douses over me. My fingers curl until my nails dig into the wood. "You can do this." I push off and head to my bathroom, busying myself with filling the tub with scorching hot water. I pour in some essential oils and petals from a mini rosebush off the counter and watch as the water level rises. It's ironic how this tub feels like my emotions. I'm filling to the top slowly, and I know that once it reaches the top, everything is going to topple over and I'm going to expose my true feelings for everyone to see. I've never been good at being something I am not. I don't last very long lying, and when I do, I feel a churn in my belly saying it's wrong. I hate injustice and want to help people who have been wronged, but when it comes to helping myself, I can't seem to find that same fight.

Pulling open the top drawer, I find a pack of matches and begin lighting the wicks of the candles that are scattered around. It is lovely in here, though not as nice as the one back in the manor. Picking up my phone, I snap a photo of the bath, now filled with crimson rose petals floating in the soapy water. I scroll through Instagram and get ready to type my second post. My fingers hover over the keys. My eyes are heavy, needing sleep that no amount of time could ever satiate.

Am I dreaming, or am I still awake?

I type out the caption… *A dream is just a nightmare wearing makeup.*

I push post and slowly remove my clothes until they're a pool around my feet. I dip my first toe into the water and wince when the sting grips me, but continue to sink my whole body in, ignoring the bites of heat. My phone begins vibrating beside me, but I close my eyes to ignore it. I've become good at disregarding that damn vibrate. Sinking deeper into the water, I allow it to wash over me, my tears floating away with the rose petals. No one will know I've been crying deep in here. There's nothing but white noise and the distinct dripping of the water falling into the tub. I arise and swipe the excess from my face, finally snatching my phone when I notice it's still popping off. I unlock and go to Instagram.

So.

Many.

Comments.

But one sticks out. It isn't because the words are kind, or that she is a friend. It's that the poster reads @Frankenstein. I curl my lip. **Are you alone, or did Samael follow you in there, too? Haven't seen him since you both disappeared into the Garden of Eden.**

I pause.

I know that realistically speaking, she can say what she wants about Sam and me. That it's no one's concern anymore. I know I don't have to worry about Brantley flipping out or calling me like a psychopath, or even worse, appearing here and causing a scene. My heart rate beats at the same tempo as the tap. I don't have to worry because I'm not his problem anymore. I'm much worse. I'm—I can't even say it.

I ignore her comment and go through the likes.

@kingmadison I miss you. A sincere smile comes onto my face. One that doesn't feel heavy or forced. **@kingtillie we're fighting.** I roll my eyes at her comment. She may not be my biological sister anymore, but blood isn't thicker than a soul bond. I hit reply to them both. **@saintvitiosis why have you both changed your usernames?** Am I missing something already? I finish up in my bath and don't slide out until the water turns cold and my fingers have aged one thousand years. I've just changed into a new set of clothes when there's a knock on my door.

I plaster a fake smile onto my face. "Come in." I have to swallow the bitterness I'm holding in my gut. I don't want to be around anyone right now. Or ever, maybe. There's something inside of me that has been taken. The light. It wasn't Brantley's darkness that blew my light out, it was the truth.

"So, we're bringing you snacks, movies, and water, because I love you, but I don't think alcohol is a good idea with the state you're in." Ophelia walks into my bedroom like she owns it, placing bags of junk food on my bed, Ivy following closely behind her. Ivy pushes her glasses up the bridge of her nose and tucks her shoulder-length hair behind one ear.

Ophelia looks between us. "Ivy is cool. She is team you."

I smile at Ivy and she slowly moves onto the edge of my bed while Ophelia gets comfortable and turns on the TV that's in the corner of my bedroom.

"So what are we watching?" I ask, taking three Cheetos out of the bag and nibbling on them.

"Some slasher-type shit."

I choke on my "food" and we both burst out laughing. I think I even saw Ivy shed a small hint of laughter.

Chapter Fifteen

Saint

All three of us fell asleep mid-movie last night. When I say mid-movie, I don't mean the slasher one, since Ophelia got scared and wanted to change it to something happy and cheerful, so we were stuck watching old reruns of *South Park*. I push off my mattress, careful not to wake Ivy and Ophelia, who are both snoring peacefully in my bed. Cheetos are tangled in Ophelia's hair, with a spoon of ice cream sticking to Ivy's cheek. The glue courtesy of Ben and Jerry. We skipped dinner last night. I would do it again and again because I've come to realize that Ophelia, and I'm hoping Ivy, too, soon, will be a lifetime friend. A forever friend. I agree that people come into your life at certain parts to either help you or to teach you, but there are other people who come into your life and you know they're there to stay. Ophelia is one of those people.

I move through the day seamlessly. Starting with working

out, eating lunch, and then Veronica pulls me aside for two hours to work on strengthening my "skill." I ask her what this looks like, and she says I will know when I can harness the voices wherever I am and whenever I want. I make it very clear that under no circumstances will I ever want to do that.

She's adamant.

I pick up the knife and fork on the table during dinner, closing my eyes and breathing in the crisp air. We're two weeks away from Thanksgiving, so the weather is cooler. Every now and then, snowflakes fall onto the green grass, and it only makes that pit in my belly ache even more. We're all sitting outside on the patio tonight, with a fire pit burning to the side as dinner begins to be served. Roast chicken, potatoes, salad, and freshly baked bread. The sun is just beginning to set behind the thick forest trees, and even now, sitting here with my coven, there's an emptiness that throbs in my belly. I miss my family. I miss my home. An invisible fist clenches around my heart when I'm reminded that Brantley won't want me back. Not now. Not even as a blood relation. Even then, I already know that seeing him again, let alone living with him, would just be a sickening reminder of what we did. We may not have known, and it may not have been our fault, but it had been done. Many times.

I swallow a gulp of Pinot from my goblet to stop the vomit from rising up my throat, swiping my bottom lip with my thumb. I need something to take away the pain. To scrub off the sticky residue that clings to my thoughts. Anything. I'd do anything to wash myself clean of that. My heart thunders in my chest, though I'm sure it will be the last beats it will do. I know what I must do.

Thud.
Thud.
Thud.

Silence.

I bring my eyes up to the person sitting opposite me at the dinner table, his glass pressed to his lips. His eyes are already on mine, flames and fire licking around the edges. I pick up my goblet and take another large swig.

Another.

Another.

Reaching for the wine decanter, I pour more Pinot into my goblet-style glass until it fills to the brink. *Blood.* Brantley's blood. I take four gulps while maintaining eye contact with Sam.

I know what I must do.

I must move on.

Dinner begins to come out in platters—mini roasted chicken, vegetables, and salad bowls for each of us. Veronica and Frankie are talking amongst each other, while Ophelia and Alessi gossip. Ivy is sitting beside me, quiet. Listening. Always silent. The other two men are on either side of Sam, losing themselves in their food.

"So," I say, trying one simple word, even though I don't want to say anything at all.

Silence.

"So," Sam urges, and his tongue drags over his bottom lip. "You feel like dessert tonight?" I don't know if the table chatter has quietened or if I'm blocking everyone out.

I breathe in and out. Steady. Patient. *Silent.* "Yes."

The corners of his mouth turn up as he leans back in his chair. "Impressed."

I pick up my goblet. "If that's true, Samael, then you're too easy for my taste…" I reply in jest, hiding the half-smile behind my glass, but I know deep down it wasn't entirely a joke. Thankfully, he does.

He laughs loudly, his head tilting back. He doesn't

recollect himself for a couple of seconds and, in my honest opinion, too long to be laughing at something that was an underlying insult. And it wasn't that funny. "Hmmm, I think you and I are going to get on just fine."

I smile sweetly at him. "I'm sure we will." I've never felt more like a Hayes than during this encounter.

∽

This is my routine for the next couple of weeks. I work out, eat, work with Veronica, have dinner and throw words back and forth with Sam, and then excuse myself to my bedroom. I bathe, and then Ophelia and Ivy come in and we watch a new movie. At first, it was partially annoying to me. I needed to be alone with my thoughts. With my tears. I didn't want people to see the pain I felt. I wanted to close my bedroom door and scream into my pillow until my throat bled. Now, I look forward to Ophelia and Ivy's nightly sleepovers. I think they knew I needed it, too. Ivy is still not chatty, but she has started smiling at me now, and her eyes. Her eyes light up whenever Ophelia and I are talking about something. She wants to engage, I'm just not sure why she doesn't, and I feel it might be rude to wait this long to bring it up. Sam and I have become comfortable with each other. Him more than me. I know he's trying to break me open. Maybe learn things about me. He makes an effort to ask enough questions whenever we're together alone—which isn't often. I asked Veronica about it one day and she said that Sam showing an interest in anything is something special and that I should be grateful. Apparently, male witches are all aloof and bitter. I can't imagine why.

Veronica is far too good at hiding her emotions. It's why I've never been able to get a read on her. But what I've noticed, especially this last week in particular, is that her mental shields are beginning to wane. As soon as I got a scent on her, she snapped those invisible walls back up tighter than a prison cell on Azkaban, and I haven't been able to get one since.

Desperation. She is desperate for me to trust her. That's what I got.

I'm making my way up to bed after dinner when Sam calls out. "Saint?" I turn around, my hand on the stair rail. He's wearing a suit. He's always wearing a suit. "Want to go for a walk?"

My routine bangs on the back of my head. The only consistency I've had since everything. Consistency I have relied on. In and out. "Ah…"

"I promise I won't keep you past your bedtime." His hands disappear into his pockets, his shoulders sagging. He looks vulnerable and at ease.

My shoulders relax. I'm being ridiculous. "Okay. I'll just grab a hoodie." I jog into my bedroom, take out an oversized Thrasher hoodie and zip it up, sending a quick text to Ophelia on my way out to let her know I'll be a little late. I make my way back to a waiting Sam at the bottom of the stairwell. "Is there a reason for this late-night stroll?" I ask carefully, following him through the kitchen and to the back patio doors. The cleaners are still packing away our dinner plates, and Veronica is talking on the phone at the head of the table with a wine glass in her hand. Her eyes follow us as we walk past her, and something slams against my chest like a fist desperate for blood. This time she doesn't send out desperation, she sends out pleasure, and this time, she wants me to feel it. She is happy I'm with Sam. Maybe she wants me to move on with someone new so that I will stay. I haven't figured her out yet.

We continue around the dwindling fire and past the garden shrubs and colosseum monuments that round the extension of the house. The pool is extravagant, with a separate lounging area that sits right at the center of it. To get there, you have to take a couple steps down and walk around the edge of the pool. There's a small fire pit in the middle of that lounging area, too, and on the other side of it inside the pool, a small bar.

"To answer your question, yes and no," Sam says, and I don't miss the way his pace slows when we hit the outside entry of the greenhouse. For some reason, I thought he wanted to go to the Garden of Eden, not the greenhouse. "Yes, because I wanted to check on you before tomorrow night. What with the opening and seeing him again—"

I pause, crossing my arms over my chest. Over the past two weeks I have been here, no one has said his name out loud. No one. I haven't even thought of it. "Who told you about that?" Bet it was Frankie.

Sam cocks his head. To anyone else, it would probably look charming, but the truth is, he isn't attractive to me. One day I might be ready to love again. But under no means will I force it. I found out something very quickly. My heartbeat isn't silent. I can't shut it off by will, or even by the most excruciating emotional pain I ever thought was possible. It will continue to beat, even with a crack all the way through it. Only now, it bleeds, too.

"Veronica. She didn't tell me everything, just a quick rundown of why you might be a little on edge tomorrow and that I should be there for you." He steps closer, and my blood turns to ice as his hand begins moving up to my face. I recoil away from it. He pauses, his hand now frozen in mid-air. "Sorry."

"It's all right." I step around him, picking up the watering can and feeding some of the drier plants. "It's just I would have told you had I wanted you to know." I place the can down, turning to face him with a fake smile, but as soon as my eyes are on his, I'm falling to the ground. Everything turns black and my head screams in pain…

"Ahhh, the carnage, my dear Saint. How we meet again. Were you worried that I had left you?" I asked her, my back turned. This time I decided to keep her in the greenroom. The place she found the most solace. "Learning more about you these past few months has been one of the most—hmmm, what is the right word?" I paused, the smile on my face too bold for even myself to admit. "Euphoric. Drug-like? An addiction?" I kept my hands buried in my pockets. I didn't need to turn around for her to know what I looked like. Her lover. Her dreamer. If only she knew the lies she had been fed. If only… though she never will. I have tried to feed off as much as I can. I can't do anymore. I finally turned to face her. She was standing behind me, her eyes fixed everywhere but on me. She couldn't face him. She couldn't or wouldn't. She was hurt. Good. I needed her pain. She would be smarter with pain. Humans always were. "Look at me, Saint."

She didn't move.

I shot forward so fast, my face nearly colliding with hers. "Look at me!" I roared so loud her hair blew around the frame of her face and her eyes squeezed clos—

I shoot up from the ground, my cheeks damp and a scream so brutal tearing from my throat that I think it might cut it open.

"Hey! Hey!" Samael wraps his arms around me, rocking me back and forth. "You're here. You're back. It's fine." For the minute, I rest into his embrace, desperate for anything to keep me anchored in this world and not inside my head. "You're here. Back. It's fine." Minutes pass. Seconds. When his arms become heavy and his presence thick, I push away from him and slowly stammer to my feet.

"Sorry…" I murmur, swiping my hair from my face. "I've got to go to bed. I'll see you in the morning." I spin around and make my way back to my bedroom as fast as I can. That was too much. Too fast, too dark, and too much. Whoever it is entering my head is evil. Their presence feels too hostile this time, yet leaves a taste of despair on the tip of my tongue.

I slam my bedroom door closed and lock it, not wanting to face Ophelia and Ivy tonight. If I'm going to see Brantley tomorrow, I need my sleep. I need enough energy to see him again.

Chapter Sixteen

Saint

I wake up the next morning with a pounding in my head that refuses to go away. Sip after sip of coffee and it doesn't disappear. I feel hung over.

"Morning!" Ophelia bounces into the kitchen, far too chipper for my mood.

I wince. "Morning. Sorry about last night."

She pours herself some coffee and falls down onto the seat beside me. "I figured you might need some space for tonight." She takes a sip. "How are you feeling about that?"

I shrug, running my fingertips through my hair. "On one hand, I get to see my brother and my friends, and on the other hand…"

"… you see him." Her voice is hoarse. She rubs the top of my hand with her palm. "Hey, I'm sorry. If there was anything I could do to help, I would."

"Know any memory removal spells?" I joke, shaking my head while sucking down another gulp of my java.

She chuckles. "Unfortunately, that kind of magik does not exist, though I could try to dig something up from the old grimoires of our ancestors? Who knows, right? Maybe… maybe they were *real* witches?" She raises a perfectly arched eyebrow at me, a smirk on her lips.

"I've never asked about your family," I say, shuffling toward her. "Tell me about them." I know Ophelia comes from big money, but I don't know much about her family dynamics and who they are, and besides, I need a lot of distractions today.

"Well." Ophelia rests her hands around her mug, the trim of her lime green robe brushing over the marble counter. "My father is the headmaster of an uptight prestigious school in Seattle, and my mother has her own law firm. Aside from those two very" —she rolls her eyes— "impressive careers, my mom comes from money, too. I have two brothers, both older and with their own families now. Neither of them live in the US, so I don't see my nieces often, and that's about all, you know, aside from my mom being heavily into the witch belief system." She cocks her head. "I would ask about your story, but I'm thinking it's a lot heavier than mine."

"Hmm." I smile at her. "You could say that."

"Morning, girls!" Veronica waltzes into the kitchen, holding a large black box with a matte black bow wrapped around it. She places it on the counter. "This came for you, Saint." Veronica moves for the coffee and Ophelia reaches forward to grab the box, sliding it closer. She snatches the card that's tucked beneath the bow and flips it open.

"Wear it." She raises an eyebrow. "Really?" she asks, turning to face me. "That's how they talk?"

My heart rate becomes thicker, and my palms turn sweaty. "Not they. Brantley."

She flicks the card back onto the box. "Well, he sounds lovely."

I reach for my phone on the counter, snickering. "He's not." Instantly, I feel a wave of guilt wash over me. He is. He definitely is. If he allows you to see it. I didn't even scratch the surface of what he hid beneath that hard exterior, though I know no one else had come closer to him than me. That's going to change now, no doubt. He's going to find someone else eventually and everything he and I had, everything he made me feel, she will feel. I shut down my thought process when I feel a rare tingle snap down my spine. Pretty sure that was a rage I had never touched before.

I type out a text to our group chat named **King Bitches**. I don't know who is going to tell Madison that the name can be read one or two different ways.

Me: What's with the dress?

The speech bubbles pop up straight away before Tillie's text comes through.

Tillie: Berta. Wear it. It matches ours but your own style.

Madison: What she said.

Me: You okay?

Tillie: She's not. You'll understand why soon.

Madison: You can't relate because you're you. And you have one.

Tillie: Chill. We're not halfway. The dress looks amazing on you. With your bump and all.

Madison: Okay. Yeah. Sure.

Me: Madison, Tillie is right. It's impossible for you to look anything other than beautiful, and even if by some

miracle you're not, who cares. You're literally creating a human being. Let your body do its thing.

Tillie: Wise, my baby sister.

My heart cracks and I leave the chat. I know it's probably habit for her to talk that way, but it still hurts to know it's not true. Thinking I had Tillie for a sister filled me with a kind of femininity I felt I needed, what with being around Brantley and Lucan all of my life. Now I don't even have that. I have nothing.

"Are you ready for tonight?" Veronica asks, blowing into her mug while looking at me over the rim.

"Yes." I push up from my chair. "I think I need to lie down." I tap Ophelia. "Can you wake me a couple hours before, so I don't sleep through?"

Ophelia laughs. "Oh, I'll wake you up four hours before because we have hair and makeup." I grab the box and empty my coffee into the sink, ignoring the feel of Veronica's eyes on the back of my skull. Once I'm back in the safety of my bedroom, almost breathless from how much ground I had to cover, I toss the box onto my bed until the duck-down-filled cover puffs around it. I chew on my thumbnail and then stop when I realize that's a habit I don't want to adopt. Rubbing my sweaty palms down my legs, I open the box and ruffle through the tissue paper until the embroidered rose gold and white material glistens beneath the light. I suck in a deep breath before carefully taking it out, careful not to touch it too much. I hook it onto a hanger and lay it out over my bed, before reaching for the shoes at the bottom. Rose gold Valentinos with white diamantes sewn over the heel.

I sigh, resting on top of my bed, my headache still lingering somewhere between the left and right of my cerebrum. I massage my temples and lie flat on my back. I should text him.

I lose myself in the art on the high ceiling. Pastel purple and pinks are glittered through clouds of ancient Greek gods. So far away. I feel so far away. "I should text him."

I grab my phone and click on his name in my messages, ignoring our old ones. The last message he sent me before finding out—I pause, swallowing the bile rising in my throat. I hold my breath as I type out the message, and I swear I almost pass out after I hit send.

Me: The dress…
Delivered.
And then read.
I'm going to faint.

Seconds turn into minutes. He doesn't reply. I wait for five more minutes, staring at my phone like an idiot before I finally put it down and close my eyes. I need rest. My muscles ache from fatigue.

This time when I sat in front of her, I was in two minds about my delivery. Maybe using Brantley's face wasn't smart.

I should have known better.

Why didn't I know better?

I knew she was going to see him again. Be around everyone again. I could feel that it was almost time. Almost but not quite. The darkness that had lived inside of me since I was a small boy throbbed to the surface. That urge possessed me. No! I yelled to myself. Not now! Not now! No, please no. Hmmm. Too late. *The urges too strong. I needed it like humans needed air. The feeling of filth against my skin.*

"Have you heard from Brantley?" I asked, resting my ankle on my knee.

She stared at me blankly, as if she wasn't bothered by the fact I came baring the skin of her lover. "No." Saint was strong. She wasn't like other people. Beneath the raw beauty and softness laid a thick pavement of cement. To have her must be—fucking marvelous. I'd find out soon.

So soon.

But for now, I needed to find out about Brantley. If he had found out what separated them to begin with to be a lie. Stupid boy.

Brantley Vitiosis would no doubt unleash his wrath amongst all and leave no survivors in his wake. He showered in the blood of his enemies and drank from the blood of those he killed. His name alone instilled fear amongst people whom he didn't know existed.

I smiled smugly. That was the power of such an elite.

She must not get what she wanted.

I kicked off my chair and made my way to where Saint stood. In the corner of the same room I'd visited her in many times before. The simple light swinging backward and forward over the table. Back. Forth. I reached toward Saint and touched her cheek. So soft.

She whacked my hand away from her, and I laughed, throwing my head back. At once I slammed her against the wall with both hands on either side of her head. She cowered, and I knew I'd got to her.

"What's the matter?" I whispered hoarsely into her ear. Though my face might look like Brantley's, my voice never had. She would never notice it, though. That was the best part. I ran the tip of my finger down the dip of her shirt, between her breasts. "Am I not dark enough for you?"

She shoved me in my chest to run away, but I grabbed her around the throat and knocked her against the wall again. No one would know I was roughing up the toy. She fought against me, her fingernails sinking into my arms.

"Let me go!" she screamed, and my eyes fired to life.

"Haven't you heard? I don't like being told no. Not even from you."

I shoved my hand beneath the front of her pants and she started to whimper. "Stop." My thumb grazed her gently. "I said stop."

I didn't. I slid one finger between her folds and groaned when she clenched around me. "Stunning. You're perfect. No wonder he's obsessed with you. The boy has taste. Thank fucking God."

I was so caught up in the moment that I didn't see her hands fly up to my face, her thumbs sinking into my eye sockets before I could get her off.

"I said fucking stop!" She squeezed, and pain erupted from behind my lids. I released her, howling in pain.

Shit.

CHAPTER SEVENTEEN

Saint

I crawl up my bed, swiping the tears from my eyes hastily. Wincing, I look down at my thumbs. I pause. Fresh blood seeped into the edges of my nails. Flying off the bed, I rush into the bathroom and begin scrubbing my fingers.

"You awake, chica!" Ophelia storms into my room and I quickly splash water over my face to hide the tears. I'm patting my cheeks dry when she stops outside the bathroom door, cocking her head. Her hair is piled on the top of her head in a messy bun, her face free of makeup—not that she needs it to begin with. She sags against the door. "Why are you crying?"

"I'm not!" I lie, walking past her.

"Mmmhmmm. You can't lie to a witch, especially your sister witch."

I drop down onto my bed and she makes her way to a duffel bag that she brought in with her. "I know I said alcohol isn't good for the state of mind you're in right now, but I've changed my mind. I will not have you feeling this way the night you see him again for the first time." She lifts a bottle of champagne to her face. "Cristal?" She flashes the gold bottle up and I smile at her.

"I don't know what I'd do without you, Ophelia."

She pulls out two flutes from her bag of tricks, and then another but places it on the office desk. She begins pouring. "Oh please. You, my little Saint, are stronger than anyone I know." She walks over and I take my glass from her. Instantly, I feel my chest loosen, the vision I just had fading. "I'm serious. If you need to talk about anything, you can trust me." She sips on her champagne, and I watch her carefully. Ophelia has the most unique green eyes I have ever seen, which only contrasts her dark mocha skin tone. So beautiful. God, but she's seriously beautiful. That kind of beauty only comes around every so often. She's the kind that everyone would stop and stare at.

"I've been having these visions." Before I can think about what I'm saying, it's out.

She turns to face me, her fluffy brows curving into her straight nose. "What kind of visions?"

I shake my head, swiping the champagne residue off my lips. "They're intense. They're—almost real. There's a man."

She rolls her beautiful eyes. "There always fucking is."

I would laugh if I wasn't still partially shaken from the last one. "He comes as Brantley…"

She pauses, then turns and grips me around my chin. "And it can't be him? Like no way can it be Brantley?" Her eyes are wide, frantic.

I shake my head. "No. I know Brantley, and I don't just mean his shell. I know his soul, the same way a dog knows its owner."

She releases my chin. "That means someone is playing tricks with your mind. Do you know how to kick them out? Has Veronica taught you that yet?"

I shake my head, another sip. "No."

Ophelia's eyes narrow, but after a second, her expression disappears. "Convenient," I hear her whisper, but she shakes it off and stands, placing her glass on my bedside table. "All right, I'm going to show you in" —she stares down at her watch— "seven minutes. Lean forward." I do, shuffling to the edge of the bed. "The error that people make with these visions is that so many who get them presume they're not real. They are. Have you heard of an out-of-body experience? See, people think it's neuroscience, and to a degree it is, because everything is science, but—" Her fingers rest on my temples. "Close your eyes." I do. "I need you in a relaxed state, almost like you're sleeping." My shoulders relax and I breathe in and out. I didn't realize how tired I was until I found myself falling deeper and deeper into a heavy haze. My eyes pop open, but this time, I'm standing beside Ophelia, where she's still standing in front of my body with her fingers on my temples. "See," she says, and I turn around to notice another version of her next to me. We both watch our bodies. "It's not a vision at all. It's all in the science of your mind. Kind of like hypnosis." "But, wait—" I shake my head. "So does that mean that the person I am seeing isn't a ghost?"

Ophelia shrugs. "Could be, but I always see more of the logical and realistic way of our kind, so I'm going to say no, I don't think he's a ghost. I wish it was more paranormal than neuroscience, but it's really not. I'm yet to actually see a damn ghost." I don't tell her that I've seen one. A lot. Hello, crazy Ava Garcia.

"So what you're saying is that someone has been coming into my room while I sleep to do this?" I scowl, my skin crawling.

Ophelia's fists clench at her sides. "Maybe. I'm not sure and haven't studied deep enough into it yet because I didn't think I would need to. We will talk about it more when you kick me out. Getting someone out of your head isn't as difficult as it seems.

You just have to find an anchor to bring you back out." I close my eyes, and just like that, I open them and I'm back in my body.

"Bishop," I say sadly. "I still have Bishop."

Ophelia reaches for her glass again, downing the rest of it. "This isn't good."

"Keep it quiet for now," I say, swirling the liquid in my glass. "I don't know who I can trust."

Ophelia nods. "Agreed. Tonight, I'll sneak in and check on you. I'll stay up all night if I have to, just to see if anyone comes in."

I nod. "That's a good plan."

There's a knock on my door, and one of the housekeepers, I think her name is Natasha, pokes her head around the corner. "Hair and makeup are here. So is Miss Ivy."

Ophelia clinks her glass with mine. "Cheers. Let's get so fucking hot that every single person in that room won't even know how to breathe without our permission."

Hair and makeup go fast. I felt a little like Cinderella getting ready for the ball with how fast they all moved around us three. By the time we were done, we were onto our second bottle of Cristal and I was thoroughly ready for tonight.

"Wow." Ophelia pauses when I stand from my chair. "Seriously impressed that they got you a Berta gown, and not just any Berta. That looks breathtaking." I move to the other side of my bedroom, in front of the floor-length mirror.

I pause.

Glamor. The rose gold gown pinches at the waist before flowing to the ground in a flurry of sequins and glitter. The strapless style is perfect, my cleavage spilling out the edges with small slits on either side of my breasts. Hello, side boob. My skin glistens with gold from the fake tan, perfectly matched for the color and style of the gown. My hair is down and straightened so sleek that it looks almost plastic, where my makeup is thick and smokey around the eyes, the edges so dark that it makes my color look transcendental.

"Okay, yeah, wow." I run my hands down the sides, ignoring how clammy they feel. Every time I remember I'm about to see Brantley again, my heart skips one hundred beats.

"I'm not ready to see him," I say, my chest closing in. I can't breathe. "I can't do this yet."

"Hey!" Ophelia places her glass on the table and makes her way to me. She grabs me by my upper arms, her bright green eyes illuminating. Her hair rolls down her back in perfect natural curls, her skin flawless. She's not wearing nearly as much makeup as I am. "You've got this." She hands me my glass of champagne. "Finish this and we will be ready to leave. Veronica is hell-bent on us making an entrance, so we're going to be a little late." I gather up my YSL bag and check my phone for new texts. Nothing. Deep down, I wanted something from Brantley.

I open a message from Tillie, with a screenshot of my Instagram photo from a couple weeks ago and Frankie's comment, which now has a lot of replies and angry Bran-stan girls swearing at her.

Tillie: Who is Samael, and you probably should have deleted this comment… See you soon.

I send her a message back.

Me: Don't laugh. A witch man.
Tillie: A warlock?! Is he hot?
Me: Does it matter?
Tillie: Good answer.

I lock my phone and slide it into my tiny trunk bag, slipping the chain over my shoulder.

Ivy stares at me with inquisitive brown eyes. So much to say. She opens her mouth, then closes it. A wide smile spreads across her face, and in that alone, I relax. Ivy has definitely slid into a comfortable friend-zone, right along with Ophelia.

Three Range Rover Sport SUVs await outside the front of the circular-style driveway, with men sporting strapping black suits. One for each SUV.

"Ahh, we're all here," Veronica says cheerfully, clapping her hands together with a trail of people behind her. I figure those people are just Sam's friends and Frankie and Alessi.

Sam locks eyes with me, smiling. "You look beautiful, Saint." He kisses my cheek, curling his arm in mine.

"So, before I forget, Saint and Samael will walk in directly behind me, with Ophelia to the right of her and Ivy behind Ophelia. Frankie, Jorge, and Gary will go at the back, coming in behind us." She names the other warlocks, as Tillie would call them, that are with Samael. "We need to form a united front. When we walk in there," Veronica says, a cigarette to her lips. How could I be related to this woman? We don't look anything alike. Even if she did dye her hair black, she is dark-featured like Brantley. "I want us strolling in there like fucking Nancy, Sarah, Bonnie, and Rochelle." She waves her arms high, her black bat-like gown breezing up in the wind. "Let's go." She smirks. "They're waiting."

We all pile into the allocated Rovers, with Ophelia, Sam, Ivy, and Jorge in ours. Veronica slides into the passenger seat at the last minute, bringing a trail of nicotine smoke with her. She pulls out a little plastic bag and dips her pink finger into it, scooping the powder onto her nail and snorting it through one nostril. She passes the bag back and we all decline but Jorge. It takes five minutes to get to the entrance of the school, this time looking a little different to the last time I was here. The gates are opened, though still old, rusted wires reaching for the dark sky. We drive in to see no one out front, as though we're really late—not just a little. A man dressed in a sumptuous Armani suit stands stoically at the entrance, an AK strapped to his outerwear. Only The Kings.

"Only The Kings," I repeat, this time out loud while staring at who I'm guessing is the valet, who breaks his hard exterior to move straight for my door.

It opens and he pauses, his eyes on me. Something similar to recognition flashes over him, just as his mouth curves upward slightly. "Ah, welcome home, *princessa*..." I take his hand in mine, offering a gentle smile. "Or should I say, *regina*..." Once I'm out of the car, he turns to face the others. "Park the cars in the back." His face turns bland. All of the affection he showed me seconds ago, he doesn't share with the others.

"I thought you were the valet, and where's my help to get out of the car?" Veronica argues from the front seat. My mouth closes.

He snickers. "When was the last time a valet was strapped with enough bullets to cut you into little bitty pieces? Get your old ass out of the car yourself." His eyes swing to the back and he pauses on Ophelia. "I take that back." He leans forward, offering his hand to Ophelia. "My lady..."

She rolls her eyes, whacking his hand out of her way. "I don't need your help, or that pretty face."

He grins at her, and I'm momentarily paralyzed by how beautiful he is. In a strange way. "Well." He grabs her hand and tugs her out of the car anyway. "This pretty face would be a good place for you to sit, too, so..."

Ophelia sneers at him. "Not even if I was desperate." She leans up on her tippy toes, pinching his nose. "Which I will never be." She pats his shoulder and grabs onto my hand. "Who in the fuck is that?" she whispers into my ear.

"—Benny, leave the fucking girl alone," Bishop's voice interferes, but it goes over my head because I'm launching myself right into his chest. "Hey, precious. How you doing?" I inhale his scent a few times, my arms unwilling to let go of his waist. I step back, holding myself up by his arms. He's wearing a suit—all black. Not one speck of color anywhere. It's perfectly tailored in all the right places, his hair styled tidily.

"You look good, brother." I smirk up at him. "You need to wear suits more often."

He pinches his collar. "Actually, I can't seem to find myself out of them lately." He gives me a once-over. "Who the fuck chose that dress? Madison. It was fucking Madison." He shakes his head, and as soon as his eyes fly over my shoulder, he tenses. A storm washes over his face, his eyes turning dark and heady. I distract him by tugging on his arm.

"Hey, this is Ophelia and Ivy. They're my friends." Bishop finally wills himself to take his eyes off whoever he locked onto behind me, resting on Ophelia and Ivy, who are standing on either side of me in their version of ball gowns. Equally beautiful, but different to mine. Silk.

He smiles tightly at them. "Well, I'll escort you all in, you know—" His eyes find that spot behind me again and I finally spin around to see who is on the receiving end of Bishop Hayes' wrath. "—for safety reasons."

Samael doesn't flinch. His eyes remain challenging on Bishop. Ballsy, I'd give him that.

Veronica sifts through us all, waving to the back. "In formation."

I raise a brow at Ophelia, who rolls her eyes. If I don't mistake it, Ivy chuckles from behind her. We make our way up the grand staircase outside and through the ancient front doors. Bishop leads us down a long hallway before he shoves open another set of doors, this time opening out onto another grand staircase that leads down onto what I'm guessing is the school hall. It's decorated with fairy lights, with a glistening chandelier hanging from the ceiling. Music is playing softly, while chattering fills the space that music notes do not. We begin walking down the steps and to where everyone is huddled when Samael comes up beside me, his arm hooking with mine.

"You nervous?" he asks, and for a split second I'm glancing down at his arm, confused as to why he's suddenly in my space.

I answer him instead. "I had a lot of champagne."

He laughs, and the sound alone makes me ease a little. Maybe he's just doing it to distract me. For that I am thankful. "A little too much, maybe?"

I glance up and him, just as we hit the main ground. "Maybe."

"Oh my God!" Two loud voices pinch through my thoughts, and I finally pull away from Samael and fling myself at both Madison and Tillie, but not just Madison and Tillie, Tatum, too. She hangs back behind them, a sheepish smile on her face.

I give her a small wave while both of the closest girls I've ever called my own wrap me in a ball with all of their limbs.

"Saint! Goodness, girl. Stay classy…" Veronica moves away from us and disappears to where a group of men are huddled around in a circle.

"Fuck her," Madison says, both finally unlatching from me. They look me up and down. Madison whistles. "Damn. See, I knew this was it. This was *the* dress." What does she mean *the* dress?

"What?" Tillie slaps her. "This was my idea for our dresses!"

I pause when I take theirs in. "We're all in white!"

They look at me, and that annoying silence I've come to know when they're not telling me something spills between us. Madison's eyes are large, and Tillie's batting her lashes. My smile is still on my face, because I haven't caught whatever they're hiding. "Anyway…" I say when they're still being weird. "Meet Ivy and Ophelia! They're good women." Madison and Tillie start small talk with Ivy and O as I step around their gowns, both so similar to mine it's uncanny, only different styles.

"I can't believe they've had no alcohol," I say to Tate, swiping a glass of whiskey as a server passes by. Tate grabs one, too.

"Oh, I know. Trust me." She takes a long gulp. "I *really* know."

I sip on mine, wincing when the strength lights my lips on fire. "How have you been?"

Her lips stretch wide, her cheeks glowing. Tatum is very pretty. She holds a classical type of beauty. "Really good. I'm here with Spyder."

"I figured," I said, another sip.

"So!" Madison grabs for me. "I know you're—"

"—there you are," Samael says smoothly, scooping his arm around my shoulder.

Everyone's eyes fall to where his arm is, mine included.

"Here I am…" I say slowly, and if anyone knew me, they'd hear the perplexity in my tone.

Samael squeezes my arm, obviously ignoring the energy I'm throwing out to him. "I think Veronica wants you."

Tillie steps forward, but Madison's hand comes out to stop her.

Madison smiles sweetly at me. "We're right here. Not going anywhere if you need us."

I cast a glance over my shoulder at my girl gang as I'm walking away. Madison, Tillie, Ophelia, Ivy, and hell, even Tate looked about ready to throw down. I recognized when it happened. I felt the shift in the room. The charge from our bodies recognizing each other. Everything moved in slow motion, and I didn't know if it was because I was about to pass out, or if it was because I couldn't move my limbs. I tilt my head up, my lips parting and ready to ask Sam what Veronica wants, but everything freezes when my eyes land on him. He stares at me from across the room, leaden and cold. His lashes somehow look darker, his eyes almost the same shade as the ebony suit he's wearing, and his hair, unlike Bishop's, is ruffled on the top of his head. His skin is paler than usual, his cheekbones sharper, and even his nose seems straighter. Maybe it's just everything is tightened, including my awareness to him, or maybe it's because we have never gone this long without seeing each other, or maybe it's because we no longer can have each other. Something tells me it's a heady combination of both.

God. Has he always been this perfect?

Yes.

Then everything crashes into me.

Half brother. Half brother.

A shudder rolls over my exposed flesh. His eyes narrow slightly as he raises a glass to his swollen lips.

Brother, Saint!

I squeeze Samael's arm involuntarily, and that's the exact moment Brantley breaks eye contact with me and lands straight on the grip I have on Samael. He pauses for a couple of seconds before he leisurely finds his way to Sam's face. The way he does it sends a chill down my spine, as if he were thinking of all the different ways he could kill Samael without even trying. The corner of his lip curls, the look in his eyes some sort of weaponry. It's not until I look beneath his table that I see Nate and Bishop holding his arms back casually, while attempting to maintain a conversation with three older men. They're keeping him tied down to his seat like an animal, stopping him from doing what? I don't know.

Veronica's face pops in front of mine. "I need you to stay near me, Saint." Her voice is above a whisper. "You're my get out of here alive card."

"What about your son?" I ask, though I realize Brantley hasn't been around The Coven lately to see his mother. I mainly assumed that had to do with me and our situation and less his hostility toward his mom.

"My son is hardly my son. We don't have a relationship; we have an agreement." Her eyes move around the room. "Samael, did you notice how many of The Kings are here tonight? Have you seen any of The Gentlemen?"

Sam shakes his head. "None."

"Wait," I say, turning to face Sam. "You know who The Gentlemen are?"

"I've seen photos, yes," he says, taking a sip of his drink. I find a white smudge in his words. I believe it's called a white lie. I release my arm from around his, stepping backward.

"Excuse me, I need to talk with my brother."

Veronica turns over her shoulder, a smug smirk on her face. "Which one?"

My fingers flex in the palm of my hand. I'm beginning to really not like that woman.

I make my way toward their table, trying my best to ignore Brantley and reaching for Bishop's hand. He pauses his conversation with one of the men, excusing himself and turning to face me. "You okay?"

"No!" I whisper toward him. I know Brantley is close enough to hear Bishop and me. Even though he's lost in conversation about money trade from China, I know his attention is solely on me. "Something's wrong."

"Why?" Bishop asks, not an ounce of worry on his face.

I look around the room. "Sam knows about The Gentlemen, yet when I first moved in there, he said he had never heard of The Kings."

The balls on either side of Bishop's jaw flex.

There's a dark chuckle that reverberates—no—violently shakes the ground under my feet as Brantley tosses back his drink. "Your precious new toy isn't as innocent as you thought, hmm?"

I pause. "What? What do you mean *mine*?" I'm whispering, but I'm well aware how dangerously close I am to yelling at him.

"Okay, you two, can we not do this right here?" Nate scowls at us, the other men who he was talking to now gone. I force myself back to Bishop. "He's hiding something, Bishop."

Bishop leans down, his mouth near my ear. "*We know*."

I step back, confused. "What?"

I turn to leave when Brantley's eyes burning the back of my head feels too hot to ignore. I retract my steps. "I'm sorry, but what is your problem?" I snap under a whisper, leaning down with my hands resting on the table. He stares at me in defiance, and I'm suddenly aware of just how angry I am with him. I just don't know why.

He leans back farther in his chair, kicking his leg out and cocking his head. He glares at me with the same interest one would have toward something as irrelevant as paint drying. "Are you talking?"

"Screw you, Brantley," I rasp out, swallowing back the pain in my chest.

He leans forward, running his tongue over his teeth manically. "You already did," he snarls. "Multiple times." I turn back around and push my way through the sea of people. I don't know what I expected bumping into him again, but that wasn't it. I find my group of girls again, Tate and Ophelia laughing mid-conversation.

"What's wrong with Brantley?" I say to no one in particular, swiping another glass of whiskey on the way. I already know I'm partially tipsy, even though our drinking has been vastly spread out.

"You mean aside from being a homicidal maniac the entire

time that you've been gone?" Tillie quirks an eyebrow. She shrugs. "Not much else."

I find his eyes again, already on mine. This time Bishop and Nate aren't holding him discretely in his chair, but they're standing obviously close to him. In fact, too close.

"Afternoon, Saint," I hear another voice from behind me and my blood turns to ice. Can dealing with too many issues and personalities at once drive you to insanity? Because if so, I might need a straitjacket before this night is over. I slowly turn to face the owner of the voice and come face-to-face with Hector and Scarlet Hayes. "Hello."

Scarlet pats Hector's hand. "Go find my son and get me a drink so I can chat with the girls."

Hector smiles tightly at us all before walking away. I don't expect an explanation. I don't expect a relationship with the man that I should supposedly call my father, but something, anything, would be better than watching his back disappear. Asshole.

Scarlet rubs my arm with her palm. "You look absolutely stunning, sweetheart." Aside from her choice of husband and her questionable taste in second chances—or ten—I like Scarlet.

Madison drapes her arm around my shoulder. "Doesn't she?"

Scarlet clears her throat as her thumb brushes over her Dolce clutch. Back and forth. Back and forth. Must be a nervous trait. "Bishop tells me you're back in The Coven?" The corners of her eyes crinkle, but there's a smile on her crimson shaded lips. I'm sure she has become quite good at concealing her emotions over the years, so I take her manner with a grain of salt.

"I am."

"Well, I would really love—*we*—would really love to get to know you a little more, but only if you're up for it?"

I look around at all of the girls, noting that they look somewhat uncomfortable.

"Sure." I smile back up at Scarlet. "That sounds nice." It

sounds terrible, but I'm in survival mode, and survival mode is agreeing to anything.

"Good," she says, just as Hector returns with her drink. "Did you find our son?"

Hector nods. "I did."

"Good." Scarlet narrows her eyes. "Excuse me, girls. I have a pair of balls to crush."

Hector follows her. I notice everywhere Hector goes, people either move away very quickly or they try to get close enough to talk to him. There's no in-between. The power one man holds without so much as breathing a word.

"She's so awesome." Ophelia sighs. "What a woman."

"There you are," Samael interrupts, coming up beside me. "Dance with me?"

I hesitate.

"Actually!" Tillie plasters on a wide, forced smile. "We were just about to head to the powder room."

"It's fine, he's my friend." I hook my arm in his and he leads me toward the dance floor. A classical piece is playing, one I don't recognize. I rest my hand behind his neck as he brings his to my hip while taking my other hand.

"Your friends always look at people that way?" He nudges his head toward where they're all standing. Tillie looks livid, Madison seems uncomfortable, but it's Ophelia that bothers me. She's watching with confusion, her brows pulled in.

"Well, no, actually. Sorry." I peek up at him. "It's a *you* problem."

He spins me around to the music and my eyes collide with evil. Brantley's jaw is working overtime, his attention solely on us. I look down beneath the table again to see Bishop's hand on his arm. Nate has one rested on his shoulder, but again, it's so discreet that no one would even notice. Veins pop in Bishop's arms, as the same ones rise to Brantley's neck. Nate shoves him down a little, and that's when I realize the strength they both must be using to stop Brantley from getting out of his chair.

Samael wraps his arm tightly around my waist and pulls me farther into his chest, his lips near my ear. My eyes remain on Brantley. I don't know why. This is torture. I feel as though every vein in my body is being filled with liquid fire, and the longer I stay here, the hotter it becomes. "I don't think your brother likes me much."

I step away from Samael, sweeping his arms off me. "Excuse me." Sweat pools at the nape of my neck. The Berta becomes too tight. My hair becomes too heavy and the oxygen too thick. I can't breathe. People move around me, but they're not moving fast enough and everything starts appearing in double vision.

I can hear Bishop talking through a mic. Loudly. "Welcome to the opening night of REU and RPA—" I stumble forward, crashing into something hard. Or rather, someone.

Hands grip around my arms, standing me up while guiding me to the back of the room. Bishop's voice drifts off in the distance until I hear a door close and a lamp switch on. I must fall to the ground because my tailbone stings.

"Saint…" Brantley kneels down in front of me, ripping open his collar and tossing his tie across the ground. "Look at me."

"I—I'm sorry," I whisper, squeezing my eyes closed. "I'm okay now. I won't. I'll leave." I stand on shaky legs and turn toward the door he brought us through, but his hand flies up and slams it closed again. I flinch. "Brantley, I can't be this close to you."

"Why?" he asks, and I close my eyes again to stop the tears from jerking down my cheek. I feel his hand over my lower belly, his fingers spreading. "Why, Saint?"

I fail the hold, unleashing tears and allowing my forehead to fall against the door. My makeup will be ruined now. "Please stop." Guilt and disgust intoxicate me, but that same magnetic surge that has always connected us will not go away. It never weakened. My heart still beats for Brantley today the same it did the first time I saw him, and I'm not sure it will ever stop. But it's something I will have to learn to live with until I find another man. "I'm going to move on to make this easier for us."

His other hand is on the door now, and I'm aware that he's caged me in with nowhere to go. "See, now that just makes me angry. You know what I'm like when I'm angry, right? Or have you forgotten?"

"Why are you doing this?" I whisper, sniffling impolitely.

His tongue glides over the nape of my neck. "Did you fuck him?"

"What?" I snap, attempting to turn around. He slams me up against the door with his hips, his hand now at the front of my throat. He drags the edges of his canines across the tip of my spine, right below my hairline. *Oh, I didn't forget.* "I said, did you fuck him? And I'm going to need you turned that way until you give me my answer."

"Brantley," I whimper, unable to move. "Let me go." The tears are dripping down onto my breasts.

"No," he growls into the back of my ear. For some reason, I feel that was a double answer.

"Why?" I sniff again, trying not to wipe my face so I won't smudge my makeup any worse than I probably already have.

"Answer me, Saint."

I don't.

He squeezes my arms and turns me around quickly, shoving me against the door. His eyes are dark and void. One eye twitches when he watches a tear roll down my cheek.

I bring my eyes up to his, his face painfully close to mine. "I should. I need to fall out of love with you, Brantley."

His lips part, and just when I think he's going to yell at me, he leans down and catches that same tear with the curve of his tongue. "No, you don't, Dea."

"What?" I rear back, attempting to push the big wall of muscle that's in front of me away. My neck aches from having to look up at him this long. "Of course I do! We can't—this—" I shake my head. "No, Brantley. I draw the line at incest."

"Saint..." he says, far too casually.

"Brantley, it's wrong!" I shake my head.

"Saint," he whispers again, his lips brushing ever so lightly over mine. *I should push him away.*

"Brantley, please, stop."

His hand flies to my chin. "Look at me."

I do, my eyes almost cross inward because of his proximity, but I do. I hold my breath.

"We're not fucking related, Saint. She lied."

My world stops spinning, and my tears dry.

"*She. Lied.*"

"How do you know?" I let out. "How can you be so sure?"

Brantley snickers. "Because Hector, though so hard to fucking believe, never stuck his dick inside my mother."

A heaviness I didn't realize I was carrying shifts off me. We're not related. I didn't do anything wrong. I take a second to recollect myself and my thoughts as a dark cloud slowly moves away from me. He backs away, but my hand flies up to his collar, stopping him. "Don't you dare walk away without kissing me."

He snarls at me. "I'm not kissing shit until you tell me that you didn't let that piece of shit near you."

"Brantley." I grit my teeth. "The fact you even ask me that insults me."

His jaw flexes. "Did he touch you?"

I shove him in the chest, reaching for the door handle and needing a desperate talk with my friends. "Shove your kiss. I don't want it anymore." I go to leave with the door wide open, but he wraps my hair around his fist, tugs me back, and slams the door closed again. He spins me around and lifts me from the ground, my legs wrapping around his waist. "Don't. Fucking. Test. Me, Saint. I've got blood on my hands from the days I spent thinking I had fucked my half sister. The rage I accumulated in those days alone could match the ones my demons created all of my life. I would not fucking play with me right now."

I rest both of my hands on his cheeks as some of that darkness dissolves in his eyes. Not all. Not even a quarter. Just a sprinkle. Enough to let me get through his rage. "I didn't touch him."

He searches my face. "I know."

I glare at him. "Let me go. You piss me off."

He bites my bottom lip into his mouth and nibbles on it. "You're in love with me? I don't recommend that."

"I am," I say, running my fingers through his hair. "And I don't know if you've noticed, but I don't care what you recommend."

The nibbling slowly turns to kissing, and I part my lips for him to enter, sliding my tongue over his. I curl my arm around his neck as he holds me up against the wall and we both lose ourselves in each other. Just kissing. Nothing more. Something so intimate that you wouldn't expect someone so cold like Brantley to be so damn good at.

He stops, slowly lowering me to the floor. "You're lucky I don't tear that dress off you and fuck you until you're blue." I begin straightening myself.

"Why don't you?" I tease boldly, though I'm glad he doesn't right now because we've still got a little while to go tonight.

He smirks down at me. "Oh, I will." He reaches for my hand, yanking me into his chest. His fingers intertwine with mine. "But you can't fuck a bride in her wedding dress before she's even married." What? I look down at the heavy cool metal that's sliding over my ring finger and pause. A rock almost the size of the entire lower half of my finger glistens back at me.

He smiles darkly at me, the corners of his mouth too fucking smug to be on a face this damn evil. "All. Fucking. Mine."

Chapter Eighteen

Brantley

Her eyes are glued to her finger, as if she can't believe that it's there. Staring back at her. But it is. And it's there to fucking stay.

She glances up at me. "What is going on?"

I curl my lips over my teeth. She once said she wanted full disclosure, and I had a lot of fucking time to think on what I wanted when it came to her, and that was honesty. Saint can sniff out a lie like a Beagle can cocaine, but I still want to be honest. "It's the opening night for the schools—*and* our wedding."

She blinks as if she still hasn't processed it.

I continue. "And Madison's wedding."

Double blink.

I run my tongue over my teeth. "And Tillie's."

"Jesus," she whispers, stepping backward until her back hits the door.

"Sorry, he's not invited."

Her eyes snap to me. "Brantley, are you all sure this is the answer to whatever it is you're all planning?"

"Don't do that," I say, running the tip of my finger down the chamber of her sternum. My cock swells against my pants, and every second inside this cafeteria kitchen is like hell on earth. I need to get beneath her. Make her scream. Fuck, it's been too long.

"Do what?" she asks, still admiring her ring. Good. It is fucking impressive.

"Second-guess whether we're doing the right thing." I step closer to her to curl my fingers beneath her chin to tip her face up to mine. "That ring, this wedding, it doesn't mean shit to me, Saint. It's all just labels and a piece of paper with some cheap two-dollar ink. Don't expect anything more than what you're used to from me. We need this to solidify our unit." Her eyes flick up to mine, and fuck, she's beautiful. It's the kind of beauty that demands to be felt by everyone.

"But how can you marry me when you're not in love with me?"

I take two deep inhales of air and count to five. Mainly for her benefit, because I already know what I'm going to tell her. I may be cold, but I'm not ignorant. I knew eventually she would want to have the discussion about love. I'm not a fucking idiot either. I know I feel a certain way about her. For instance, that "way" usually leads me down Murder-ville Drive whenever I think she's either in danger or touching another man, but love? Shit. "Love will never exist with me."

She keeps her focus on her ring, but I catch the way she tugs the corner of her bottom lip slightly into her mouth and nibbles on it. I notice her nervous trait and bring her face back up to mine with my finger. "But the way I feel about you will last a lifetime after love dies out. You once said that would be enough for you. Does that still count with a ring on your finger and a new title as my wife?"

She finally brings her eyes up to mine. "You are more than enough for me, Brantley."

I smile weakly down at her, but it doesn't reach my eyes. My smiles never usually do.

She sighs. "Do I even want to know what is happening tonight? Aside from our weddings? And what about Veronica finding out we're married and that we know we're not related?"

I chuckle, grabbing her hand while pulling open the door. "That's all for the finale." When we break back into the main area, the crowd has thinned tremendously. I find Bishop and Nate near the corner with Tillie, Madison, Tate, Spyder, and Saint's two friends, Ophelia and Ivy, beside them. I trust my people with Saint. Never an outsider. But something about the way Ophelia guards her makes me feel at ease. Maybe one day I'll trust her and Ivy.

Maybe not.

Madison is smirking at Saint, and Tillie has one raised eyebrow. Hector is talking on the stage, everyone watching him carefully. Good. Because it keeps eyes off us.

"Oh, so you just couldn't wait…" Bishop clucks his tongue as we approach.

Saint rubs her thumb over her ring. "Was no one going to tell me until the last damn minute?" She growls, reminding me of a cute little pussycat, before her fist is flying into Bishop's arm. It's scary how much the two of them slipped so effortlessly into the brother-sister dynamic. "A heads-up would have been lovely."

Tillie grabs her by the arm. "Let's fix your makeup and I'll fill you in." All of the girls disappear to the bathroom, and the three of us don't stop watching until they're through the doors. I search Benny out and nod at him; he blows me a kiss as he moves to the front of the ladies' bathroom. Benny and I have become closer since Saint has been gone. Before, I pushed many of my family members away because I didn't trust them around Saint. Their intentions. You should never trust a Vitiosis. But Benny, though he and Nate are a walking fucking UFC fight waiting to go down, is loyal. He has become closer to our circle since Bishop took the gavel. It's good. He's going to be one of our stronger outside allies.

"Did you tell her everything?" Bishop asks, shoving his hands into his pockets.

I shake my head, snatching a glass of bourbon from a tray as a waiter passes us. "No. Have you both told Tillie and Mad?"

They both take a sip of their drinks before Nate answers, "No." He cracks his neck. "At least we will all be in the doghouse together and they won't find out until we're up there. That way, they won't cause a scene."

"Eh," I argue. "Pretty sure your girl doesn't give a flying fuck about an audience." Nate's face pales.

"Actually," Bishop murmurs, and we both turn to face him. "I told Madison a little bit. Just enough to warm them up before, but not the whole truth."

Nate sighs. "My balls just ran away."

Chapter Nineteen

Saint

I never thought much about my wedding day. I'd watch them on TV and think they were a waste of time. Why not skip all of the trouble and just sign the paper? If it really was only about love, why did you need to spend thousands to prove it?

"Your makeup is fine," Tillie says, dabbing a powder brush into her compact. "That motherfucker made you cry. I need to fuck him up."

Ophelia chuckles from the toilet stall where she's taking care of business—with the door open. Have we all just bonded that quickly that it's almost too natural now? "I got your back."

"Well, I don't!" Madison says, her hands flying around the place. She turns to face the mirror, running her finger over her lips to correct her lipstick. "He still scares me."

Tate slides up onto the bathroom counter, her legs dangling

off. "Once upon a time, we'd all be snorting lines of coke off this impeccable marble." She runs her hand over it. "How times have changed."

Madison chuckles. "Just, and thankfully." I'm glad I missed that era.

"So, do we know why we're getting married tonight?" I ask, opening my clutch and pulling out my lipstick.

Madison places her hand on top of the counter, sighing. A long finger taps against it and I feel like I'm holding my breath waiting for her to answer. "I don't know *why* tonight, but I know this world enough to know there's a reason. I will say this—we have to be a united front. Our circle has to be impenetrable. A girlfriend is a liability and weakness. But a wife? A wife is a weapon in this world. A wife is *unfuckwithable*. A wife in The Elite Kings' world is a damn queen. There's a level of respect that comes from being the wife of a King all on its own." We all stay silent for a while, because what she just said made some sense.

"I guess I'm still learning," I say truthfully, opening my bag. Ivy shuffles on her feet in the corner, watching us all attentively.

Ophelia places her hands under the faucet, her eyes on mine in the mirror. "I just have to say something." She turns, drying them with paper towel. "Whenever one of us would fall out of line, Veronica would lock us in our rooms and wouldn't let us out until we'd fasted all of our sins out. My worry with this, is that she's going to punish, well, the rest of us."

"What?" I gasp, shoving my lipstick back inside my clutch.

Ophelia shrugs. "I mean, we're all used to it. We know the rules, and if we don't follow, then there are repercussions." I can't believe I didn't pick up any of Veronica's toxicity when I first met her. Her emotions have always been a challenge to me, but I haven't felt the other girls' unease around her.

Tillie stares at Ophelia. "That's weird. You know that's weird, right? And that's coming from someone who owns an island filled with nocturnal humans who live on little forest roads and wear fucking clothes from the fifteen hundreds."

Ophelia raises an eyebrow. Ivy hides behind a small giggle.

"Okay, listen." Madison takes control, grabbing mine and Tillie's hands. "We marry the boys tonight together. We do it because none of us are going to be marrying anyone else." She clears her throat. "Let's be real, they would never allow it either, but let's make a promise?"

I think about arguing her point, but come up with nothing. "What is the promise first?" I say, knowing these two entirely too well.

"A promise that in twenty years from today, we all rewrite our vows. Our way. Properly. A real wedding. If I can't look sexy today, damn straight I will in twenty years."

I stare at her blandly. "My wedding present to you will be glasses."

Tillie smacks her with the back of her hand, and then sighs, massaging her temples. "How old would our kids be then?"

"They'd be starting Riverside Elite Uni."

Our eyes all connect, flying between each other. I nod. "Deal. Twenty years, we do it our way."

The smiles on both their faces tell me that our soon-to-be-husbands should be terrified.

We all make our way back out of the bathroom after another round of pep talks. The girls don't know any more than I do, which makes me think there's another reason why the boys want us all to get married tonight. Or maybe it's just about making a statement like Madison had said.

Ophelia grabs me by the arm as we're passing the man I mistakenly assumed was the valet. "I need you to keep me away from him."

"Oh, you like?" I ask, wagging my eyebrows suggestively at

her. We sidestep away from him as she continues to drag us to the back of the room where all the boys are waiting.

"No!" she grumbles. "I need you to keep me away from him so I don't accidentally kill him."

I don't get a chance to demand her to elaborate because we've caught up with everyone.

I can feel Brantley's eyes on me like a hot iron hovering over my skin.

"This is going to go fast, efficient, and sorry, girls, but rather fucking coldly." Bishop smirks at Madison. "Hope you weren't wanting your dream wedding."

"Just to not be fucking pregnant would be nice." She snickers her response.

"Personally, I don't care." Tillie wraps her arm around my shoulder. "We made a pact, that in twenty years from today, we're all going to do it again, only *our* way."

Bishop's face drains of color. "Of course you would."

I turn to face Brantley, finding his eyes still on me. Blank and expressionless. My heart pounds in my chest when I think he's, once again, pissed at me. My palms become sweaty and I hate the way I've allowed him to affect me. But then he dips his head, his eyes hooded while hiding a smirk behind the back of his hand. *Right*. Veronica is still here and can't know that I know we're not brother and sister. I wonder at the kind of restraint he's testing right now. Brantley is patient with his wrath. He doesn't unleash it all at once or out of control; he uses it as a weapon and guides it to where he wants it to go. That's what makes him so terrifying. I already know whatever he has planned for Veronica is going to be disturbing, and that should bother me, but at the moment, it doesn't.

"Before you all start bitchin', our parents all got married this way, as did their parents and so on. It's how we do things."

"Never fucking brought this up before," Madison snaps, her anger radiating toward my brother.

He simply turns toward her, and I almost step between them because the look on his face is feral. "Actually, I was about to. You know, that final riddle I texted you before everything blew up?" He takes a simple step into her space, and I'm pretty sure we all hold our breath as her shoulders vibrate and her lip quivers. Not from anger, but pain. Her face becomes animated. Everything she is feeling in this moment shows in the way her eyes turn heavy, and the muscles in her arms relax. He remains fixed on her. "Let me refresh your memory." I swear we all stop breathing. "Riddle me this, Kitty. What's round, smooth, and is home for a sparkling stone?" He grabs her hand with his and tugs her into his chest. It's not until Madison looks down that she gasps loudly, and we all follow her line of sight. A large oval-shaped diamond blinds us. "A fucking ring that should have been on your finger years ago."

"Bishop, I—"

He shakes his head, his finger pressed to her lips to hush her. "Nah uh, don't go soft on me now. You know fighting with you gets my dick hard." *Gross.* "And you're about to get it real hard tonight…"

"Okay, enough…" I whisper. "Please." My stomach rolls, my hand covering my mouth.

Bishop chuckles, mouthing sorry to me before continuing, "In short, we go up, sign, say the basic vows, and then, Saint, you're going to play a song—" I blink, bringing my eyes to Bishop. He continues, "any song on the piano. The girls will stay near you." I was frantically searching my mind for a song that I didn't realize he was now directly in front of me, a finger on my cheek, turning my face to his. "Ophelia and Ivy are your friends?"

I nod.

His pupils dilate, and that's when I know the wedding tonight isn't just for us, or for making a statement. It's a distraction. I just have to figure out whether it's a distraction for us or for someone else. "Anyone else?" His jaw is set, unmoving. He leans down. "You know what I'm asking you."

I swallow. "Please. Just keep it to those who deserve it and *do* not touch the girls."

Bishop leans back, searching my face. "Not even Frankie?"

I shake my head. "Bishop, you know me. Please…"

"Fuck," he curses under his breath, finally dropping his finger from my cheek.

"Ah, what's happening?" O steps beside me as the lights turn soft around us.

I exhale, squeezing her hand with mine. "Revenge."

Ophelia shuffles on her feet, and just when I think she's going to fight it, she crosses her arms. "She deserves it, Saint." I know she does. But there's a big question that is still hovering over my head. *Who has been pulling me under all this time?*

I lean into O. "Is there a chance that whoever has been giving me these visions can do it without touching me?"

"What are you talking about?" Brantley asks, his eyes narrowed on me.

How is he listening? "Nothing." I almost hold my breath while I wait to see if he's going to fight me on not elaborating or let it go.

Bishop comes back from answering his phone, his face tense as Hector takes center stage. He shoves his phone into his suit jacket, his eyes going between O, Ivy, and me. "They've disappeared. *Fuck.*" His shoulders rise and fall as he squeezes the top of a chair. His head lifts. "Lucky for us, we specialize in finding people who want to *run* away—" He slowly drags his eyes to Madison, and the look he passes her almost makes me cower.

God! He must have been awful to her when they first met. Too bad he's in love with her now.

Madison flips him off. "Not fast enough, though, huh?"

Bishop glances between Brantley and Nate, shaking his head as Brantley bares his teeth, a feral hiss escaping him. He turns and throws back the rest of the whiskey that was in his glass but remains silent.

Bishop begins. "This wedding is an elopement. The people who are here right now are direct lineage to The Elite Kings or work very closely with us. This is how it's going to go. The six of us will be on the stage, we will exchange vows, and then, Saint, again, you'll play a song on the piano. The girls will follow you and watch as you play, but Ophelia and Ivy don't need to be up there with you anymore." I know I should ask why that is. I have to figure out if they're trying to distract us or someone else.

Hector interrupts, tapping a mic at center stage. A single light beams on him and the crowd silences. There has to still be around fifty people here.

Hector glances out. "I know it has been, well—" he finds Scarlet, who is sitting near the front of the stage, "—a long time since we've had this happen, but the truth is, tonight is a double-edged event." Hector clears his throat, gesturing toward us. Another light shines down on us. "It's a triple marriage ceremony. The three Kings are here to unite their other halves within themselves, and this world." Bishop begins walking with Madison gripped around his arm. Then Nate and Tillie.

I stare at Brantley beside me, hooking my arm in his. My fingers look minuscule clenched around his bicep. My heart races again and sweat beads down the back of my neck. My head throbs and people around me start disappearing in and out.

"What's wrong?" Brantley whispers to the side while we continue to walk to the front stage.

"I don't know," I answer under my breath. Reaching the

stage, I stand beside Tillie and opposite Brantley. He continues to watch me with worried eyes as I turn over my shoulder, relieved to find Ophelia and Ivy behind me, watching with worried eyes. Something is happening.

O steps closer, her hand on mine. Tate is behind Madison.

O must sense my discomfort because her brows pull in as she starts searching the crowd. Everything flies over my head when Scarlet steps forward, carrying a knife. The blade is sharp and long, but the handle looks to be made from bone. It looks old and *very* used. Hector opens a book in front of him, worn leather with no title. He flips through pages until he reaches somewhere in the back. Scarlet raises the blade up while Hector reads a passage in fluent Latin.

"But what is love if not the substance that pumps through our veins. But what is love if not sacrifice. For you will find this especially in this world; that love does not exist, but blood, blood flows forever." Hector takes the blade from Scarlet and I follow Madison, Tillie, and the boys when they all place their hands out. Brantley is opposite me, with Tillie and Nate and Madison and Bishop. We stand in a line, with our hands out, waiting. The urgency is gone, but the feeling of betrayal is still emanating from somewhere. I just need to figure out from where. *Who is feeling guilty?* Hector continues, *"So take this oath for what it is, and that's not a marriage of two, but one of six. When others fail you, your family will not. When you're hurting, they hurt. When you're struggling, they struggle. You take the future steps together. You're in this together."* Hector starts at the top of the line, taking Bishop's hand and cutting him through his palm before moving back down. Once we're all cut on both hands, Hector is now at the opposite end.

"Repeat after me while taking each other's hand," he says, holding the knife up beneath the light. *"On this day, I choose* blood. Today, tomorrow, and forever. Blessed be the EKC." We repeat the words after he repeats them.

Hector smiles. "You may now kiss your brides." None of us move. Hector rolls his eyes, and the movement is so foreign that had I liked him, I would have found it amusing. "Or you can kill each other," he mumbles, turning back around to the crowd while adding, "Probably a higher chance." He raises his hands up into the air. "The ceremony is finally completed. Please, enjoy the rest of your night."

The ceremony is finally completed.

All of us girls freeze. I can feel Tillie brush against my arm and Madison's anger reverberating off her beside me.

Minutes pass and the boys still haven't said anything.

"Hold up!" Tillie's the first to break the silence because, well, it's Tillie. "You're telling me that you *used* our *motherfucking* wedding day to complete the ceremony for Bishop?"

"Not just for Bishop," Nate says to her. He tries to step forward, but her hand flies out. "For *all* of us, Tillie. The changes we have been saying that need to happen in order for us all to move with the current times start here. This is part of those changes."

"Meaning?" Madison fumes, grinding her teeth. I remain frozen on the spot, but I can feel the pitter-patter of blood falling from my open wound and dropping to the ground. Music continues in the background while people go back to their socializing, as if nothing just happened. As if we didn't just go through what would be considered a major life event.

"Meaning," Bishop says, grabbing a roll of bandages and snatching her hand in his. The snarl never leaves his mouth. "*You* are all safe. People will know exactly who the fuck all three of you are before this night is over. In fact, I wouldn't be all that surprised if word has already been spread to the fucking Yakuza in Japan."

"But it was part of the ceremony, Bishop!" Madison snaps at him. "Meaning you used us all to seal it."

Bishop shrugs. "Tough shit, Kitty. If we had told you all, you would have thrown a fucking tantrum."

Tillie hands me a Band-Aid, but I shake my head, remaining focused on Brantley. "You used me to get me here so that this could happen…"

Brantley's eyes weaken, but yet somehow still intensify. "What?"

I bring my hand up to my mouth.

His jaw clenches as he follows the movement.

I flick my tongue over the bottom of my palm, licking the wound before sucking on the tip of my middle finger. He growls softly, taking a step forward.

"Jesus Christ." Nate groans somewhere, but I can't seem to care. Because I'm *pissed*. If he had told me this was going to happen, I wouldn't have cared. It was the principle. He told me he wouldn't lie to me, and I believed him. I'm beginning to think he told me that just so I didn't need to dig deep to find his lies. They knew I could sniff them out so instead, they baited me. I am such an idiot.

I step away from Brantley. "I have a song to play."

I turn quickly and make my way to the piano that's on another makeshift stage in the center of the room. Taking a seat on the stool, I flex my fingers over the keys and close my eyes. Breathe in, breathe out. No one stops what they are doing. I appreciate that. I don't want all eyes on me. I play the first song that comes to mind. An angry storm of emotions and betrayal spray over the keys with every flick of my fingertips. By the time I'm finished, I stand up and rush to the back of the room. I'm tired, my muscles ache, and my mind is in a tailspin. I need sleep. I jog up the stairs at a speed I didn't know I could wearing heels, rubbing the tears from my cheeks.

Madison rushes over to me once I'm back in the school foyer, out of breath. "There you are. Tillie and I are leaving, you want to come?"

I nod, just as my eyes fly over her shoulder and land on Ophelia and Ivy, who are still down below. "Yes, with Ivy and O."

Pulling into the long driveway of the manor, I feel all of the past memories crawl up my throat, cutting off my air supply. *Goddammit, Brantley.* I want to fight him, swear at him, yell at him, but the closer I get to my home, the more I feel myself ease.

"Hey." Ophelia's hand is on my knee. Ivy sits opposite us, watching our exchange quietly. "It's going to be okay. Ivy and I can go back to my parents' house tomorrow."

I shake my head, resting my hand on hers. "No, please, you can both stay for as long as you want. I'm just sorry that you got caught in-between all of—" I wave my hands around, "—this, and now with Veronica out with the knowledge she has." I pause, swallowing past all of the overwhelming emotions that are threatening to choke me. She could be anywhere, waiting and ready to attack. "At least until after we've found Veronica, I really want you both to stay here."

A look passes between them, before Ivy nods, her brown hair brushing against her collarbone. Ophelia gazes up at the manor, one perfectly dark eyebrow raised. "No offense, but this house is scary. You know that, right?"

For the first time since marrying Brantley, I laugh, pushing the door open and climbing out. "I know." After we left the opening tonight, Tillie and Madison decided to drive their cars here instead of riding with us so that—in their own words—they had a way of escape when the boys got home.

"Can you believe you're married?" Ophelia hooks her arm in mine and drags me up the stairs as if she owns the house.

I'm still smiling when my eyes lock onto the lion door knocker. Everything inside my gut feels empty. Uncomfortable. Unsettled.

I push open the door just as Kore and Hades come crashing down the stairs in a whirl of black and orange.

"Oh my God!" Ophelia screams, jumping back behind the front door and closing it slightly. "Do they bite?" she asks, poking her head through the gap.

I lean down and squeeze both dogs into my arms. "Not really." I giggle as their tongues slide all over my cheek and neck.

"What do you mean *not really*?" Ophelia yells. "Saint, honey, I need a yes or a no, and if it's a no, I'm out."

There's laughing behind Ophelia as Tillie pushes the door open. "They don't bite if you're with her or Brantley. If not, then your ass is dog meat."

Ophelia's silent, so I nudge my head at her from over my shoulder, just as Madison and Tillie make their way farther into the house. I smile at her. "They won't attack."

Both Ophelia and Ivy step out from behind the door, closing it slowly. Ivy steps forward and starts scratching Kore behind her ear. Kore rolls over onto her back and exposes her belly while Hades glares at her. He's never impressed with how easy she rolls on her back for other people.

"So, let's go hide out in the theatre room and snack out. Sounds like the perfect honeymoon to me," Madison grumbles, stomping into the kitchen with a deadly frown etched on her face. I stand and swipe my hands down my thighs while Tillie follows behind her.

"I'll show you to the rooms you can stay in." Both Ophelia and Ivy follow me up the stairs, with Hades and Kore not far behind. Once I hit the second level, I turn down the opposite wing to mine and Brantley's room, the guest side—that has never been used except for workers.

"There's bedding in the cupboards and your own

bathrooms." I push open both doors. "I have a big enough closet for all three of us to live happily for an entire year without going shopping. What's mine is yours." They both thank me and I leave them to it as I make my way back downstairs to Madison and Tillie. I'm rounding the corner when Tillie exits the pantry, hands filled with potato chips, peanut butter, Nutella spread, and— "Are those pickles?"

She places them all onto the counter as Madison pours hot popcorn from the microwave into a large bowl. It smells like a cinema in the kitchen. "Yes. Don't ask."

"I don't have to because I'm pretty sure we all feel the same way."

Madison growls, "I'm so mad."

"Are you, though?" Tillie asks, an eyebrow quirked. She sighs, leaning against the counter. "Okay, so they made us marry them *right now*." She looks between us. "Remember, we planned to marry them eventually anyway."

"It's not that with me," I say, reaching for the bag of Lay's. "It's that they did it as a ploy, and for what? I don't know. We still don't know because they're all very good and capable of keeping secrets from us, which, by the way, I said I did not want and Brantley agreed. I feel like Brantley only told me that he will be honest with me so that I *didn't* go searching for truths by using my curse." I pop open the jar of Nutella spread, bringing it to my nose and sighing. I love Nutella. I grab a couple of chips and dip them into the spread. "I wanted to know everything." I bite into the chocolate-dipped chip. "I'm mad about that, but I also know there's a chance I'm being unreasonable, but I can't help being so *mad*." I run the edge of my thumb over the rim of my bottom lip, sucking off the gooey residue.

"What is it you're mad about?" Madison asks, reaching for a chip and following what I just did.

I run my tongue over my teeth, sighing. "I don't know."

We get halfway through our second movie when the girls all fall asleep. Madison and Tillie are spread out on the lazy boys with their feet hanging over the side, and Ophelia and Ivy are laid out over their blankets on the floor. The movie is still playing. *Pulp Fiction.* I massage my temples in an attempt to subdue the throbbing headache I've likely caught because of all the sugar. I'm in nothing but an oversized Riverside Prep hoodie and fuzzy white socks that reach just below my calf. My hair is tied into a high pony by a big white scrunchie, but it still almost falls to just above my tailbone. Hades and Kore are on either side of my chair, resting quietly. I need the silence to think. Tillie is right, we all most likely would have married them eventually, but they took away our control. *That's* why I'm mad, I decide.

"Roughly how long are you all going to be mad?" Bishop interrupts my silence from the door, and I turn to face him, hitting pause on the movie with the projector remote.

"I don't know."

He continues walking in until he's beside me on the chair. "Ophelia and Ivy going to stay here?"

"Yeah," I say, crossing my arms in front of myself. "At least until Veronica is accounted for. I don't trust that she won't punish them." I turn to face him. "What is it that you're all keeping from us?"

Bishop shakes his head. "Saint, I love you. I do. But there are certain laws that we still have to abide. I get that all three of you, though vastly different, all agree with one thing, and that's you *think* you want to know what happens. And maybe you do truly want to know, but what it still can't change is that you won't." Bishop is good with twisting his words and making people think they got an answer without actually giving an answer. Poor Madison.

"I know he kills people, Bishop," I whisper softly, my eyes glassing over as I fight my tears to stay down.

"But that's all you know, and that's all he wants you to know." Bishop kicks out his feet. "Did he tell you about the sort of shit that happened to him when he was a kid?"

"Not really. I know things did happen to him because sometimes he would come home with blood on himself, but I never asked him what."

"That's what he needed, Saint," Bishop says, his eyes on mine. "Someone who never asked him *what*."

I sigh, resting my head back against the sofa.

"How mad is she?" Bishop nudges his head over to where Madison is sprawled, her long brown hair trailing behind her.

"Mad, mad."

Bishop smirks, his eyes darkening. "Good."

"She's pregnant. Be nice," I scold him, leaning up off my chair to reach the back of Kore's ear.

"I'm never nice. And if I was, I wouldn't have caught her attention."

"Leave them here for tonight. Let them come home when they want. Give them some control."

Bishop scoffs. "Fuck no." He stands and makes his way to where Madison sleeps. I glare at him, but he ignores me and scoops his arms under her body, picking her up effortlessly. "Night, *princessa*."

"Night." I shake my head at him in disapproval as he disappears through the door.

Nate comes in next, but I don't ignore the fact Brantley is right behind him. I roll my eyes. "You know you're all terrible."

Nate winks at me and picks up Tillie the same way Bishop did Madison. Just as he has her mid-air, her eyes pop open and she slaps his arm. "Put me down. I don't need you to pick me up. I have fucking legs."

Nate swears, placing her back onto her feet. "You're fucking impossible, you know that?"

They both leave, and now it's just Ophelia and Ivy who are snoring on the floor. Brantley hasn't moved farther into the space, and I haven't brought my eyes up to his. Truth, I'm afraid. The only thing worse than knowing you love someone irrevocably is feeling your sanity leave your soul anytime he looks at you. That's what Brantley does to me. Anytime he's near, I feel his heat against my skin. Anytime he talks, the words that leave his mouth find a home in my bones, and every time he looks at me, it's like a shot of paralysis being pushed through my veins. He's well-aware of the power he holds over me, and instead of being a gentleman about it, he uses it as ammunition and shoots me in the heart.

I stand from my chair and make my way toward him, keeping my eyes a safe distance away from him. I just don't want to do this in here, near O and Ivy, and risk waking them up. I'm passing his chest, ready to walk into the kitchen, or hell, outside, when his hand flies to my arm and he slams me against the wall. There goes that idea.

I groan, my eyes closing. "Stop."

He's in front of me, I can feel him. I can feel the warmth from his deep breaths fall over my lips. The unspoken words that haven't passed his lips yet. "I don't like being ignored, Dea."

I turn my head away from him. "I'm not ignoring you. I'm just—"

"—upset?" He leans down and brushes his lips over mine, sending a surge of electricity straight to my core. "Good. Get upset, but you do that shit in front of me, not behind me."

Finally, I turn to face him. He's so close that all I can see are his dark eyes. Smoldering heat. *I can't breathe.* He leaves burning embers in his wake, but I'd follow in his footsteps anyway.

"Why are you upset with me?" he asks, searching my eyes. He rests one hand up near my head and leaves the other to his side. "Because you married me, or because you preferred it better when you knew you couldn't have me?"

I snap back in shock. "What?"

He pushes off the wall and leaves, walking up the stairs. I stay for a few moments before I realize I need to follow him up. By the time I reach his bedroom, his door is closed. I contemplate knocking. Then think about barging in and demanding that he explains what he's talking about. My mouth opens and I rest my hand on the doorknob but hesitate.

"Just do it," Bailey says, and I turn to face her. She's leaning against the wall where the staircase separates the two wings. Her eyes are rimmed red, and she sniffs, swiping beneath them. "Honestly just do it. He loves you, Saint."

"Are you okay?" I ask, ignoring what she just announced. She may be his cousin, but she doesn't know him the way I do. She doesn't know that he is incapable of love, and I don't say that lightly. "Have you been crying?"

Bailey closes her eyes and pushes off the wall, folding her arms across her chest. It's a ridiculous question because I know she has been. It's obvious. "I'm fine." She gestures to the door. "Make things right with him. You're going to need each other." She disappears around the corner and I stare back at his door. The black to my white. I fall backward, sliding down my bedroom door while keeping my eyes on his. How many times have I found him in this exact position over the years, right outside my door? Brantley may not be able to love, but that has never stopped my ever-growing feelings for him anyway.

His door swings open and our eyes collide. He's shirtless and wearing nothing but gray sweats that hang off the tight curve of his abs. His hair is damp, and droplets of water slide down the deep lines of his muscles. "What are you doing?"

I rest my head against my door and lean up to look at him. "I don't know."

He steps forward, standing over me. He brings his hand beneath my chin and tilts my face up to his. I try to ignore the way his fingers wrap around the entire bottom half of my face, or that in this position, looking up at him from the floor, is a pretty questionable position to be found in if Bailey decides to come back up. He runs the cushion of his thumb over my bottom lip. "The next time you run into my arms I won't be letting you go, Saint, so be careful with which door you choose to walk through." His hand drops down to his side and he disappears down the hallway, until I hear his footsteps fade down the stairs. I know what I want. I've always known it's him. I think deep down that's not the battle I'm fighting. What's he going to say when he finds out the secret I've been hiding from him? That someone has been sneaking into my mind, wearing his face, and tormenting me every night.

I stand and glance between the two of them, before taking the step I knew I would take.

CHAPTER TWENTY

Brantley

Dad was in his office, talking with Uncle Hector. Usually when they were in there, I didn't go in. All their talk of Elite Kings' business wasn't a place for me right now. At least not yet. I pushed my way through the hallway anyway, desperate to hear whatever the fuck it was they were talking about.

"That girl will be in danger all her life," Hector said, placing a cigar in his mouth.

"Mmm," my father mused. "I'm sure Brantley will make sure she's safe."

"And his mother?" Hector probed. "What does he know of her?"

"The truth. That she's dead." His answer was clipped and burned with a bitterness that couldn't go unnoticed.

I paused, reaching for my phone in my pocket.

"Thank Christ for that."

I stepped backward and dialed the number on my phone, stepping out to the back patio and rounding the pool. I needed to put a safe distance between my father and me if I wanted to have enough time to end this conversation.

"Yes?" Her voice broke through softly and I relaxed.

"How did you pull off your fake death?"

She didn't answer, allowing seconds to pass between us before finally whispering, "Because he's evil and I had enough need to stay alive. You give someone enough reason to do something, and they make it possible. I stayed low, paid off the right people." I swallowed the saliva that was in my throat. "You trust me, you don't ever trust him, Brantley. You know what he does to you. The kind of acts he makes you do to all those girls, too. What kind of man would do that?"

"I know." I took a seat on a lawn chair, running my fingers through my hair. I could already feel the frustration and anger bubbling beneath my skin. I trusted her more than my father, and painfully close to how I trusted my brothers. From the first ever phone call I got from her, to now, she has done nothing but look out for Saint and help me with Lucan.

I heard her shuffle in the background. "Never tell him that I'm alive, Brantley. Because when you need me, I won't be here. When she needs me, I will no longer be here." She paused. "And she will need me." I hung up and tossed the phone on the chair. I already knew Saint held the curse, so I knew Veronica was right. Eventually, she's going to need the guidance of my mother.

Hector sits on the sofa in the corner of my sitting room. I want to push away the thoughts of what door Saint decided to go into and focus on Hector and why he's here, but it is all I can think about.

"What is it you want, Hector? Or are you here to beg me not to kill you one day?" I walk further into the sitting room with a bottle of water up against my mouth. I fall down on the sofa opposite him, turning the fireplace on with a simple push of a button. I run my fingers over my abs.

His eyes fall. "Do any of you ever wear shirts?"

"I'm in my home. You're lucky I'm wearing anything at all."

Hector chuckles, throwing his leg over his knee. "I heard your house is rather full as of late. With Bailey and Abel always around, and then the two new witches you've come to acquire."

"What can I say?" I bare my teeth. "I like collecting weird shit."

Hector leans forward in his chair, the flames from the fire burning against his cheek. "Do you understand why I was taking her to Perdita now? Why I defied the plan during the ceremony to get her away from Veronica?"

I think over his intentions. His *always* intentions, not just his now intentions. In Hector's own way, I do see why he was taking her to Perdita, now that I know my judgment of my mother was severely wrong. She had dug her nails deep inside my head from a young boy and groomed me to trust her. "What I don't understand is why. Why would she go through all of this for Saint?"

"That's something I don't know, son. Sorry." I stand from my chair and make my way to the alcohol cabinet. "The good thing is, no one has ever outrun us before, so we should be able to find her."

I laugh into my glass, sipping on the burning liquid. "Something tells me she's going to be the Katerina Petrova of our world." I swirl the liquid in my glass and keep my eyes on the fire. "Do you know what her gifts are?"

Hector flexes his neck. "I do not, but I know she doesn't just hold one, but two. She has never disclosed to anyone what they are."

"Well, what could they be? Realistically."

"Realistically, son, dark magic does exist. It's in the mind of those witches. The more they believe, the more dangerous they are."

"And what's going to happen to Saint?"

"Well, The Coven will either be burned or she will have to think about taking it on."

I clench my teeth. "And what about The Gentlemen?"

"You all have a meeting with the new capo." Hector stands from the sofa. "Try to hear him out, too, Brantley. I know your vendetta against them runs deep, but Danny is different. He's not like his uncle and cousin. He plans to co-exist with us and settle the beef." I grit my teeth as Hector comes closer, squeezing my shoulder. "I—"

"—You motherfucker!" Bishop comes flying into the lounge like a fucking tornado and I step backward, careful not to spill my drink. I almost thought he was coming for me when I realize he's going straight for Hector. His fist is flying into his father's face before I can stop him.

"Son!" Hector dodges his next swing and grabs him by the arm. Hector's shoulders tighten, his chin lifting. "Sit the fuck down and talk like a fucking *King* and not like a fucking street rat."

Bishop's nostrils are flaring, his shoulders rising and falling as he breathes. "You gonna tell him, or should I? Hmm?" Bishop raises an eyebrow, and I take that as my cue to place my glass down onto the bar and slowly make my way to them.

"What are you talking about, Bishop?" I ask, but my eyes stay on Hector.

"You may be my father, but I will not hesitate to kill you if you go after any of ours, and by the sounds of it, you have."

"What are you talking about, son?" Hector asks calmly. I'm still taking calculated steps, ready to move when I need to.

"You let Veronica out last night." As soon as the words leave his mouth, I feel my body tense. I swear I can hear the loud fucking thundering of my heart in my chest. I'm going to kill him. Bishop fists Hector's collar, pulling his face closer to him. I've never seen Bishop face-off with his father like this, but I have seen him lose it a few times. This is different. I have no doubt that, if needed, Bishop would put his father down. For Saint, he definitely would.

Hector shoves Bishop off him, dusting off his suit. "First of all, I'm going to break your fucking nose for throwing down before getting facts straight. Have I not taught you anything at all? Second of all—" He sneers at both of us, his lip curling but his demeanor still clean. Tight. As if he's allowing us to see his anger while remaining completely in control. "Have you ever wondered *why* I haven't just killed Veronica to begin with?" He unbuttons his jacket and lowers himself onto the sofa, while gesturing to the other opposite him, his jaw tense. He is pissed. *So the fuck am I.* I'm sick of finding out all of the shit he has done *after* he does it.

"You have five minutes," Bishop replies calmly. Too calm.

"Three," I correct, falling to the spot beside him.

Hector stares between us. "Veronica has put a bounty on Saint's head. She's had it active for a while, from what I can see. She doesn't know that I know this, but I've known for some time."

Squeezing my fist in the palm of my hand to stop myself from completely losing it, I manage to grit out, "How long and explain."

"I've known she was alive all along, Brantley." My mouth opens to ask another question, but he shakes his head, clearly wanting to continue. "The bounty she has on Saint is known by all six gangs in New York City. She kept it local, so it's manageable if we can get them all together."

"What's the fucking problem then?" I'm dancing dangerously

close to losing my shit. She has a fucking bounty on Saint, and I let her walk right into the bitch's arms. "Why the fuck haven't you worked all these years to get it off her?"

Hector tilts his head to the side. "Have you forgotten what one of the four gangs is?"

"The Gentlemen." Bishop sighs, massaging his temples. "You couldn't get them to sway, even if you fucking paid them before."

"Correct, but now it's different because Danny is capo. I do feel he can be bought, though I'm not expecting it to be cheap."

I grimace. The whiskey isn't helping me right now. If anything, it's making everything worse. I push my glass away on the coffee table and lean forward. "We will handle the meeting with them all, Gentlemen included."

Bishop's hand rests on my shoulder before he looks back at Hector. "Sorry, Dad. I fucking flipped."

Hector stands from his chair. "Son, I respect the hell out of you and am proud of how far you have come and the direction in which you're taking The Kings—" He buttons up his jacket, pausing when he reaches us. "But either of you try to ambush me like that again and I'll fucking cut you." He leaves the same way Bishop arrived, and as soon as he's out of the room, everything suddenly feels too heavy. I fucking pushed her into Veronica's arms and believed every word she fucking fed me. I took the damn bait. I've never trusted Hector completely. I always knew there were too many secrets hiding behind all that fancy hair. But now, I see it. I see his intention for Saint and how wrong I was to allow Veronica to take her. He had tried to stop it from the fucking beginning, and we all assumed he was working against us. I practically forced her into that coven, thinking my mother had every intention of keeping her safe.

How fucking wrong I was.

"Don't start that shit." Bishop's voice is low, his arms crossing in front of him. I forgot he was still here.

I run my hand over my face and let out a frustrated growl. "It's my fault."

"Shut the fuck up, Brantley. You did what you thought was right. We know now, and she's safe. Let that shit go, brother." He stands, patting my shoulder. "If you need to revise it after we put Veronica down, fine. We will all sit in The Palace and fucking hash through it all, but you're not carrying that shit on your own. I'll see you in the morning." I don't answer him, and it's not until I hear the front door close that I backhand my glass off the coffee table and watch as it flies across the room and explodes against the wall. Leaning on my elbows, I close my eyes and start counting to ten. By the time I hit eight, I've realigned my priorities and am on the same page as Bishop. He's right. We need to remain vigilant. *We will fucking win this.* Flicking off the light, I make my way back up to my bedroom and see she's not where I left her when I get there. I go for her room first, because if she's in there, I'm dragging her ass out and into mine. As if I really gave her a damn choice. Do I look like fucking Bishop?

I shove the door open until the handle hits the wall on the other side.

Empty.

The corner of my lip slowly curls up when I turn and realize she's made the right choice.

Stepping forward, I swing open my bedroom door and find her body wrapped in blankets horizontally. She's fast asleep, with her arm covering her forehead and her leg dangling off the bed. She looks like an angel, but she sleeps like a fucking menace. I take a moment, just watching her sleep. It's not until my eyes fall down to Hades and Kore staring up at me from the foot of the bed that I make my way into the bathroom to brush my teeth.

Slipping under the covers on my side, if you can even fucking call it that, I snake my arm around her waist and yank her into my body. She wriggles in my grip. "Tired."

I sink my teeth into the back of her neck. "Don't care."

She moves onto her back and rests her hand on my cheek. "It's not because I married you tonight." I pause. I don't want to have this conversation with her right now.

"Not what I wanted to talk about. Go back to sleep."

She ignores me. "It's—there's something I need to tell you, and you're not going to like it."

Instantly, my hackles are fucking arching to the high heavens for the second time tonight. Fuck. "What?"

She tries to shuffle away from me, but I tighten my grip around her waist, pulling her flush against my chest. She sighs when she realizes she can't fight me. "You know those texts I was telling you I started receiving?"

I nod.

She bites her bottom lip. "And you know how I told you about seeing you in the limo after the ceremony?" My grip tenses around her waist. It'll bruise. She brings her arm around the back of my neck, and that's when I know whatever she's going to tell me, I'm going to fucking flip.

"Before you try to tell me that I have some fucking twin brother, I don't."

She shakes her head. "No, I know. It's not that. It's, I've been seeing someone every time I close my eyes. Sometimes my eyes aren't even closed." She pauses, pushing off my chest and turning onto her back. This time I let her. Her eyes are focused on the ceiling. "At first when I saw him, I was confused. I thought maybe you did have a twin brother."

"Wait, he looks exactly like me?"

She turns her head. "He doesn't just look like you, Brantley. He *is* you." My fist clenches. I can feel the familiar thudding of my heart as it begins racing. "In the beginning, he stayed away from me. A good distance. I'd see him when I was first in The Coven. Once or twice and it was very brief. I thought it was you those times because he was so far away and I thought you were in the limo with me. Then he started showing me weird things inside my head." She turns back to face me, tucking her hands beneath her cheek. I don't have the will to grab her because I know I need to snap something. Anger and frustration are swimming inside of me and I know that if I have her in my arms, I might fucking hurt her. "I think he didn't come close to me those two times because he knew I would know it wasn't you. The first time I saw him inside my head, I knew. Though he looked like you—a replica—it wasn't you. He was too—simple. But by this point, he didn't care. He almost wanted me to know that it wasn't you."

Before she can continue, I ask, "So this is who has been sending those texts?" I'm leaning up on one elbow now, glaring down at her.

She flinches. "Yes."

"So he's real? As in, I can feel his blood spill over my hands when I fucking kill him?"

She stares up at me. "Yes."

"Fucking good. So who is he?"

She breathes out, her eyes turning dim. "Well, I don't know. That's the problem."

A deep growl escapes my mouth and I swing my legs out of bed, tearing the covers from my body and reaching for my phone on the bedside table. The light from the screen blinds me, but I search Bishop's number and hit dial.

"Brantley," Saint whispers from behind me, but it's too late. All I see is fucking red. "Just give me enough time and I'll figure it out."

"What?" I snap, shoving her hand off my arm. "As in allow this fucker inside your head to do whatever the fuck he wants to you?" I stand, hitting dial on Bishop again. I start pacing back and forward. "Nah, fuck that. He knows that's the only way he can get to you. You're motherfucking untouchable every other way."

Bishop finally answers. "Fuck, Bran. The fuck?"

"Someone's inside Saint's head with her visions. Someone who is fucking appearing as me."

Bishop grunts and I hear blankets shuffling in the background. "I missed the days where our problems didn't involve ghosts."

"Not a fucking ghost."

"So hypnosis? Telekinesis? What?" Bishop asks, suddenly wide awake.

"Fuck knows, but it's something."

"All right. Meet at The Palace in the morning. Seems we got a lot of shit to talk about, but I was thinking at the home tonight that we might need to get the girls onto Perdita. It's the only place that's safe, at least until we figure out what the fuck is going on."

"We can't leave Saint there. She's the key to it." I turn around and squeeze my eyes closed. "B, he's *inside her head* every time she closes her eyes. How the fuck can I stop that?" I'm aware my breathing is rigid and the veins in my neck are pulsing one hundred beats a minute.

"Meeting in the morning. Try not to think too much into it. Fuck, you're just not used to having no control over her."

"Fuck you," I snap, hanging up on him and flinging my phone across the room.

"Brantley," Saint repeats. I grind my teeth. Needing something. Anything to release the angst in my bones. "It's fine." *It's not fine.* I'm about one more revelation to snapping. Bodies are going to start dropping if I find out *one* more fucking thing.

I back up against the wall, needing some distance between us. "How's he getting in?"

"We don't know." She crawls up the bed, wrapping her arms

around her legs. "Ophelia is going to find out. She knows more about it than me. Can we just worry about it tomorrow?"

I fall down the wall and hike one knee up against my chest while resting my arm over top. "It's cute how you think I'm getting any sleep tonight. Or fucking ever."

She slides out from beneath the covers, sliding the scrunchie out of her hair and tossing it onto the floor before curling her fingers beneath my hoodie. She pulls it over her head and drops it onto the floor, tilting her head. "What about now?"

Her swollen breasts move with every breath she takes. I push up from the floor. "You win." I wrap my fingers around the back of her thighs when I reach her, throwing her onto the bed. She arches her back up as I spread her knees wide. So fucking responsive.

She wriggles beneath my grip, but I tense.

I lower my mouth down onto her inner thigh, sucking her skin into my mouth hard enough to leave the notorious mark of *you're fucking owned*. I continue to suck and kiss my way to her clit. She's panting and moaning, cursing at me every time I blow on her.

"Brantley!" she screams. "Put your damn tongue on me!"

I chuckle deeply, running the tip of my nose up the slit of her pussy. "Okay, baby, damn… chill…" I then stroke her clit with my tongue until she comes in my mouth.

CHAPTER TWENTY-ONE

Saint

I'm running on the treadmill the next day—because Brantley won't let me out of his sight long enough to run the dogs—when Madison pushes through the gym doors, wearing a sports bra and small shorts. Her belly is perfection. A small round, tanned bump. She ties her hair up into a high pony, making her way to the treadmill beside mine.

"So they're trying to ship Tillie and me to Perdita until this bitch is found." She pushes some buttons and begins walking.

"That's a good thing, though, right? Brantley says it's safe there?"

Madison smiles softly, but it doesn't reach her eyes. "Beautiful isn't an efficient enough word to use when describing the overall aesthetic of Perdita, but beneath all of her beauty, there's a darkness that will never wash away. And aside from that." She ups her speed and I double check to make sure she hasn't bumped it too high. The girl is carrying twins. My nieces or nephews. "I don't know if anyone told you this, but I had a brother. A twin brother." She rubs circles around her belly. "It's why I'm having twins, I guess."

"Oh, no one has told me." I quiet, leaving enough silence for her to speak. Friendship is a gift. An expensive one. You can't just give it to anyone. There are times when a friend needs someone to talk to, and there are times when they need to be talked to. Right now, I'm guessing she needs someone to talk to.

She takes a swig of her water, upping her speed again. My eyes dart between her and the number on her treadmill. Crazy woman. "They won't. No one likes to talk about Daemon. He was so special, especially to Tillie and me. I found out he was my brother on that island. He was raised on that island" —she sucks in a breath— "he died on that island. I didn't know him long, but as soon as I met him, we were inseparable. Tillie had a deep connection to him, too, so I guess that's why neither of us is in a hurry to get back to Perdita, and aside from that, Tillie has history there. As does Nate." She sucks in deep breaths and I reach forward to lower her speed, glaring at her when her mouth opens and she's about to fight me.

"I'm sorry to hear about your brother. I can't even think about losing Bishop." I wince at the thought, my eyes tearing up. "Nate has history there?"

Madison rolls her eyes. "I love him. So much. But the boy stuck his dick in places that he should never have stuck it."

I chuckle, bumping down my speed to a walking pace. There's no way I can talk and run without passing out, and since I didn't end up getting much sleep last night, despite Brantley riding me into a coma, I don't want to test my chances. Even with the bite marks on my inner thighs still fresh. "He loves her, though."

"Oh, more than anything ever. They fought for their love. They fought hard."

"Who fought hard?" Tillie interrupts from behind us, biting into a glazed donut while sneering at the gym equipment as she passes. She pauses her chewing. "See, this is why I'm bigger than you with one baby. Because while you're exercising, I'm eating."

Madison frowns, gesturing to the other treadmill. "Then exercise if it'll make you feel better."

"Fuck no." Tillie continues eating her donut, taking a seat on the bench. "This is my chance to chill. Got lots of time to be fit, but during pregnancy is not it, and anyway, the boys are kicking us to Perdita." She places her hands on her lap. "Maybe that's why I'm stress eating."

I turn off the treadmill and wipe my face with a towel. "It will be safer with you all there."

"Mmmm." Tillie sucks the frosting off the tip of her fingers. "You wait until you meet our replacement who is running the island right now."

Madison tosses her towel at Tillie. "Stop acting like you would actually *want* that job."

Tillie muses over her words and then shrugs. "You're right. I absolutely wouldn't." She looks to me. "Where are your other two girls?"

"They're down having breakfast, where we should be." I call out while passing her, making my way down to the kitchen with both pregnant bellies in tow. As soon as I round the kitchen corner, the smell of fried fat hits my nose and puts my head in a spin. My hand flies up to cover my mouth as I dash back down the hallway and into the guest bathroom, flipping open the toilet and expelling everything I ate last night. I swipe my mouth with the back of my hand and flush, knocking the cover down and taking a seat on top. Sweat beads at my temples as my stomach rolls.

"Can he do this, too? Make you sick?" Brantley interrupts from the doorway, filling the space completely.

I shrug. "I don't know. Maybe." Reaching for the mouthwash that's on the counter, I take a swig while pumping soap into my palms and scrubbing. "Ivy can go with them to Perdita," I say, after I've spat and rinsed my hands.

Brantley stares at me, and it's the first time I've noticed the slight dark circles under his eyes. With anyone else, it would look exactly what it is. Rough. Drained. But with Brantley, it just makes him look more like a damn vampire. Scary. Deranged. Volatile. Which he is. Usually he's so assertive and staunch, but since telling him about my visions last night, he's more on edge.

"Done. But Ophelia stays. We might need her."

I dry my hands and lean against the sink. "You should go get some sleep."

"I'm fine."

I close the space between us, lifting his heavy arm and placing it over my shoulder. "You should go and get some sleep." Looking up at him hurts my neck.

"Bacon is ready!" Ophelia calls out from the kitchen.

Brantley moans. "You do realize all of these people, including Tillie and Madison, are only allowed in this house because of you, right?"

I tilt my head while keeping my eyes on his, pressing my lips to his arm. "I know." I step out from under him. "Please get some sleep. I can't imagine you grumpier than usual." The bacon smell doesn't hit me as hard as before as I pull out one of the stools beneath the kitchen island.

"Can he make me nauseous?" I ask Ophelia as she scoops scrambled eggs into a large bowl.

She peers up at me from beneath her lashes. "No. Remember, it's not paranormal. It's science, but—more." I know Ophelia believes in the science side of everything, but I've seen things. How can she classify me seeing a dead girl as science?

Tillie smothers thick spread over her toast. "I swear boys make you hungrier than girls. I was never like this before."

Before I can ask her about her last pregnancy, the boys pile in and start loading their plates.

"Hey." I turn in my seat, looking at Bishop. "Where's Eli?" I haven't seen him since the ceremony.

Bishop tilts his chin, a satisfied grin flashing over his mouth. "Busy."

"Okay…" My stomach rumbles, but the sweat is still sticky on my shirt from my run, so I tear it off and toss it to the other side of the room.

I take a plate and move to the dining table, listening as they all talk about normal conversations that don't include crazy witch mothers and rich covens.

∽

I watched her carefully this time. A little more than usual. I'd begun to look forward to the times I could attach myself to her. I fed off of it. Needed it. I didn't want it to ever stop. She was looking down at a gravestone in the Vitiosis cemetery, her hair down over her shoulders and her eyes weak. She was in a dream state. Not knowing what was happening to her, but not caring either. This was the part where I knocked on her head and got her to let me in, but they were catching onto what I was doing. They weren't far behind. I wasn't at all surprised by this. I knew every step I took was just one copied.

Her arm reached out toward the stone, her fingers grazing the fuzzy moss growing through the cracks. She curled her finger and a high pitch shriek bellowed when she ran her finger down, dirt catching itself beneath her clean nails. I wanted to follow her tonight. Maybe see where her subconscious wanted to take her.

Feel where she wanted to go when not being forced to be with me. Her movements stopped. Birds flew out from the trees and insects that were once loud were now silent. Something was wrong. Her head moved like static, half of her hair falling over her back. Her eyes came to mine. White. Completely white. No color.

I stilled, looking around myself. Something wasn't right. What was she doing?

She raised her hand and pointed one finger at me. "You're going to die."

"Stop!" Ophelia grabs my arm as I fly off the bed, sweat slick over my skin. It has only been a few hours since Tillie and Madison flew off to Perdita with Tate and Spyder, but I wanted to get started straight away. Brantley, Bishop, and Nate are in the room with O and me, so I know I'm in safe hands. Safe enough to do this.

Ophelia wipes my sticky hair from my forehead. "We can't go too hard. He read that something was wrong."

"Do you know who he is?" Brantley seethes, sitting beside me on the bed. Bishop is on the other side and Nate is standing at the bottom of the bed.

"No." Ophelia sighs. "He's still appearing as you."

Brantley kicks off the bed. As he heads toward the bathroom, he slams his palm against the wall before disappearing inside.

Nate whistles while looking up to where there's a fresh hole. "He needs to kill someone. Preferably whoever is in your head. We have roughly—" Nate looks to Bishop. "Twenty hours to find out who this person is before we're all in danger from him."

"I'd say ten hours," Bishop grumbles, shaking his head.

"This person." Ophelia searches my eyes. "He has to have a connection to you to be able to do this. Who did you make friends with when the texts started coming through?"

"No one," I say, shaking my head. "I don't know if you've noticed, but I'm pretty sheltered."

Ophelia curls her lips beneath her teeth to stop from laughing. "Okay. So it can't be that. Maybe they're using another line to you, but that would mean whoever he is using would have to be very close to you. It all works that way when you're an empath—an especially strong one like you. We feed off of emotions, whether we want to or not, and we form connections to people, whether we want to or not. I fear this may have been what has happened here."

I shuffle up the bed to rest my head against the abundance of pillows. "The only people I'm truly close to are Brantley, Bishop, and Madison and Tillie. That's all."

Ophelia stands, hand on her hip while she begins pacing the room. "It has to be one of them." She runs her fingers through her long hair, brushing it back. "There's no other way he could possibly put you under like that."

"So let me get this straight." Nate takes a seat on the only chair in the corner of my room. "He's using hypnosis and then visiting her in her dream state?"

"Yes," Ophelia says. "It is possible. But you have to know what you're doing."

I rest back against my headboard. "This is getting tedious."

Chapter Twenty-Two

Brantley

I'm known to be unreasonable when it comes to Saint. I'm aware of that. But every single fucking night that she goes to sleep, I can't rest. It has been three fucking weeks and we still have no lead on whoever the fuck it is that's playing mind games with her, and on top of that, both leads we had on Veronica have run cold. The Coven is completely cleaned out, except for the furniture, and I've sent Benny on a mission to find the other two girls who were in The Coven with Saint. I want them both caged until I know exactly what their part was in all of this. They're on borrowed time if they were in bed with Veronica. One thing I'm thankful for during all of this, is there's no Kings' business bringing more heat to our plate. I haven't let my mind travel to that place where I've locked away my guilt because I know it can consume me. I need Veronica dead, and I preferably need to be the one who does it. I don't kill women, children, or old people—unless they're fucking rapists and pedophiles. But I'll make an exception for her. First, I need to know why.

I lean down and touch the unmarked headstone, swiping the green vines that wrap around the edges. "If only dead men speak. I could do with a hint of what the fuck Veronica Vitiosis ever wanted with Saint." Lucan was a piece of shit. He more than hurt people; he destroyed them, and I was just another product of his carnage. But if there's one thing I found odd about him is that he never, ever ratted out Saint. He never spoke of her to anyone. At first, I assumed he did that for Hector. Lucan Vitiosis was absolute with his undying loyalty to The Kings. I was happy with that. Fucking glad. He may have been a perverted pedophile who preyed on young people and got off on watching his son deflower virgins, but he had one redeeming factor: his loyalty to The Kings and his willingness to destroy anything to protect the Vitiosis name.

I realize how fucking stupid that sounds. If Lucan didn't give a fuck about anyone and anything but himself, it would be easier for me to hate him—and I hate him—I hate him with every single fucking ounce of what makes me, me. I don't need more reasons to hate the man, which is why I have no issue admitting that. Veronica is different. Did she and Lucan plan this all-a-fucking-long? Did Lucan always know she was alive? No. Can't be. The mind of a Vitiosis is an endless pit of confusion. They're the snake in the grass you don't want to step on. Every single movement they make is calculated and thoroughly thought-out. I'm just like them. To my very core, a fucking Vitiosis, but I'm working hard to use it in a different way. Not how they always did.

My loyalty to The Kings is unmatched, but my loyalty to Saint is lethal. I'd walk through flames for her before I ever allow her to so much as feel the heat of pain.

When I met her, I was fascinated, but when I came to know

her, she was my obsession. I treated her as my possession because if I looked at her as a girl, I knew I'd fuck her. I could never trust myself with her. Not even in my thoughts. So I blocked it all out. I blocked her out. I became void, which was easy. I was a Vitiosis, after all. I became the snake in the grass that curled around her feet, waiting for someone to come too close before I'd bite.

"Didn't think I'd find you out here." Just the sound of her voice is enough to disarm me. I don't like her being so close to Lucan, even if he's dead.

I turn to face her, leaning against his headstone. Her eyes float down, her head tilting. "Whose grave is that?"

I squeeze the stone, decaying rocks crumbling to the ground. "No one."

Her brows pull in. When I gather she's not going to stop staring at the headstone, I feel my muscles tense, and the longer time passes, the more my blood boils. I push off the stone and grab her by the hand, pulling her into my chest.

She peers up at me from below. "I'm sorry I can't help. I want this over as much as anyone."

I run my tongue over my lip and move her hair away from her shoulder. "And I'm sorry I can't kill him. But I will." My jaw clenches, my fingers tightening around her small chin. I force her eyes to mine. "I fucking promise you I will kill him."

She smiles sweetly up at me. So fucking sweet. Too sweet. I can't believe I ever deprived myself of her. I know why I've been void for so long—because I needed her to fill the parts that were stolen from me as a kid. "You don't need to do that. But just so you know, Ophelia hasn't left the bedroom in days, and I'm beginning to worry this is consuming her. She has grimoires spread out over her bed, and papers upon papers on *What people don't want you to know: Scientific facts about how powerful the human mind can become*. I think I even saw a paper with the words *'how to know if you're using all of your brain.'* I've been taking food into her, but she refuses. As if she's too lost in her train of thought to come up for air."

"Leave her be, Dea. That will be how she—" I wave my hand, "witches, or whatever." The afternoon dips behind a large black cloud in the sky as thunder rumbles deep through the forest.

Saint looks around the cemetery. "It's weird when I think about it," she says, shaking her head while stepping away from me. "How often I dream about this place. How many times you've found me here."

She runs her hand over the headstone, her long white hair pulled to the side. Over the past few weeks, her body has filled into her clothes. I don't know if that's just her changing as she gets older, or if it's from her obvious peak of appetite.

I'm fucking here for it.

The curve of her ass and the dip in her thighs when she bends over to pick a dead flower from the ground has my cock swelling in my jeans. She turns, looking up at me with the faded orange petals pushed to her cheek. "Maybe I like dead things?"

"You like me, so it makes sense."

Her eyes are on mine. "I love you, Brantley. Not like." She turns her back on me, dropping the dead flower to the front of Lucan's stone. She doesn't know it's Lucan, because it's unmarked, but it still fucking pisses me off that she's petting it. Enough to ignore the fact she's suddenly mad about something.

She turns back to face me, resting her hand on my chest as she goes to pass. She pauses. "I'm aware that you will never say those words back to me. I don't care about that." When I refuse to take my eyes off that fucking dead flower she placed on Lucan's headstone, her hand comes to my cheek and she forces my eyes to hers. She's getting bossy. "But I want you to know that loving you has been the easiest thing I have ever done. It's natural to me, Brantley. I think I loved you before I even knew you existed, and that kind of love is strong enough for the both of us." She's about to continue back to the main house, but I catch her hand before she can leave.

She looks over her shoulder as I run my thumb over her bare knuckles. My mouth opens. *What the fuck are you going to say to that?* I run my tongue over my teeth. "Come here."

She ambles back to me, back into my arms where she belongs. Her eyes fall to the necklace around my neck. The same chain she has, only hers is her coven's crown. The very fucking emblem I thought would protect her has ended up being the very thing that has put her in danger. Her fingers glide over the new pendant on mine. "What's this?"

I look down to the small vial that's clipped around my Cuban chain, before smirking up at her behind hooded eyes. "Hmmm, not sure you'd want to know…"

She shuffles on her feet, running the cushion of her palm over the small bottle filled with a drop of blood. A single drop. "I do," she whispers, and my heart fucking smashes against my rib cage when I see a blaze of fire behind her innocent gray eyes. It's not a bright blaze. More like a heavy wave of flames, strong and demanding to be felt, more than seen.

Fuck. Me.

"Your blood."

She doesn't flinch. "My blood?"

"Yup." I pop the letter at the end.

"Now I want yours."

I pause, intertwining her fingers with mine and bringing them up to my mouth. I bite down on her index finger. "That's not even the worst part."

"I assumed so," she said, her eyes glassing over as she watches my tongue flick over her finger.

"Can you guess where this blood is from, Dea?"

She licks the bottom of her lip and my stomach drops to

the ground. If this turns her on, I'm going to fucking pass out. "Probably."

I chuckle, grazing one of my canines down the inside of her finger. "Still love me?"

"Worse," she says, her throat flexing when she swallows. "I want you to fuck me." I see fucking red. I pick her up from the backs of her thighs and she wraps them around my waist as I back her up to sit on the headstone behind her. My mouth is on hers in an instant, because fuck, who would have thought I'd love kissing so much. With her, it's different. She raises her hips up and grinds against the swell in my pants. "Brantley. Hard and fast. Please," she begs into my mouth. Between her sweet kisses and the gentleness of her tongue, she whispers something fucking gnarly and I Eat. It. Up.

"Hard and fast, huh?" I say, grabbing at the waistband of her pants and yanking them down. She raises her hips up quickly, while forcing the button of my jeans off and pulling down the zipper. She rubs her hand over my cock and I groan, biting her bottom lip as my fingers find their way to her middle. I brush my thumb over her clit, down her slit, and increase pressured circles.

Her head falls forward onto my chest. "Brantley. Fuck me. I'm serious."

I grab my cock and direct it over her wet slit while my other hand tangles in her hair, tugging it back so she looks at me. "Seeing your virginity on my neck turns you on?"

She bites down on her lip.

"Admit what it made you feel like and I'll fuck you so hard my cock will think it has a new home." I rub the tip against her clit, ignoring how wet she's dripping off me. "Truth, Saint."

She moans. "Yes! Okay! Yes! It turns me on."

I squeeze the back of her neck and force her lips to mine. "Why?"

"Oh my God, Brantley," she whimpers, directing herself

closer to my cock. I'm going to fucking explode if I carry on, but what can I say, I'm a masochist.

"Why?" I repeat, teasing the entrance of her tight gap.

"Because I've marked you! You're mine. *Just mine.*"

Sweat spills from my temples and drips down my neck, over the pulsing veins that are prodding through my skin. I grab her by her ass cheeks and slam inside so fast she screams. "Good answer." Pulling out, I drive into her hard and fast, just as she wanted, biting down on her neck to silence my own groans. I'm fucking obsessed with her. Everything she is I will always be. I know this. I fucking married her. *She's mine.* I grab onto her throat and squeeze as I pick up the pace. Her body bounces off mine hard as cries of pleasure leave her soft lips. Her walls clench around my throbbing cock, licking the rim like a fucking suction vise. I know my obsession with her is deadly. I'll kill people. My friends. The old fucking lady walking down the street. Suddenly, my kill code is faulty when it comes to her safety. If anyone so much as breathes near her in a threatening way, I'll fucking kill them. Her legs tighten around my waist as I lick the blood on her neck.

She lets out one more soft whimper as she throbs around my dick. Just as she's coming down, I pull out slowly and slam into her so hard her teeth clatter. And then again. Tears pool in the corner of her eyes when I unleash all of my anger, my resentment, my fucking feelings for her until the intoxicating explosion erupts around my balls, shooting through my veins.

We stay like this for a few more seconds, until we catch our breath, then I slowly, and not willingly, pull out of her, tossing her pants to her first before tugging up mine.

"I'm obsessed with you," I say, keeping my eyes on hers while tucking my still hard dick back into my jeans. "And that should terrify you."

CHAPTER TWENTY-THREE

Saint

There was an old clock in the center of the room. I couldn't see it. But I could hear it. The distinct sound of time running out. A reminder that no matter how untouchable we thought we were, time was the one thing that could reach through at any given moment and take us. Like a Grim Reaper, gliding through purgatory and choosing his next victims.

This time was different. I was in my head. Not in his head. I liked this better, because I could study him closer now. Maybe he didn't want me in his anymore; maybe he knew we were close.

I shuffled across the dusty floorboards, but they creaked beneath my feet.

"I'm trying to work something out," the voice said. The one I had come to realize was his. The voice that gave away everything. "You think I'm dead?"

I turned, straightening my shoulders. I didn't want him to

think I was cowering. I didn't want to give him that power. "No, I think you're alive." The room was unkempt. As if we were on the second level of an abandoned house. There was a crib in the corner with cobwebs through the bars, and a single mobile hanging above. He moved toward the crib and turned the dial until the tune began playing. I recognized the lullaby as "Ring-a-Ring o' Roses." Only it sounded flat. As if the batteries were almost dead. The lullaby itself was haunting when you looked at the history and origin of it.

"I do wonder why that is, Saint. Is it because maybe you want me to be alive, so that your—" he paused and leaned against the railing of the crib, "—charming husband can make do on his promise?"

I folded my arms over my chest, breathing calmly. "Who are you?"

He didn't answer. He simply studied me carefully. "You think you have this all figured out. All of you."

"Where's Veronica?" I snapped back quickly before Ophelia pulled me out of my sleep. I already knew he must have been working with her. I didn't need his confirmation. She would have been helping him all along; I just had to know why.

He ran the tip of his finger over the wound on my neck and smirked. It was almost too painful to be this close to him this time. Touching Brantley's mark. His favorite spot to bite me just below my ear. "Riddle me this…" I gulped. "What's neither here, nor there, but a place that has caused all a little despair?" He breathed over my lips and I had to stop the bile that rose in my throat. "The time starts now; the games have just begun."

I whacked his hand off me. "Tell me why."

He seemed surprised by me hitting him. "I'm not working with Veronica, Saint. In fact, you should ask your husband why it is that they haven't killed her yet? I'm sure he can fill you in. When you come back to me, I might just be ready to talk."

I fly off the sofa with my fists clenched.

"What?" Ophelia asks, her hand on my forehead. "What did you get?" It's just her and me this time, with the boys away briefly. They didn't leave us without doubling security. I told them we would be fine, that the house alone is security, but they didn't budge. Whatever dragged them away from here is obviously important, and I didn't want to make a big hassle about it since their focus has solely been on me since Tillie, Madison, and Tate flew to Perdita. It has been three whole weeks. I feel guilty that everyone is separated on my account, and to make matters worse, Madison is three months away from giving birth, with Tillie not far behind her. "Please tell me we didn't just defy orders for nothing."

It's true. Both Bishop and Brantley demanded we don't do anything until they're home. I couldn't wait. With that same guilt living inside of my head rent-free, I need to find Veronica and get to the bottom of whoever this person is that has been invading me for months. "Not nothing. This time was different."

Ophelia hands me a glass of warm milk. "Drink it. Warm milk is comfort for the soul."

I take a sip and sigh when I feel it slide down my throat and settle in my belly.

"See…" She smiles at me. She must have showered today, too, since she's not dressed in her pajamas. That's another reason why I feel guilty. What this is doing to Ophelia and Ivy, who still hasn't said a word to me and hangs out in her room more and more every day. Occasionally, she'll give me a gentle smile, but that's about it. It's weird. She says nothing at all, but I still have come to trust her. Words can be deceiving, actions can, too, but energy speaks from the soul.

I smile at her, placing the mug onto my lap while wrapping my fingers around it. "I—" my words are cut off when an explosion rings through my ears. As if a village of women are screaming. I drop to the floor, covering my ears. Dust and shattered plaster burst in front of me, the milk from the mug I was sipping on spills over the old wood floors. A piercing sound deafens me so badly I can almost taste it. I tremble to my feet, coughing. Someone has blown up half of the house!

"Ophelia!" I scream, pushing through the rubble and ruined furniture. "O—" A hand slams over my mouth and pulls me backward. I'm being dragged farther and farther away from wherever she may be, and it's not until whoever has me is outside the house that I see the carnage. The entire right side of the house looks like it has been torn off and flames lick up the sides.

Whoever is behind me removes their hand and yanks on my arms instead to pull me back. I launch forward. "Ophelia!" My tiny wrists slip from their hands as I run forward, desperate to check on her and Ivy. I'm about to hit the first step when a sharp crack explodes from the back of my skull and I'm falling forward. Tangy metallic liquid squirts up my throat and spills down the sides of my lips. I can't walk. I'm falling. The concrete is getting closer and closer to my face.

Everything is black.

It's nice here.

Quiet. The world, my problems—they don't exist here.

Just peace. Silence. *Peace.*

CHAPTER TWENTY-FOUR

Brantley

She's too good for me and I'm not enough for her. I know this. But it still doesn't stop me from fucking her. Didn't stop me from chasing her, and it sure as fuck did not stop me from marrying her. I've protected her all of her life, but I missed an obvious villain I should have kept her from all along.

Myself.

But you give a villain something worth fighting for and he won't just fight for it, he'll kill for it. Why do you think villains are so feared? It's not because they're evil. Sure, they can be, but no, that's not it. It's because they—I mean—*we*—have no boundaries. At all. It took two days for us to go through all six of the most deadly gangs in New York. In order to lift the bounty that Veronica had placed on Saint, we had to offer all six of them something they *wanted*. They knew we were good for it. Hell, if you were worth us knowing about, you would know we were good for it. The Russians, Italians, The Rebels, and The Circle were easy enough. Even gangsters have something they want but don't have. The trick is to find it and use it. The Rebels will always have a beef with us, but we knew they wanted money more. We knew The Circle wanted off our radar. Since the whole Nate and Tillie fiasco, they wanted to lay low and didn't want us to start spraying bullets—like we were planning to do one day. We knew granting them that was a risk, since they're so fucking inconsistent, so Bishop threw an easy three million at them to shut them the fuck up. Three times the amount Veronica would have placed on Saint's head. But Veronica was smart. She didn't just go after any gang in New York, she went after all of the ones who would *love* to take us down a notch. Stupid bitch forgot the power of greed. We knew what they all wanted from us before we walked into their territory. Was it convenient? Fuck no. We didn't like being at a disadvantage, but it was for *her*. The two who were not easy were the MS-13 and fucking Midnight Mayhem. Who would have thought this fucking cult dark sex show had such a fucking pull with the underworld? Newsflash, they fucking did. Thank fuck for Eli and selling his dick for a good cause, so we didn't actually need to meet with them. He was living his best life. We had just come from the meet with the MS-13, delivering them their fucking one wish. I was fucking tired. Ever since the ceremony, everything has been all go, especially today from jumping around and meeting with all these fuckers. Meet after meet, all I did was picture them being the one to kill Saint and it made me fucking *feral*. I'm over playing fucking genie and granting one wish to these fuckers to not kill Saint. So here I sit, right where I never fucking wanted to be. In the ass middle of a fucking meeting with the new head of The Gentlemen and his two henchmen. Truthfully, my patience is hanging below zero, and I already hate these motherfuckers, so all it will take is one. Fucking. Thing. To tip me over and start dropping bodies. I'm all the way fucked-up. Suddenly, I understand all the bullshit that Bishop and Nate go through for Madison and Tillie.

I fucking get it.

I fucked up. I should have told her those three words. I was wrong. I can love. But I can only love her. She is the exception and will always be the exception.

I need to see her.

"Are we done?" I ask, looking up at the new capo of The Gentlemen, Danny Dale. Danny is just shy of twenty-four, so around our age, and, if we want to believe the shit that's coming out of his mouth, is wanting an alliance with The Kings. That's all he wants. This has never happened in the history of Kings and Gentlemen beef. Not even with The Rebels, who are still going to be rebelling just for the fuck of it.

Danny looks over at me, his pretty blond hair curling around his neck. He stops running his finger over his scruffy beard, all his tattoos on display beneath his shirt and jeans. The patch he wears on his leather vest is the same as they always have, in bold coloring with a single tie beneath their name, only where the tie ends, a blade begins. "I am willing to forgive you for killing my uncle and cousin, and wiping out a quarter of our *best* soldiers, yet you still sit here and insult me, Brantley."

I run my tongue over my lips and both Nate and Bishop are silent as I lean forward, resting my elbows on my knees. "Danny, I'd wipe my ass with your forgiveness before I'd ever consider an alliance with you. Your uncle and cousin deserved the spray of bullets that pierced their flesh like a hot knife to butter. In fact," I say, looking up and down his now rigid body, "I often replay the scene in my head when I'm having a bad day. You know, just to make me smile."

Danny chuckles, but the air is suddenly tight. He glares at me. "You don't smile."

"Oh, I do, and I did." I tilt my head. "Especially when I unloaded those bullets."

He flies off his chair and his right-hand man, Anakin, has his palm pressed to Danny's chest. Anakin is the opposite of Danny. Big, strong, wise. He's older, and he's more levelheaded. I know this because Anakin "the mighty warrior" came through on a job of mine. I hadn't taken it. I put his name in the reserve for a rainy day. Truth was, I knew I might need him one day. And I will need him. Maybe not today, but maybe in the future, and boy, is it good knowing you have leverage on someone who resides in the enemy's camp. I only have one name in my reserve folder, and that's his. I fought backward and forward with Hector about my reasons. He eventually gave it up. But now with Bishop ruling the pack, I no longer have to worry about the politics of trying to get him to see reason.

"Enough," Bishop snaps, putting a cigarette in his mouth and lighting the end. He sucks in for a second longer than usual before blowing out a thick cloud of gray smoke. "None of us have seen *our wives* in a while, so we're all on edge." He points to Danny with his finger. "Your uncle and cousin deserved all of those bullets, Danny Boy. You know we don't act unless needed—" Bishop puffs on his smoke, unaffected, "Right?" When he doesn't answer, Bishop then points to me. "If you want to continue your beef with Brantley, you go ahead and do that, but I remind you: his reputation should be enough of a warning for you. There is another thing that makes him smile, too, which is why we're here."

Slowly, Danny shrugs off Anakin. "What I want in exchange for her safety might surprise you." He sighs, and my muscles tense. "I don't want us to have to worry about bullets flying from either of our sides. Bishop, Nate, I know both of you are expecting children, and I just so happen to be, too." He tosses a photo at Bishop. "My wife. I'm not worried about hiding her from you all because I'm well aware that if you want to find anyone, you're equipped to do so. I'm showing you this to offer an olive branch. I know who all of your women are, now you know mine."

I pause. "Poor chick." Snatching the image off Nate after he's taken a look, I glance down at it. It's a photo of Danny and a young woman around our age. Her eyes are the color of the ocean right when the sun hits it. They look incredible against her dark skin and mocha colored hair.

"Fuck you," he hisses, glaring at me.

"She's too pretty for you." I flick the photo back to him.

His eyes don't detach from mine, a wicked snarl fresh on his lips. "I have no doubt at all that you would tear my head off, Brantley Vaden Vitiosis, but make no mistake, I won't go down without a fight, especially for my woman and kid. So, you ask yourself if you want your little precious Saint to be walking this earth without her big, bad protector."

Nate's knee starts to jiggle under his weight. I already know what he's thinking, and under normal circumstances, I'd be all for the bloodshed, but right now, and I hate to admit this, Danny is right.

"I want peace between both of us so we can reside on each end of Riverside without the fear that one of us is going to kill each other's family."

"Danny Boy, you will not need to worry about any bullets coming from me." He relaxes slightly. "For now." He snarls. I smirk.

"You're a real piece of work. You need to go back into that hole you crawled out of."

Nate's leg gets increasingly faster.

I look up at him, unaffected. "Oh, you mean hell?"

Bishop laughs, stubbing out his cigarette in the astray. "All right, that's enough, you two. We get it, you're never going to like each other, but can we form this alliance for our offspring, and Brantley, for the safety of Saint?"

I stand from my chair and look out over the city of New York through the glass of Bishop's downtown office. This is where we conduct most business meetings, but The Palace at Nate's is where we have our Kings' meetings. "Stay out of my way, Danny Boy. For now," —I turn to face him— "and forever."

"We will stick to our side, and you stick to yours," Danny says, nodding.

"And if this treaty is broken?" Nate asks, and I have to hide my proud smirk as I lower myself down onto the window seat.

Bishop reaches for the paperwork that he printed off. He takes out a knife from the drawer beneath his desk and cuts his thumb. "If the treaty is broken, the next time you bleed near us will not be to sign a blood oath, and it won't be only your blood."

Danny steps forward, giving his hand to Bishop, who drags the blade over his palm. "This oath covers our families, too. We do not go after them."

"We do not," I say, making my way to Bishop with an open palm.

And then Nate.

We all squeeze a droplet of blood beneath our names, including Danny's henchmen, and then shake on it. "The treaty has begun."

Danny and his merry men leave, and as soon as the door closes, Bishop's office phone starts blaring.

We all look down at it. The fuck. That thing never rings.

Bishop hits the answer button. "What?"

"Bishop!" Ophelia cries on the other end. "She's dead. She's dead. She's dead."

Chapter Twenty-Five

Saint

I think we are all wired to fear death. The second we come into this world, we start finding ways to dodge it. I thought over this as she slowly wrapped her arms around her small body and rocked back against the wall. She hadn't seen me yet. I would wait. She would probably never understand why I did what I had done, but there was no point trying to hide now. I was ready to bare it all to her. I was out of time.

I watched and patiently waited as she brought her eyes up to me. Her brows pulled in. I didn't see her injury, but I gathered it was on her head, since I had a godforsaken migraine, I couldn't get rid of. "You're alive."

I noticed when she recognized my face, because all movements stopped. Her head was no longer shifting, and her eyes were wide open.

My mouth curved. "What is it, Saint?"

She still hadn't moved. "No," *she simply said. A range of emotions shifted over her face. Exactly what I expected and why I didn't come in my true face to her until now.* "No."

"Yes," *I said, unbuttoning my suit jacket.* "Say my name."

"No," *she shouted. This time her voice cracked and whimpered in pain.*

"Say it!" *I screamed, flying off the chair and falling down to her face. I squeezed her cheeks with my fingers.* "Say my name!"

Her mouth opened, and right when I was caught off guard, expecting her to whisper it, or not say it at all, she arched her back so high until her head tilted backward. "Lucan!"

"Wait, Saint—"

My retinas are like rings of fire, begging to be put out as I fly up from the position that I am in. My throat burns and my limbs are weak. Concrete walls with moss growing through the cracks, a single bed, no windows, and one door. Unlike the last time I woke up in a strange place, this one reeks of danger.

"Where the hell?" I bring my hand up and wince when the lump on the back of my head echoes through my mind. I need to tell Ophelia that it was Lucan inside my head all this time. We were wrong thinking he was alive. It was another case of Ava Garcia, only smarter. Like a snake, slithering into my mind. Aside from my throbbing head, I don't feel pain anywhere else, so I move off the bed and try to find an escape. Anything. An old vent, a crack in the wall, a hidden window, but I come up short. Turning around, I lean against the wall as drops of water slide down my arm.

Footsteps echo outside and I begin stepping backward, when I recognize the sound of heels. I already know who it is before she appears.

The door unlocks and Veronica stands at the threshold with Sam at her side. "Morning, Hecate! Did you have a good sleep?"

She moves deeper into my bedroom and grabs my wrist, yanking me closer to her. "Time to follow me." I don't fight her because I know I can't. I'd rather she assume I'm not going to put up a fight and loosen her grip, allowing me to pounce when the time is right, then jump around like a hellcat and give away all of my tricks. *"When it comes to fighting back, you have to meet it with patience, or you'll lose every time."* Brantley.

I swallow saliva and continue to follow her down the damp hallway. Cell after cell passes by, all empty from what I can see. "Where are we?"

"In the place where they will never expect you to be." Veronica nudges her head at Sam. "Follow behind her."

He moves behind me, not a single word spoken. Not one word since she barged into my room, and I don't know why, but it makes me uncomfortable. I think deep down in the back of my brain, I had thought it was maybe Sam invading my mind.

Oh, how wrong I was.

"Why are you doing this to me, Veronica? What did I do? Why?"

Veronica doesn't say anything until we reach the end of the hallway and she's pushing open yet another door. It widens into a large room that looks more like an igloo, with doors branching off. There are chairs in a circle, with a boy I don't recognize on the other side.

He seems young. Too young. Very pretty looking, too.

He's wearing a suit, immaculate, and his hair is dyed blond. He nods at Veronica. "You have twenty-four hours before we will need to move her across."

Veronica waves him off. "Go and do your little duties. Your rebellion is appreciated." Veronica takes a seat on one of the many chairs and gestures her hand out to another. "Take a seat, Saint."

I do, slowly lowering myself down. Sam follows. Still silent.

Weak. He was obviously in on this all along. I should be shocked, but not much shocks me anymore.

Veronica lights a cigarette. "I'm thankful there's so much anger happening on this *very* island right now, sweet Hecate, or this wouldn't have been possible."

"Where am I?" I repeat, though I'm getting tired of not getting any answers.

Sam remains still by my side.

"Perdita," Veronica says. "It's where we have been all along. The Lost Boys are so desperate to get their new queen 86'ed."

Perdita.

"Does she know you're here?" I ask because I need all of the information I can get.

Veronica crosses her long legs, leaning one arm on the back of her chair as her cigarette dangles between her two fingers. "Of course not. I'm still alive. The queen is deranged." She shakes her head.

"Where are Frankie and Alessi?" I know she could lie to me, but again, I'm gathering as much information as I can. *"The next thing I need to tell you about revenge, Saint, is to learn all of your information before you attack. They'll assume you're buying time and forget to be careful with their answers. Watch how they answer. Find their lies."*

Veronica's eyes come to mine. They widen. "Dead."

My heart cracks in my chest. I don't believe her. I don't want to believe her. I *cannot* believe her. "You lie."

"Do I?" she asks, her head tilting. "You're the empath. You tell me, Saint." She leans forward while tapping her stiletto on the concrete. "Do I look like I'm lying to you?" She finally leans back and rolls her eyes. "They were always a liability. You took the good ones, what was I supposed to do with the trash? Put a pointed hat on them and call them my witches?" She stands from her chair and moves around the room. There are seven doors.

The one directly opposite me is the one the boy went through. I'm going to assume that's the way out. The longer I stare at the doors, the more I get confused with which one it was he walked through, though.

I squeeze my eyes closed. "Why go through all of this trouble?" I don't tell her about me finding out it is Lucan inside of my head. Now that I know who it is, he won't be able to enter. That was one of the first lessons Ophelia taught me. I can put a mental shield up against the energy he sends off.

Veronica takes her seat again. "I guess I've thought a lot about how this conversation would go. You were supposed to come to *me* when you were a baby, not to Lucan."

"But why?" I cross my leg on top of my other one. "Why did you need me?"

She doesn't answer, her eyes shifting all over my body, as if she wasn't sure if she was going to answer me. "Because you were to break our generational curse, if you were gifted. I found out that you were gifted as soon as you started sleepwalking into the cemetery. I needed you to break the curse that had been put on my coven from my own actions. You see…" Veronica stands and walks to the back of the room. She picks up a small jewelry box that I didn't notice was there and brings it back to where she was sitting. She pops it open and I almost hold my breath as I wait for her to take out a chain. Identical to mine. Even the pendant is the same. It dangles from two of her fingers and she catches it in her palm. "We haven't been able to breed a true *Child of the Night* since I had Brantley." I try to wrap my head around the information she's unloading on me so quickly, but struggle to catch up.

"Curses aren't real," I say softly, and I feel Sam's arm brush against mine. I flinch away from him. The traitor.

Veronica tsks, waggling her index finger at me. "Neither are witches."

She has a good point. I continue to listen.

She places the chain back into the box. "By the time I found out, it was too late. I was already eight months pregnant and ready to give birth. I was the leader of The Coven, so essentially, I didn't owe any of them an answer as to who the father of the baby was." My stomach coils. "The Coven and Elders were furious when they found out that it was not only not conceived by our code, but by an Elite King. You have to understand, there are stories of the time Humphrey Hector Hayes was alive. The Kings were not who they are today, and most of the witches kept them to that standard. Everything you know about them is minuscule to what they were back then. Anyway," she says, taking another cigarette out of the pack and lighting the tip. She inhales and exhales. "My sisters were furious, as was I with my pregnancy. They performed a ritual in the garden the night I gave birth and then tied me to a cross, much like the crucifixion of Jesus." Veronica leans forward and flicks the ash off her smoke. "They cut him from my womb and sent him to be destroyed, Saint. I helped them because I wanted to earn back their trust. He was to be sent straight to The Lost Boys for execution." She leans back in her chair and I have to stop the visuals from flashing through my head. I feel sick to my stomach, thinking of Brantley as a sweet baby, being carried off to be executed. "Obviously, he was saved by someone, but the witches never knew by who."

"Wait!" I stop her with a single word. "Who saved him?"

She stares off into the distance. "I still don't know." Her mouth twists and the furrow lines between her brows deepen. "But I have my suspicions."

"You sent your baby to be killed?"

She flicks her nails and shrugs. "Yes. I would do what I had to do. Lucan was a mistake."

"You're disgusting. Lucan found out, didn't he? About your plan to kill the baby."

"Ah, Brantley was right about you. So smart. Yes, he found out, but it's not what you think. Lucan wasn't evil. My son, he is evil. Lucan is not. Lucan is simply soulless. I thought I was free when they took him." She blinks, her dark lashes fanning out over her cheeks. "Of course I found out later that Brantley wasn't killed at birth and was living back with Lucan, so I did the next best thing; I got close enough for him to trust me."

Curses, witches, and warlocks. It's all folklore and fantasy, and deep down, I wonder if Veronica is unstable, at best. But then I remember what I've been through with Ava Garcia and now Lucan. Maybe I'm just psychic. It doesn't explain the witches she recruited or the history of The Daughters of the Night, nor does it even touch the subject of said male witch seated beside me.

"I knew I could never set foot near Lucan again without him burning my eyes from my fucking sockets, so I went straight for Brantley. He was hard to crack at first, but he grew to trust me. Literally." She sighs, stomping out her cigarette butt. "When I learned of you, I knew you had to be the riddle to crack the curse code. You were half-King and half-witch, though not my daughter—" She smirks, running her tongue over her teeth. "I thought the black hair would have been a giveaway that you were not my child." She rolls her eyes before continuing, "I mean, surely someone carrying the Hayes' curse had to be the one to break the curse, right?" She stands, running her hands over the doors in the room. "See, your curse is something you hold all on your own. The Elders don't care that I was with a King. The problem was that I didn't partake in the ritual of The Hunt and conceive the correct way by our laws." I don't want to interrupt her since she's spewing all of her tales. Veronica studies me closely and I'm painfully aware of how close Sam is sitting beside me. "How is Tillie doing? I've got to say, I would have loved to see her run this island. Maybe give her something else to run except her mouth." Her hands run over the skirting of the doors.

"She is fine, and I'm sure she will be handling this island the same way she does *her mouth*. With teeth."

Veronica chuckles. "So cute." She jumps back into her story time. "As years went on and you grew older, I knew you were it. I knew I had to continue to keep Brantley close to me in order to stay close to you, too, because when the time came and I needed you, I knew I would need to go through him first."

"To break the curse?" I say, confused.

She smiles sweetly. "Yes." *Lie.* Every single time she talks about this "curse," waves roll off her and smack me against the chest. She's lying.

"How?" I'm humoring her at this point.

"Well, by killing you, of course, but only after you've given me exactly what I want." Her eyes flick down to my belly. "That."

Her lips curl beneath her teeth, but her eyes spark with a kind of light I never thought I'd see through the darkness she carries so well. "Because you, my dear little Hecate, are pregnant."

"What?" I gasp, my hand protectively going to my belly. "No, I'm not."

She slinks back in her chair. "Yes, you are, and even more so?" Her head tilts. "Is that you're going to stay right here until that baby is born, and *then* I'm going to do what I should have done all those years ago but couldn't." She stands from her chair, clapping her hands together. "So, are you hungry and what for? Congratulations. You've earned whatever you want to eat for the remaining—" her eyes fall to my stomach, "six months."

I don't answer. My mouth refuses to move as she laughs her way out of the same door the other boy went out of. When she's gone, I turn to Sam. Sam, who I thought was my friend. "Is what she is saying true? I'm on contraception. It's impossible."

Sam doesn't look down at me, keeping his eyes trained in front of him. "Whatever I tell you, you won't believe me."

"Try me, traitor," I mumble, suddenly nauseous. *I have been spewing lately.* I still, my muscles frozen. *And eating weird food.* "Oh God…" I thought I wasn't getting my period because of the pill. It would do that sometimes; they were always irregular. *"Oh my God!"* I stand from my chair and begin twisting the door handles to see which ones are unlocked.

"There's no point. They all lock from the outside and only one leads up to the mainland."

"I don't want to talk to you, Sam." I turn to face him, my breathing ragged. I need to get out of here. I try to swallow everything that has happened to me over the past couple of months but fail when a tear slides down the side of my cheek. I swipe it away angrily before Sam sees it.

He makes his way to me and grabs my hand.

"Hey!" I snap at him, pulling out of his grip, but it's no use, because he's dragging me to a single door that *isn't* locked and shutting it behind himself. We're inside a room now, with a bathroom and a small kitchen. No windows again.

"Madison and Tillie are here. I'm going to get you out, but you have to be patient."

I squeeze his arm. "I don't know what you're talking about. Let me go." I turn to reach for the door handle when he slams it closed in front of me.

"Saint, listen to me very carefully, because when we're not in this room, there are eyes and ears on us." I hold my breath. "I work for The Kings."

I swing around, my fist flying into his cheek. Pain erupts in my knuckles when he stumbles backward, his eyes ablaze. "I don't believe you!"

He grits his teeth. "I don't fucking care if you don't believe me, Saint, but—" He lifts his shirt, exposing a scar on his bottom hipbone. The mark of a King. I hadn't seen it before today, but I gather it has to do with The Kings since it's their emblem. "I am not a King, I am an ally to them." He drops down on the bed. "Hector got me in as soon as he found out that you were gifted. He knew we would need someone on the inside, and he was right." His eyes come to mine. "Saint, if I wasn't who I am and you got an *actual* stupid fucking male witch, he would have raped you the night of The Hunt—but you and I, we didn't have sex."

"So I didn't break the curse like she says I did?" I ask, tilting my head.

He rolls his eyes, and it looks weird on him. "There's no fucking curse. She's barren and cannot have more children, and the daughters who came through before just didn't get pregnant, didn't have sex, or practiced safe sex. The curse, as she says, is all in her head."

I move closer to him. "Sam, I need to get out of here."

He peers up at me. "I know. I'm going to get word to Madison and Tillie."

"No!" I shake my head. "They're pregnant."

He smirks up at me. "Tillie, and you, are Perdita blood. The Lost Boys are rebelling right now because they have not taken to Valentina. They don't see her as their true queen, but Tillie?" His eyes flicker with thirst. "Tillie, they know, respect, and would kill for." He stands from his bed. "I will get word to them. Just keep yourself busy and don't drink anything she gives you." He makes his way to the door. "Now I'm really sorry I have to do this." Leaning forward, he unbuttons my jeans and yanks them down slightly, wrapping my hair in his fist and pulling the door open. He shoves me through the door, but not hard enough that I fall.

"Next time, you're pissing on the floor." I don't get to ask Sam why he's doing this. Maybe these allies The Kings have do things because they're born to do it. Or maybe it's because they want to, or they owe them. But I've been a part of their world long enough to know the likelihood of Hector having something on Sam is high. He pulls out a set of keys from his pocket and directs me to yet another door. Unlocking it, the door swings open and he pushes me inside. "This is your room. You stay here until I allow you out." Then the door slams closed and I'm left alone with the information I've just been fed.

Chapter Twenty-Six

Brantley

Fire burns through my veins as I lean against the wall. It has been four hours since she was taken. *Four hours.* I move through the rubble with Ophelia behind me and the rest of The Kings outside.

"She's not anywhere close, Brantley. I'd feel her."

I nod, aside from the ever-burning rage that's swimming in my gut, Ophelia is one of the good ones and I know she wants to find Dea as much as I do. She was lucky to survive the explosion herself, with a broken arm and a bruised head.

I look up to the ceiling and pause. "Who else was home?"

Ophelia steps up behind me and follows what I'm staring at. "Just us."

I shake her off and turn toward the door when I hear Bishop's footsteps. "I just got off the phone with Madison. She's not fucking happy and she said if we don't find her in one hour, they're both flying back."

"Fuck." I grind my teeth, unable to contain my anger. I shove them all out of the way as I make my way outside, stepping over splintered wood and the garden that Saint spent years flourishing. It almost breaks me right then and there, seeing her flowers and greenery burned to ash. I step over them with my heavy boots, unable to bring myself to step on them. Reaching for my phone, I pull it out and dial Hector's number.

He answers instantly, "I know. I'm working on it."

"Well, work fucking harder!"

He sighs, closing a door in the background. "You know when I gave the gavel to Bishop, it meant I didn't have to deal with this anymore."

"Bullshit," I snap at him, dropping down onto the stone bench seat. "You love Saint and you know it."

"I do," he says, and I hear a flick of a lighter. "Which is why—and you're not going to like this much—but it's why I put Sam in."

I fly off the bench, just as Bishop and Nate walk in behind me. "You what?"

"Put me on speaker."

I do, squeezing my phone in my hand.

"I put Sam in as soon as I noticed that she was gifted. I knew Veronica would come for her eventually."

"How would you know that?" I fume, squeezing my phone.

"I didn't want to have this conversation now, but Veronica has always had her eyes on Saint. Your mother is so caught up in the riptide to the delusions in her head that she actually deems them true."

"What are you talking about?" Bishop's eyes fly to mine, his jaw set and his shoulders straight. I know that look. I know if it came down to it, he would probably do what we have to do when it comes to his father, but I also know Bishop doesn't rule like Hector. He has a conscience.

"She has had it in her mind that Saint could break a curse that has existed within The Daughters of the Night since she gave birth to you. It was a punishment, you see, for her sleeping with someone who was not a witch."

"Why?" Bishop questions. "Why is it not allowed for them to be with another man?"

"Just one of their laws, son. On top of her with another man outside, she went with a King. When The Coven first moved into Riverside to live and work *with* The Kings, we drew up a treaty. If the treaty was broken, the witch who breaks it would ignite a curse that would live within her coven forever, until—"

"—until what?" I grind out. "I'm getting impatient."

"There's a riddle…"

"Of course there is," I seethe.

"The only way the curse could be broken was by a Swan born by a Hayes." Hector clears his throat. "As you can imagine, that would never have happened, and if it did, she would die because of our own laws. Until recently." He pauses. "*A Swan and the Devil. One pure, one evil. Neither can exist with the other, until one is born with wings that fly.*"

"That's a shit riddle. It doesn't make sense." Nate pulls out his pack of smokes and I have to fight with myself not to take one.

"It's not when you think about it." Hector pauses. "I'm trying to get in touch with Sam and have tried for a couple of weeks now to no avail."

I squeeze my fist. "Is there a chance he could have flipped?"

"Not a single fucking one," Hector announces. "If he can't get through right now, it means that one, she's found him out and killed him, or two, he's unable."

"Tracking?" I grit.

"I'm on it now."

"Good. Call us when you've got something."

Rage burns through my veins like lava as I end the call. I find myself having to do something. Anything to keep busy. I move through the rubble and find Ophelia and Ivy on the front doorstep. Ophelia is holding Ivy in her arms, sobbing. Guilt weighs down on my shoulders. Saint fucking loves these two. For her, I'd do what I need to do.

I reach into my pocket and take out my keys. When I'm on the last step down from the front door, I turn and toss the key to Ophelia.

She swipes the tears from her eyes. "What's this?"

"A key to one of my rooms in the city. Both of you go stay there."

"But what about Saint?"

I bring my eyes to her. "Saint will be home within the next twenty-four hours. That's a fucking promise."

Ophelia scrubs her eyes with the backs of her hands. "I'm sorry I passed out and didn't help her."

"Not your fault," I mumble. "It was probably a good thing you did. Veronica would have killed you otherwise." I hear a car pull up behind me and turn over my shoulder to see a black Range Rover.

Benny steps out, straightening his suit while flicking a toothpick around in his mouth. "I heard about your goddess. What can I do to help?"

I turn to face Ophelia. "You can take these two, the dogs, and Medusa to my penthouse and watch them until we have Veronica in fucking shackles." Thank fucking Christ the explosion didn't hit our half of the house and the animals are safe.

Benny leans to the side to look over my shoulder, his mouth in a wide grin. "Well, shit." He moves forward, flicking his jacket back, but my hand flies up to his chest.

"Aye!" I shake my head, glaring at him. "No. Not right now."

"What? I don't know what you mean."

"For the record, Nate is inside, and I don't know if you haven't noticed, but he's still not over the little kidnapping act you pulled on Tillie."

Benny smirks, licking his lip. His piercing moves with it. "Ah, but wasn't it great?"

"Benny, you're not here for that right now."

He rolls his eyes. "Fine. You have my word."

"I mean it." I shove his chest a little. "Those two are important to Saint, which means they're important to me."

Benny slaps my shoulder, sidestepping around me. "I got it, I got it. Don't fuck her. *Yet.*"

I turn and watch as Benny helps both of them into the SUV. I move to the end room in the house to get Kore and Hades and Medusa's travel enclosure. Benny packs them all into his Range Rover and drives off down the driveway, just as Nate walks up beside me.

"Still hate him."

"I know," I say, turning to find Bishop on his phone, his eyes ablaze. "What?" I mouth.

"Yeah, we're on our fucking way." He hangs up his phone and grins at me. "Fire up the jets. We're on our way to Perdita."

Chapter Twenty-Seven

Saint

I miss my dogs. I miss the way their short fur feels beneath my palms every time I pat them. How sassy Kore is and how domineering Hades is. I miss Medusa. How she slithers up my arm with her black body, a complete contrast to my white skin. I even miss her little attempts at eating me.

I miss my home.

My home that's probably no longer intact. My stomach rolls as I toss and turn with uncertainty. It feels like it has been hours since Sam left me here.

The lock on the door moves and I stand, waiting to see who is on the other end. I don't want to be met with Veronica.

I don't want to see her vile face again. She could have killed someone, or my dogs and pets. The door doesn't budge, and suddenly, it's being kicked in and Tillie stands on the other side, blowing her pink hair out of her face. "Told you I still have it."

Madison rushes through and pulls me into her chest. "Come on." She pushes me out the door. "We're getting you out of here before the bitch gets back."

"How did you know where I was?"

Madison pulls out a gun and hands it to me.

I admire it. "I've never shot one before."

"I'll fix that, but for now, you will not hold one." She shoves it into the back of her pants, and I glare at Tillie, who shrugs as if *that's just Madison*. I had no idea Madison carried guns.

Tillie flexes her fingers and I catch the knuckle busters on her hands. "Am I the only one without a lethal skill?" I whisper as we make our way through to the main room and finally through another opened door.

"Your lethal skill is your husband, honey. Trust me on that." I pause when we come to stairs that lead up to what looks like a trapdoor.

"What is this place?"

Tillie sighs. "It's our other home, and fortunately for us, we get to raise some hell."

"But how did you get in?" I ask, when Madison is pushing open the lock.

"Well…" Tillie shrugs. "Let's just say they like me better here, and Sam, who is right now distracting Veronica."

I don't want to think about what he's doing to distract her, but I follow them up. I squeeze dirt and earth as I pull my body up to stand, brushing my palms down my legs. Trees reach for the sky, with flowers and gardens planted all around them.

"Wow." It is beautiful. I have never seen a forest like this. It looks like something out of a fantasy movie.

"Perdita is unique," Tillie says as we begin making our way through the slender saplings. They obviously know where they're going, so I follow their lead. "Wait until you meet the people. Nocturnals."

"They don't like me," I say, my hand resting on my belly. I almost forgot all about everything that was revealed to me earlier, and subconsciously, I still don't believe it. Not until I take a test.

"Why do you say that?" Madison asks. I step around the flowerbeds that are sprawled out everywhere until we come to a clearing of dirt. Solar lights line the edge of every path. "Because I met one. He came down when I first got there and didn't care."

"He didn't know who you were, Saint. No one here knows that our crazy mother had another daughter." Madison's phone rings in her pocket and she swipes it unlocked, bringing it to her ear.

Her eyes fly between Tillie and me. "Okay. See you guys soon."

"They're coming?" I ask, just as we reach the end of the road. I haven't missed the little streets that veer off the main road, or the tiny signage that points down with unusual Latin road names. It almost feels like Hobbiton.

"Oh, they're coming, all right."

We make our way onto the main street. Shops line either side, perfectly symmetrically, but all of their doors are closed. I remember Tillie saying something about the people who live here being nocturnal. I bring my hand up to shade my eyes from the sun that's setting over the mountains that are tucked behind the shops. It is possibly the quickest kidnapping event ever.

"Is it safe for me to be walking down here so casually?"

"Yeah, we're heading into the big mansion right there. It used to be our mother's, but now Valentina resides inside." Tillie's distaste for this girl is obvious with the way she spits her name.

"And I take it we don't like Valentina?" I ask, just as a store across the road catches my eye. *Perdita Convenience Store.* I pause. I don't realize I have stopped walking until Madison and

Tillie are in front of me, glancing back between the bright, very open lights of that one shop and me.

"What's wrong?" Madison asks, her hand on my arm. My lips curl beneath my teeth as I fight with myself. They're my closest friends. I should be able to tell them the news Veronica tried to hide. If I do, it will make this easier. We can get the test and take it all before Brantley is even here, and I can tell him for sure if I'm pregnant based on a test instead of some spiteful words out of a hateful woman's mouth.

I blink slowly. "I think I might be pregnant."

There's a small gasp. Tillie squeezes my other arm. "You think?"

"Well, Veronica said I was. She wanted to keep me there until I had the baby. The woman is seriously unstable."

Madison is already storming across the road. We both jog after her as she pushes her way through the front doors. "We're not doing the guessing game."

After searching the aisles, we find the right one and I grab the bright pink box that spells the words I need. After Tillie pays with her actual presence, our stroll down the main street suddenly turns into more of a sprint. Tillie pushes open the gates as we pass the guards sitting at the front. "Valentina isn't here right now, so let's just get this over with." The house is extravagant. It drips an opulence that no amount of money in a mundane life could ever afford. The walls on the outside are marble, the trimmings gold. She pushes open the door and it spills out onto a lobby with an imperial staircase that leads up to the second level.

Madison grabs my hand as we jog up the stairs, bypassing photography. Women after women. "Is it just women who run Perdita?"

"Yep!" Tillie smiles. "I love this place. More than Nate would like to hear." Her smile falls, but she guides me down the long hallway, to the end where a bedroom is.

She pushes through the door and closes it, flicking the lock. Madison's phone blares off in the background and she answers it instantly, waving me toward the bathroom.

Suddenly, I don't want to. It makes it real.

"Hey!" Tillie takes my hand and guides me to the doorway. "It's going to be okay."

"Tillie…" I shake my head with a heavy sadness. "Brantley will never want a child."

"You don't know that." She rubs my back. "That grumpy motherfucker will probably make the best dad in the world."

"He would, but he won't want it."

"Take the test. We will go from there."

Chapter Twenty-Eight

Brantley

I already knew about the curse and Veronica's obsession with it. What I didn't know was the length she would go just to "break it." I trusted her. I fucking trusted her. The only person outside of my circle I trusted, and it wasn't just any trust. It was a kind of trust that only came from years and years of labor.

"Madison is acting fucking weird." Bishop ends the call, tossing his phone on the table that parts both our aisles.

"Is that uncommon, or?" Nate asks, sipping his vodka. "Just saying, Tillie has been the same."

"Nah." Bishop grinds his teeth. "She's hiding something from me."

"Why do you say that?" I ask, watching him carefully. This jet is filled up with all our front-line soldiers, excluding Eli. Spyder is near the front with his right hand, and a couple of

Rebel members behind him. Yeah. Never would have thought I'd see the fucking day that a Rebel, well two, were sitting in the same jet as us. Who would have known?

"She was in a rush to get off the phone. Distant."

"You have PTSD, bro," Nate says, flicking his fingers up and down. "She's run too much." The sides of his jaw flex. I know Nate just hit the fucking point. I ignore them both and settle back into my seat.

"Shouldn't you all be pissed that they went and saved her without you?" Spyder calls out from his chair. He and Tate have been flying back and forth since they landed in Perdita. He's probably thankful she's not with the girls right now and tucked away back on common ground.

Bishop answers smoothly, "No. I trust they'd keep each other safe. Ain't no one love those girls more than us but each other."

I know Saint is safe, and that's enough for now. The next thing I have to think about is how I'm going to end Veronica.

Landing in Perdita isn't for the weak. The plane always needs to dip and turn and twist. At one point, it feels like we're about to tilt over. Nate hates it every time we come. The pretty little psycho has a fear of flying.

"Question," I ask, kicking up my feet. We're traveling straight to Valentina's in the limo-style Hummer. These roads aren't for the average car, considering we have to trench through bush to get to the mainland. They made it this way on purpose to protect the people. "If Tillie wants to take over this island, would you let her?"

Nate looks up from where he's staring at the ground, his eyes coming to mine. "Never." His head tilts. "Would you with Saint? Seems her speed. Seclusion, quiet…"

I clench my fist in my hand.

He chuckles and sits back in his seat. "Exactly."

The trip continues, and twenty minutes later, we're driving down the main strip of Perdita, heading right for the famed marble gates. The sun is beginning to set in the distance, and when we arrive, the guards who man the entry let us in with a nod. The gates separate, and right there standing on the front steps, ready to welcome us home, are all three of our women.

CHAPTER TWENTY-NINE

S<small>AINT</small>

M<small>Y</small> THROAT DRIES AS THE BLACK H<small>UMMER</small> PULLS DOWN the drive, stopping outside the doors. Tillie squeezes my hand. "Should we tell him now?"

I shake my head. "No. He needs to be focused. This will stress him out."

"Just to be clear." Madison clears her throat, speaking from one side of her mouth. "I'm not very good at lying when Bishop is around. He can sniff out lies from my lips before I even speak them."

"If you manage to slip, it's fine. But please try. I'm—" Sweat beads around my brows, "simply not ready to tell him."

They both squeeze my hands reassuringly, and I'm, once again, thankful for both of them. I sometimes wonder how I survived without them for so long. I understand what The Elite Kings' world is like. How their rules work and boundaries are pushed. Maybe our connection isn't all sexual like the older generations were, though I'm aware how close things have gotten between Nate and Madison and Tillie and Brantley. But maybe with us, it's about a soul connection and not a sexual one.

The door opens and Brantley is the first to step out. I freeze. Suddenly, I'm afraid he can read my mind, or even see I'm hiding a bump. Shit. How far along am I? Would it be possible to even have a bump yet?

He takes the steps up to me and wraps his arm around my waist, pulling me into his chest while his hand is on the side of my head. "I've had about enough of people hurting you and getting away with it, Dea." His tone is almost too calm for the words he spoke.

"I'm okay." I smile up at him, resting my hand on his chest. "Because of the girls and Sam."

Brantley grunts, his hand sliding down my arm and to my palm. After taking the test, Madison ran me a bath and Tillie cooked some food. I'm now in a pair of ripped boyfriend jeans that belong to Tillie and a Slasher shirt of Madison's. I couldn't find two of the same sides to wear but managed to find the perfect one from each.

I squeeze his fingers with mine until he looks at me from behind his shoulder. I always feel small beside him, but even more so when he's angry. "I'm fine."

He ignores me, turning back to face Bishop and Nate, who are jogging up the stairs. "Where is she?"

"We can't get ahold of Sam. Hector is tracing him now, but while we wait—" Nate hooks his arm around Tillie's neck and drags her into the house. "I need to fuck my wife."

Tillie throws up deuces and they both disappear upstairs. Bishop and Madison still seem tense around one another, but the love they have for one another is louder than the way they hate each other. It's what makes their relationship so real, seeing them this way.

"Hungry?" Madison asks, sidestepping away from Bishop and making her way through. We follow behind them and into the kitchen. The atmosphere feels heavy, as if Brantley is barely containing his anger.

The kitchen is at the rear of the house, adjacent to the main living room. The architecture is articulate and classy, with windows that overlook the greenery in the back yard. No pool. Though I didn't suspect there would be, as it's so cold here. Not an obvious cold, more of a comfortable one. As if the rain only trickles, not pours, just enough to leave a constant mist in the air. The kitchen is a loud red that makes me uncomfortable, and the stools that are tucked beneath the varnished wood counter are pulled together with cream leather. I'm not sure what she was thinking when decorating this area, but I'm assuming she wasn't at all.

"I know what you're thinking," Madison fills the silence as Bishop and Brantley meet with whoever else they came over with in the living room. "This kitchen is ugly."

"Maybe." I stifle my laugh and watch as she pulls out a capsule from the fridge and pops it into a large bowl-shaped mug.

She pours cold milk over top and then places it into the microwave. "It's your mother, by the way." The microwave beeps and she takes out the mug. The smell hits me instantly. Cocoa, cinnamon, and honey. She slides it over to me while stirring. "She cared more about sex than she did about anything else."

"Sounds amazing." I widen my eyes at Madison and smile.

"One of a kind!" Madison mocks back.

I take the first sip and groan. The harsh notes of cocoa beans mixed with the sweetness of the honey and spices taste almost exotic, or something I should not be eating. Otherworldly. Forbidden.

"Right? They have the best chocolate ever in Perdita. You can't get anything like their chocolate anywhere." I place my mug down and rub my temples. I don't know what I'm doing. I feel guilty for asking the girls to keep this secret from Nate and Bishop, and then I feel guilty for keeping it from Brantley and everyone, too. But I'm scared. I'm scared because Brantley and I are already so volatile. I just need to know if this volatility is something that is part of our relationship or if it's a product of him not being happy about something.

Bishop enters behind us with Spyder. Spyder is Bishop's first cousin and has dyed blond hair. They seem similar, but it's not obvious unless they're standing side by side or if you're really looking. His brows are pulled in and Spyder shuffles beside him. Brantley is nowhere to be seen.

"What's wrong?" I ask, sensing the unease between the two of them. This right here is another reason why I don't think announcing I'm pregnant is a good idea. There's too much going on.

Bishop pulls out a stool beside me and rubs his hands over his face.

"Bishop, spit it out, please. I can practically taste your emotions."

He smiles at me, reaching forward and brushing my hair out of my face. "I just got off the phone with Dad."

"Okay?"

"Seems there's been an incident back home." He breathes in and out, and I automatically know this isn't going to be good. Not just the words he's saying, but the way he's saying them.

"My dogs?" My hand is on my stomach as a range of emotions forces their way up my throat. I think I'm going to be sick.

He shakes his head, his eyes on mine. Pained, but serious. The muscles in the sides of his jaw flex a couple of times before he takes my hands with his. "When the explosion happened, it wasn't just you, Ophelia, and Ivy at the house."

"What?" I pause. White noise fills the gaps between him. I think I stop breathing altogether.

He blows out a breath. "It's Bailey." I don't hear anything else because I shove back from my chair until I'm standing upright, only it happens in slow motion. "She was in her bedroom when it happened. She didn't make it, princessa, I'm so fucking sorry."

I shake my head. Sadness spills into the cracks of my mind as I try to wrap my head around Bailey not being here anymore. "No. She can't be. I just saw her the other night. It can't be."

Bishop pushes off his chair and takes my hand with his, wrapping two of his fingers around my chin to bring my eyes to his. "It was her, Saint. I'm so fucking sorry." The ball that was clogged in my throat explodes as pain, loss, and sorrow sink their nails into the marrow of my bones and begin tearing away at me from the inside out.

"No." Tears stream down my face, but I don't bother to wipe them away. I can't seem to care.

Madison sobs in the background, but I don't hear anything else. Bishop pulls me into his chest and wraps his arm around my waist. "I'm sorry, Saint."

"It was my fault." The words that leave my mouth are foreign. My stomach rolls and my chest contracts as an ugly guilt settles inside of me. Like rot, it's going to spread.

"No, it wasn't," Brantley says, his fingers intertwining with mine from behind. For once, he doesn't force me out of Bishop's arms. Instead, he presses his lips to the back of my head. "It wasn't your fault."

I swipe the tears from my cheeks, turning and burying my face into Brantley's arm. "Fix this."

He directs my face up with a gentle tug of his finger, his eyes searching mine with a force I have never experienced before. In this moment, he is like a magnet, calling me. "I don't know how to fix this, but I promise you that I will make things right." The corners of his eyes soften, his mouth in a hard line. I see the fight he's struggling with. To mourn his little cousin, one of the only people who has held him accountable, or to not allow that barrier to lower.

I bring my hand up to his cheek. Skin so soft, yet cheekbones so prominent. "You don't have to hide anything, Brantley. We know you cared for her."

The muscles beneath my palm tense. "I did."

"Veronica dies tonight," Madison says, breaking through the tense and somber atmosphere.

I look toward her as Brantley pulls me into his chest. Madison nods, swiping away her tears. "Bailey deserved better. Tonight, that bitch dies. I'm sick of her games."

I nod in agreement. I don't wish death upon anyone, but it's hard to be against revenge. I know it's not healthy. I know I will most likely live with both of their deaths for the rest of my days. I squeeze my eyes closed. "She deserved better."

Brantley's arm tenses around me before he falls down onto the stool I was on, pulling me onto his lap. He nudges his head up at Spyder. "Get those two fucking rabbits out of their room so we can start this hell raising."

CHAPTER THIRTY

Brantley

"Saint's still in The Coven?" Bailey asked, rounding the large sofa in the sitting room. "I take it by the almost empty bottle of whiskey on your lap, that's a yes." She flicked her hand up and down my body before falling down beside me, curling her legs under her ass. She gestured to the bottle and I shook my head, handing it to her. She takes a long pull without so much as wincing.

"Well, you're definitely a Vitiosis."

She stared at me beneath her lashes. "Did you expect otherwise?"

"No," I answered, already not wanting to get into a conversation with anyone tonight. Just not tonight. Because tonight I found out that Saint cannot be mine. At least not in the way I needed her to be. If I couldn't have her in that way, then I didn't want her in any way. The old whiskey stung the back of my throat and I hissed, my eyes finding the fireplace. "She's my sister."

Silence, then Bailey laughed so loud that I glared at her. She snatched the bottle out of my grip. "I'm not even sorry, but that girl is not your sister. I don't care what bullshit you're being told."

"Her visions." I snatched the bottle back from her. "Are never false."

She took it back, narrowing her eyes on me. "I didn't say her vision was false. I'm saying that maybe it's being manipulated. And how do you know that evil witch isn't lying?"

"I just know."

Bailey sighed, kicking her feet to rest on the coffee table. "I call bullshit. That woman has been planning this all along."

"You're too paranoid."

Bailey glared at me. "Am I? Or am I right?"

I hate I never got the chance to tell the annoying little shit that I'd always protect her. I hate she died thinking that I couldn't stand her, because I actually could. I wouldn't have let her fucking live with me otherwise.

"How's Abel?" I ask Bishop, grabbing the AK that's lying on the table and loading up.

Bishop's face tightens. "Not good. He was already fragile. They were fragile."

"You don't say," I mutter, flicking the knife up and putting it into the holster on my jeans. "I heard a couple of their fights."

"They were toxic. Abel isn't built like all of us. Bailey gave him something he could call his own, but it was Bailey, so no one could own her." I flinch at those words, because nothing could be truer. She was a Vitiosis through and through. "She was excited for the twins, and for Tillie's baby."

"Would have been the most annoying aunt ever." I chuckle, taking a seat at the dining table. Nate walks through, running his hand over his face. We had already told him the news after Spyder dragged his ass out of Tillie. He's fine, Tillie not so much. "Where are the girls?"

"Upstairs," Nate says, his throat bobbing when he swallows. He leans over and clutches the edge of his chair. "Getting real sick of people fucking dying."

"It's inevitable in our world." I wait until he slowly brings his eyes up to mine. "One day, we're all going to fucking die. We just have to make sure we die before the girls."

Nate chuckles, pushing off the chair and reaching for a shotgun. "And make sure we leave a fucking ruthless army of legacies behind."

My face scrunches. "Fuck no. I'll leave that to you two."

Nate snickers and Bishop laughs. He points at me with the tip of his pistol. "If you so much as think you won't be getting her pregnant, then fuck, I don't know you at all."

"I don't want fucking kids, so I'll make very sure that doesn't happen."

Bishop rolls his eyes and Nate shrugs. "Well, you can be the moody uncle that kills all of their dates."

I shiver at the thought.

"Hey." Bishop leans over his shoulder and I follow his eyesight to Saint, whose eyes are on me. "You all right?"

She looks pale. More than usual. I tilt my head. "What's wrong?" Stupid question. She just found out Bailey is dead and she thinks it's because of her.

Slowly, she shakes her head, a smile on her lips, but it doesn't reach her eyes. "Nothing. I was just about to tell you that Valentina is here."

∽

"Do what you must," Valentina says, walking back and forth in the kitchen. She's wearing a long gown that you can one-hundred percent see-through, a metal crown twisted on the top of her head, and her long ash blonde hair is twisted in a braid at the nape of her neck.

"Why didn't you tell us that The Lost Boys had been rebelling?" Bishop asks, rolling a cigar between his fingers.

"Because!" Her hands fly up in defense. She sighs, dropping onto the single sofa in the corner of the room. "You would see that I'm having trouble and might think I'm incompetent."

Nate watches her carefully, though he doesn't bother to take note of her obvious fucking display of nipples through her gown. I do. I notice them, but they do nothing for me. She never has. "You still should have told us, Valentina. We could have put a stop to it earlier rather than later."

"I know." Her shoulders sag, holding his stare. "I am sorry, Nathanial."

I shuffle in my chair. No one calls him by his full name. She's lucky Tillie didn't hear it and go all *your kingdom, my king* on her again. Fucking cavewoman.

"Well, I don't give a fuck about any of this. This is your area," I say to Nate. "And don't you dare look at Saint. This island is yours and Tillie's responsibility. Handle it." I stand from my chair, cocking my gun.

Bishop glances up at me. "Where the fuck are you going?"

"I'm not waiting anymore. Because *this* is my responsibility."

"We all carry this," Bishop corrects me, twisting his neck until it cracks.

Nate stands next.

I turn to face Valentina. "Make sure the girls stay indoors. We will leave Spyder here to guard the door with your guards. No one leaves or enters this house. Understood?"

Valentina nods. "I haven't been over to that side."

I clench my jaw, annoyed because she, once again, proves

that she hasn't got a fucking clue how to run this island. She's going to need some help, whether Nate likes it or not.

"If we come back a man down, you make sure the girls don't know until they're safe."

"It's just Veronica, isn't it?" Spyder asks, and we all fall silent.

I shake my head slowly. "How do you think she has survived this long? Veronica Vitiosis has allies."

"Who?" Spyder asks, full of disbelief.

Bishop checks the bullets in his pistol. "Every single enemy that Lucan had."

The ATVs are parked at the front of the house. Enough for all of us to drive into the woods. Sirens blare out in the distance. I need to tell Tillie to change the tune. Listening to *The Purge* siren is probably going to put more fear into people than keep them home. Especially since it's dark. I'm sitting shotgun, Bishop's driving and Nate, Cash, and Hunter are all in the back of ours. In the one beside us is Spyder's right hand and a couple of Valentina's strongest guards, along with Cash, Ace, and Jase. Whenever we need backup, that's who we call. Whoever can make it in from our original crew. Even if they're busy doing whatever they had been sent off to do to fill in for their fathers now that it was our turn, they'd come if they could. Trees slap past us as Bishop floors it forward. We fly over small hills and branches, with the other ATV following closely behind. I tighten my plain black bandana around my face and flip my hoodie over my head, bringing the AK up to rest on my shoulder. I look through the scope, turning on night vision. More and more movement catches my eye the deeper we venture to the other side of Perdita that *no one* wants to go into.

"Any idea why she didn't take Saint to this side?" Bishop asks over his shoulder.

I shake my head. "No. I'm guessing it's because she didn't want them to know."

"Or that she wanted us to find her, and then to enter The Devil's Pit on our own fucking accord."

"Knock, knock, motherfuckers." Nate smirks, raising his shotgun up and pointing it forward. He pumps up and starts firing. Bishop doesn't let up the gas until we're crashing through the iron border. I grip onto one of the bars and raise the AK up with my other. As soon as we crash in, I start spraying. Bullets are flying everywhere.

Every. Where.

The Devil's Pit is laid out identical to the main street of Perdita, only where everything is clean, wholesome and bright in Perdita, it's all darkness and gore here. Where the shops are in Perdita; there are jail cells here. Flames burn down the pathway of the main road that's lined with dirt. This side of Perdita is the prison of the island. They stay in, or they get shot. Criminals don't get to walk free—ever. That is the rule. Some choose to come in, because they don't want to live amongst the people of Perdita. They're too sterile. Too perfect. All of these fuckers contained behind this wall are scum. Rapists, murderers of their own people, thieves. And now, they're all gassed up and ready for us.

Bishop was right. This was a setup and we just rode straight into it.

I squeeze the trigger and aim my gun sideways, unloading a whole clip into who is shooting. Bishop directs the ATV down, running over people on his way. We were lucky there were still a couple of guards who work *for* Perdita, so they gave us an in. But the people inside are rogue. Ruthless, and they don't give a flying fuck who is at the other end of their gun. You give these crims something to do and they'll do it. Especially if it's chaos.

A single strip of road is doused in dried blood and ridden with dirt, reminding me of the old cowboy era.

I aim. I shoot. I aim. I shoot.

We get to the end of the road and Bishop drives straight through the wired fence that blocks off the prisoners from the home. No one runs this side of Perdita but the guards. No one.

The ATVs kick up dirt as we slide to a stop. Guns no longer popping off. The silence is unnerving.

"Everyone good?" Bishop calls out over his shoulder.

They all nod.

I climb out, heading toward the front door. It's an abandoned house, but when I look closer— "Someone has been living in here."

Bang! A single shot blares out and we all duck. "Fuck!"

I turn slightly. "Who got hit?" Someone is lying on the side of the ATV, clutching his stomach. *Please be a fucking guard.*

When he turns his head, I already know it isn't. "Fuck!"

Bishop runs toward Cash, holding his hand over his stomach. "Hold it there. Hold it right fucking there and don't you dare close your eyes. We fucking need you." Cash shakes his head, harsh and desperate. "Hey!" Bishop shoves Cash as Hunter finds his way to him, too. "We need you."

"I'm sorry, B." Cash coughs and blood spills down his throat. Rage fills my veins and I reach into the back of the ATV, grabbing another shotgun and pumping it before swinging it over my shoulder. I raise the AK up and shoot out the windows I can see, while walking straight through the front door. I see fucking *red*. Enough people have died because of her.

Nate is firing shots behind me, but all I can see is the tunnel in front of me. As if everything to the side is blurred and all I need and want is *blood*. I raise my gun up just as someone comes flying down the staircase. I pull the trigger and he falls instantly. Another comes down, and again, I point and shoot. I move into the sitting room behind the stairs and on a single white sofa sits Veronica, a cigarette in her mouth and her body completely naked.

I snarl. "I'm not going to make this easy for you."

"Ah!" She raises her finger and twirls it, signaling for me to turn around. I do. Samael has Nate locked into his arm in a chokehold, a devious fucking smirk on his face. "Oh, how unfortunate. And if you're wondering why the rest of your army hasn't barged in here, it's because they have an extra little dot directed straight to their forehead."

"What do you fucking want, Veronica?" I lower my gun. No point in keeping it on her. I'm not going to do anything to jeopardize anyone else's life.

Yet.

"Ah, the question you're all wanting to know." She stubs her cigarette out in the carpet. "I want Saint, Brantley. As I was to have her until you decided to destroy all of that by falling in love with her. You know I knew I couldn't get her through Lucan, so I knew I had to get close to you."

I pause.

"Why Saint?" I ask, confused. I take a small step closer to her. Enough, but not too much so she doesn't notice. "Why her? Why the obsession with her all these years?"

She laughs, crossing her legs. "Well, I guess I should expose it all to you." She cocks her head, her long black hair covering her tits. Thank fuck. "Saint is not my daughter. That was a last-ditch effort to pull you both apart, which is ironic really, since the reason I became close to you to begin with was to get close to her. Shame on me because your bond is even stronger than the possibility of incest."

"Hold up," I seethe. "We already know we're not related, you sick bitch. We wouldn't have married had we thought that was true."

"Ah, how disappointing. I thought that was quite impressive."

"You would." I raise my eyebrows. "You're disgusting."

She laughs, her head tilting back for a brief second.

Another step. Turning my head slightly, I notice Sam watching Nate instead of me. I still can't get a read on him, whether he's working for us or for her. Confusing fucking bastard. I'll put a bullet between his eyes anyway, I decide. Just for making it so hard for me to read him.

"There was a reason Hector brought Saint to your father instead of me, Brantley. It's because Lucan, though he is who he is, cares about one thing. The Vitiosis line continuing. Hector didn't bring her to you to raise; he brought her to you to fuck." She slants her head. "Why do you think he had you have sex with all those girls? He wanted you to impregnate one—or all—and got his rocks off while doing it." I hold my breath, my shoulders tight. What she's saying makes sense, but she's no better than Lucan. "Your father was smart. He knew with her being Hector's child and being a Swan, she would be worthy of more than just your spawn one day, so he allowed you to raise her how you wanted. The reason he never outed her was because of this fact. Even in his final hours. Even as much as you hated your father, he still protected you. Even her."

I raise my gun to her head. "Shut the fuck up. You don't know shit about that piece of shit, and I know more than you think."

Veronica shakes her head, unfazed by the gun now pointed at her. "She broke the curse, Brantley. One of the girls fell pregnant during The Hunt that Saint was present in. She carries the gift from the original Hayes' witch, passed down from her father. It's the only reason why I wanted her."

"She has them because she has—I don't fucking know—psychic abilities. It's not fucking magic."

She tsks, wiggling her finger at me. "Such a skeptic, son. I knew after you told me about her first sleepwalking encounter that she was gifted. I knew right then I needed you to trust me so that when the time came, you would allow me to take her under my wing." She smiles up at me, and I know right here and now. I know I didn't inherit my malice from my shitty father. It was all from her. She is why I am the way I am. She is why I will *never* reproduce children. And Lucan, obviously. "Lucan sniffed me out when I was ten years old. He was already in his early thirties. I was pregnant before my twelfth birthday, birthed you that same year." Her eyes glass over. "I hated your father, and you were a constant reminder of all I endured. That he made me love him in his sick and twisted web of darkness. I always found myself wanting to please him. Do better. Even though I hated him."

I pause.

Her mask slips back up as a loud cackle roars out of her. I have to fight all that's inside of me not to kill her right now. "Every step I took was to earn him back. He eventually came to me. Helped me. We kept the lie that you thought he thought I was dead, because it would be easier for me to play the victim if you knew your father tormented me. He put everything in motion the day that girl walked her bright little soul into the darkness of our manor. I walked from you, from him, to fulfill this, and Brantley, it will be fulfilled. Your father was a powerful man in all the right places. While The Kings were playing god, he was getting dirty with scum, but the scum is what made this happen." She can't look at me as she speaks. She's lying.

"Why. What's it to Lucan?" I start counting in my head. I can't be standing here for minutes longer. The more she talks, the angrier I become, but I need answers—and I need all of them before I make a move. A move I don't even know yet.

"Let me ask you something." Veronica leans forward, gazing up at me. "All those girls he made you have sex with. All the boys. The videos he made. What did you think that was for? Aside from trying to impregnate girls?"

I hear the beating of blood being pumped through my veins. "What?"

Veronica smirks up at me. "The Vatican, Brantley. They were for The Vatican."

"The fucking orphanage that Saint was in?"

"Yes."

I pause. "You told me that she was to wear that emblem. That it was to keep her safe."

"I lied," she whispers. "That was just a simple step to see if you trusted me. One of the many steps."

"The fucking Vatican. Wait." I squeeze the handle of my gun. "Are you saying she was brought to me *for fucking that*?"

Veronica shrugs. "Hector, in his defense, didn't know what The Vatican did with your father. He put Saint in when she was a baby, thinking they would keep her safe. The Vatican called Lucan right away to collect her, that she was to be protected. They urged Hector to take her to Lucan, feeding off of the fact Lucan only cared about the continuation of his bloodline. But then you became fierce over her. Like an animal, unhinged. Lucan couldn't whisper her name without you flipping your shit, so we had to play it safe and allow you both to come together organically. I wanted Saint, Lucan wanted her to be with child."

I start pacing because if I don't, I'm going to kill her and everyone in this house. Fuck if my brothers die. "What do they do to them when they're in The Vatican?"

"Some are sent to covens, but mostly, they all die if they can't be sold."

"Virgins are worth more money. Doesn't make sense why he would make me fuck them before."

"Not every man wants a virgin, and you didn't get them *all*."

Saint was sent to me from The Vatican without Hector's knowledge.

To be a recording.

But Lucan knew she was more worthy than that.

I keep my tone neutral. I don't want her to notice she has thrown me off-balance. If Lucan was sending them to The Vatican, then that means he had his nails deep into witch business way before we even knew about Saint being gifted. "Why did he do this?"

Veronica shrugs. "The Vatican had an agreement with Lucan. It fed his addiction, and The Vatican got paid. Lucan never took money for his dealings, though, and the leader of The Vatican got the one thing they wanted. Power."

I think over everything she has told me. "You've taken over what he did since he died."

She nods slowly. "But worse."

"How so?" I snarl, baring my teeth.

She opens her mouth. "I run The Vatican, too. Always have."

I've peaked. Tapping out. I'm done playing this fucking game. "I knew you were full of shit with this cursed shit," I snap, dropping down to her eye level. "See, I knew *everything*."

She pauses but doesn't offer a fleck of unease at the way I'm moving fluidly without restraint. Good. "I knew you ran The Vatican. I found out the night you tried to say Saint was my sister." She opens her mouth, but I raise my hand to silence her. "I knew she wasn't my sister all along. You think I'm stupid? Or even worse, your lack of education when it comes to The Elite Kings is even more humorous than I could give you credit for. I admit, watching this fucker put his hands all over Saint, and having to play along with the brother act was one of the worst fucking things I've gone through, but Veronica?" I reach for the knife that's in my pocket and unclip it. Her eyes fly around the room now. I lower my voice. "Ah, I see it. Now you're scared, right? Have you finally figured it out?"

Her brows curve in, shading her eyes. I rest the blade in my hand. "This has always been our game, and you played right into our riddle." I hear the footsteps behind and don't have to turn over my shoulder to know who are all behind me.

Veronica shakes her head. "No. Impossible. You can't have known. No way. My plan was flawless! Confusion and knots that not even you could untie!"

I chuckle, running my tongue over the front of my teeth. "You underestimated us, and that—" I flick the knife around my fingers before sinking the tip into her knee cap. She cries out a scream that has a direct line to my fucking insanity. "—was your biggest mistake. Now it's my turn to talk. I trusted you, yeah. I trusted you when you told me all of my life that you ran a halfway house for children that didn't have a home. Hell, I even believed every single fucking time you told me that you were nothing like my father. That you were pure, good, too good to be around him, which was why you left him. You said you knew you couldn't take me away from him, and I believed that. I believed all that shit for most of my life. *That* I will give you. Because, make no mistake, there's no way you would have come near Saint had I known." She pants desperately as I yank the blade out of her. "Now to fast-forward, before you came to the house, spewing the bullshit about Saint being my sister, we were tipped off." I turn over my shoulder and flick my blade to Samael. I bring the tip to the edge of her jaw. Exactly like mine, only smaller. "We *all* knew of the lies." I lean down to her ear and whisper, "Saint included."

Veronica shakes her head. "She didn't. I would have known."

I run the pointed tip over the curve of her jaw. She wriggles backward and forward, sweat dripping down the side of her neck. "Because of your *gifts*? You've been living in your bullshit little world of covens, witches, and Elders for so long, you actually believe the shit you talk." She screams once I get to the end of her chin. Blood trickles down her neck. "Just off subject." I tilt my head. "Have I ever mentioned to you that I know exactly how to make someone bleed out without killing them?" I smirk.

"Oh, come on," Samael grunts in the background.

"There's an art to it. You just—" I lean beneath her chin to see the parting between her skin and her muscle. "Have to make sure you don't cut too deep. Back to my storytelling…" I stop my cutting, standing straight. "We all knew she wasn't your daughter, but with her own stubbornness, and with the argument of Samael being in The Coven, she said she would be safe. Learn what you were planning. Stay close to you. Fuck, I was mad about this. I think I almost lost all of my control and dragged her back by her hair. Lucky for you, I prefer her hair on her head, where I can grab hold of it." I glide the knife up to Veronica's cheek. "The Kings are always three steps ahead of everyone. Remember that when you're reunited with Lucan."

She laughs, blood still trickling down her throat. "About Lucan. Were you prepared for that, too?"

"You mean the fact he was getting into her head?" Her face pales. "Yeah, well, she and Ophelia figured that out. Mental blocks or something now stop that from happening."

"Ah, so interesting that not even her walking out to his unmarked stone showed you that your father was tormenting her and has been for a lot longer than she even knows. *Years.* Even."

I know it's Lucan, I should have fucking known he was probably doing sick shit to her.

"Admit it, Brantley. We hit you at angles you didn't expect."

"Really?" Bishop says now, coming up behind me with a cigarette in his mouth. He blows out the smoke. "'Cuz the way I see it, this doesn't look like a scene that would be played out by people who didn't expect it. Now, you've killed two of our people."

"The Kings are a dying breed," she says, spitting blood onto the floor. "Even with you all having children."

Bishop pulls out his gun, aims it at her foot, and squeezes

the trigger. She screams in pain. "Don't ever fucking talk about my kids and think I won't shoot."

"We don't usually kill women," I say, cracking my neck. "There has been only one exception in the past. Now you're the second."

I turn to face Nate and Samael. Nate nods.

"Do you have any last-minute requests?" I say, cocking my head while wiping the blood off my blade.

She blinks up at me, and I see it. The exact moment she realizes it's over. She and Lucan's long tirade of evil is coming to an end. "You think you won't be the exact product of your father and me when it comes to your child, Brantley?" She laughs, her eyes darkening. She's ready for death. Good. Because she's not going to get it quickly. This is personal. Between her, Lucan, Saint, and me. When I walked into this, I knew this death wasn't for anyone's hands, only for my own. But it has to be more than that.

"Lucky for me, because I'm not ever having a child." I take the steps needed until I'm face-to-face with her once again, kneeling at eye level.

"Ah." She clicks her tongue. "The sweet little Saint didn't tell you."

I blink, and all of the blood that was erratically pumping through my veins at the mere scent of death turns to ice. "What?"

"Well, I can die happy now. I've surprised you one last time."

CHAPTER THIRTY-ONE

Saint

"Being pregnant makes my stress levels difficult to deal with," I say, standing at the window on the top floor with the curtain pulled back. It has been three hours since they've left. In those three hours, I've decided I know what I'm going to do about this baby. I'm going to tell Brantley. I shouldn't have held it from him to begin with.

"Tell me about it," Madison mutters, glancing down at her phone nervously while waiting for the call. Her belly has grown a lot over the past couple of weeks. Not a lot that she looks like she's carrying twins, though, as Tillie will always remind everyone.

Valentina is quiet on the sofa opposite Tillie and next to the door. They've not so much as blinked at one another. Tillie, once again, is being unreasonable with her beef, but that's Tillie. She's protective of the people she loves, and that should be something that's praised, more than taken as a threat.

Madison's phone lights up and she jumps off the sofa as my heart knocks so hard in my chest it winds me.

"Bishop!" She holds her breath for a few seconds, and then sighs, falling back onto the sofa. "Okay, we will see you soon." Madison hangs up the phone, looking to Valentina. "Bishop said your guards pulled through with their promise."

Valentina nods, breathing a sigh of relief. "I knew they would."

"You still have to handle The Lost Boys, Valentina. You can't allow them to run around on you and make you a fool." Tillie finally addresses her. Now I kind of wish she didn't.

Valentina's eyes water. "I know, Tillie. They're just so wild. I find it very difficult to keep them in line."

"You need to make one your pet, Valentina. Has my mother not taught you anything? She had Daemon. That's how she kept them under control. Not because she was queen, The Lost Boys don't care about that. They do, but not to the extent that others here do. You need to take one on. Find the strongest. The alpha of them all." Tillie stands from her chair. "And if I ever hear that you've not told us any of the updates happening on this island, mark my words, I will take it back." She leaves the door wide open in her departure.

Madison ignores Valentina, resting her hand on my shoulder. "Come on. We should wait for them downstairs."

"Be down in a second." I pat her hand before she moves out of the room, following Tillie. I wait until I know they're both out of earshot.

"I hope you take her threat seriously." Valentina's eyes travel to mine. I know she's been knocked around emotionally since we've been here, but I need her to understand. "I need you to do as she says, and do it very well." I stand from my chair. "I don't envy you at all, and could probably come to like you, but I need you to listen to what she says. Handle this island. Because if you don't and this happens again and she *does* take it back from you, that will draw a rift between her and Nate. That will destroy their relationship." Valentina blinks, watching me with wide eyes. "And if you do that, I fear I cannot guarantee your safety from any of us." I offer a small smile. "Thank you for opening this home to us and for helping. If there's anything I can do for you in the future—" I make my way to a table in the corner, picking up a pen and making my way back to her. "This is my number." I scribble my phone number on her arm. "Come down and see your guards home."

I knew as soon as they walked through the front door that something was off. I could smell the war on their hands and it had nothing to do with Veronica's blood.

"What happened?" I ask, looking amongst all of them. Nate goes straight for Tillie and wraps her in his arms. Brantley doesn't so much as look at me as he makes his way into the living room with Jase and Hunter. Hunter who has red-rimmed eyes.

"Where's Cash?" Madison glances around the room. The guards move to Valentina to update her as my hand flies out to Madison's. I've known all along how close Madison truly was to The Kings. She doesn't need to be worried about being a great mom; she's already been the best one to all of these men. She's a natural at sitting beside Bishop. I squeeze her fingers with mine because I already know what has happened.

Bishop's eyes are on hers, and only her. I see the swell in his chest as he takes a deep breath. "I'm sorry, baby."

"No." She shakes her head. "No. No, Bishop. You will not say those words to me. You will go out that door and come back in with better words."

"I can't," he says, stepping closer to her. I back away, giving them space. "I can't, baby, and I'm so fucking sorry I can't do that."

She begins falling to the floor, but Bishop catches her by wrapping his arm around her back. Her whimpers fade out all the way up the stairs, and then it's just me standing in the foyer with nothing.

Nothing but another death on my name and Brantley being distant. I wrap my arms around myself and make my way to the left side of the house, needing space and silence. Usually, I have Bishop to cry to when I'm feeling this way, or Brantley. But not now. Right now, I have to cry to myself. I find a hallway light and flick it on, following the path to the end. Past the abstract artwork hanging on the walls, and toward a door. I push it open and pause when I'm met with a bar. Of course there's a bar in this house. It's big enough. A long wooden bench lines the side, seats tucked beneath. Sprawled around the room are small booths, each with a pole on the tables in front of them. A strip club. There are records hanging on the wall, and a large picture of Scarlet hanging behind the bar. A paparazzi obviously took it, with Scarlet and Hector climbing out of a city car at a red-carpet event. They look younger than what they are now, and the image is filtered in sepia.

I rest my head in my hands after taking a seat in one of the booths. It's dim, with nothing but the green neon lights offering what they can. The death and loss that I've come to live with is overwhelming. Frankie and Alessi didn't deserve what they got, not like Veronica did. *Bailey.* Tears spill from my eyes and land straight on top of the table. Ongoing. One after another. I can't stop them, even if I tried, but I don't. Crying is therapeutic. Like releasing your sadness into the universe and allowing the pain to go with it. Unfortunately, it doesn't work that way. I don't know how long I sit in this same spot, but the tears have dried and I'm ready to go back out. I need to tell him.

I stand, turning around to head back out the door when my eyes connect with Brantley, who is sitting in one of the booths behind me. He hasn't changed his clothes, the black bandana still resting around his neck. With all of that willingness to find him, I'm now left with no words at all.

He still hasn't looked at me, his leg stretched out in front of himself and his hoodie resting around the back of his neck. The lighting casts green shadows over his jawline and high cheekbones, but I can still see how angry he is. Enough that he hasn't said a single word.

"Were you ever going to tell me that you're pregnant?"

Oh.

"Yes," I answer truthfully, "I was."

"When?" he bites, his eyes colliding with mine finally. Now that I have his attention, I just want to give it right back to him. "When you were four months? Six? Hell, after you had the baby?"

I swallow the bile rising in my throat. For the first time, I'm nervous around him. I can't move. My feet are cemented to the ground. "No, I was going to tell you when you got back."

"And what if I didn't make it back, Saint? Hmm? Because Cash sure as fuck didn't." He winces and looks away from me. Right now, a smart person would retreat from Brantley. They'd read the signals he's setting off and stay away. You don't walk into a lion's den after it tried to eat you, right? Apparently, I would.

I slide into the seat beside him. He doesn't move. The whiskey in his hand is halfway full. "But it wasn't you."

"It should have been." He shakes his head. "That's all I kept thinking when it happened, was that it should have been me. Cash matters to people. He has parents who care about him, and a job that is important." He brings the bottle to his mouth and takes a hard swallow. He hisses, "I have no one. No family. No important job. In fact, I'm almost certain that people would live without me here for that job. Literally." He turns to face me. "But then I was told that you were pregnant." His eyes travel down to my stomach. "And do you know what that does, Saint? It makes me weak. Because now I do have something."

"Listen to me," I say, grabbing his cheek and turning him to face me. "Even without this child, you still had a family. You have people who love you. Everyone loves you, Brantley. Your duty with The Kings, it's what you've been raised to do. If you don't want to do it, I'm sure Bishop will work around that for you, but here's the fact." I take a slow but deep inhale, running my thumb over his cheekbones. "I love you. And if it was you who died tonight, I wouldn't have been too far behind."

His eyes narrow. "You would fucking kill yourself? If you say yes, I'll do it for you right now because that is *not* fucking happening. Ever."

I shake my head. "No, but my heart would literally break. We're darkness and light, and one cannot exist without the other, or what is the point?"

"I don't deserve you," Brantley whispers, his eyes losing focus.

"You deserve so much more than you know." I lean backward and rest against the chair. "I'm sorry about Cash."

"Yeah," he whispers. "Me too." I shuffle around to look at him, curling my leg under my other. "We can talk about this baby when you're ready. I don't want to rush you into having the conversation."

He runs his finger over his upper lip, his eyes not moving from mine. My neck always aches at how high I have to look up at him. "How long have you known?"

I stifle a sarcastic laugh. "Since yesterday. Veronica knew somehow, and then when the girls got me out of wherever that was, we stopped off at the convenience store on the way here. I took a test and swore them not to tell."

He rolls his eyes. "So they've all been hiding it, too?"

"They have, only because I asked them to. They didn't want to and warned me that they can't keep secrets from Nate and Bishop."

"And can you?" he asks, and the smooth tone he allows his words to wrap around makes my stomach flip.

"Can I what?" I play dumb.

"Can you hide shit from me?"

I rest my head on his outstretched arm, shaking my head. "It only made it easy because so much was going on."

He takes another swig of whiskey. "I can't right now, Saint. I can't have this conversation. I can't even—" He clenches his jaw. "Meet me upstairs. We're sleeping in the room opposite Madison's."

"Brantley, I—"

"—Saint? Please. I just need a minute."

My mouth closes and I pull back from him, giving him his space. When I climb out of the booth and make my way to the doorway, I know whatever is going on inside his head right now is a war that only he can fight.

I drag my tired body upstairs. The house is quiet for how many people are sleeping inside of it. I find our bedroom and drop down on top of the bedcovers, not even bothering to shower or to get beneath them.

⁓

The mattress sinks beside me and I turn onto my side, wincing when my legs feel numb from pins and needles. I don't know what time it is, but I'm guessing I had a decent amount of sleep, so it's either really early or really late.

He's shirtless and wearing nothing but his briefs, sliding under the covers. I don't speak. Nervous with what to say to him. His hand finds me as he wraps me in his arms, pulling me into his chest. I sigh when I feel his skin against mine, and it's not long before we're both drifting off. Without noise. Without the need to speak. Just in comfortable silence.

I fling my arm onto the other side of the bed the next morning, hoping to find Brantley there, but I'm met with an emptiness big enough to deepen the void inside my heart. It's just after six a.m. Why is he awake?

I swing my legs over the side of the bed, brushing my hair away from my face when there's a knock on my door. "Come in."

"Morning," Tillie says from the threshold. I look up to see she's carrying a longboard filled with food. I cross my legs beneath myself. Did she just bring me breakfast in bed?

I wave her onto the bed, patting the puffed-up blankets. "What have you got?"

"Well," she pipes up, placing the breakfast platter on the bed sheet, just as Madison strolls in swiping a towel over her face. She's dressed in gym clothes, a sports bra and tight little spandex shorts.

"Have you been fucking running?" Tillie asks, throwing a piece of bacon at her as she snuggles into the blankets of my bed.

Madison closes the door, picking up the discarded bacon and biting into it. "Tillie, I'm pregnant. That doesn't mean my love for fitness stops."

Tillie rolls her eyes. "I love you, but no."

Madison kicks off her runners and sits at the bottom of my bed. "How are you feeling?" She chews on the single piece of bacon, her eyes on mine.

I run my tongue over my top lip and reach for one of the egg muffins. "He's not okay. I think he's upset with me about the pregnancy, but I just don't know if he's upset because I'm pregnant or because I didn't tell him that I was pregnant." I sink my teeth into the muffin and stifle a moan when salted butter slips down my throat. *God.* Has food always tasted this good, or does pregnancy just make you think it is?

"He will come around," Madison says, tapping my leg. "If there's one thing I have learned from being with Bishop, it's that sometimes it's not easy to love them. Actually, I would go so far as to say that they're probably the most unlovable men walking this earth."

"Geez, Mads. Tell us how you really feel…" Tillie's fingers wrap around her hot chocolate.

"No, I'm serious," Madison says, picking at the family of grapes on the platter. She slips one between her lips and chews slowly. "They're not easy to love, but that's what makes their love worth it in the end. Because you both had to fight for it. Blood, guts, gore, and at times, barely hanging on by the edges of your claws. You hang on to them because, even when they don't love you back, what they give you is enough until they do." Her eyes come to mine. "Brantley is by far the worst of their kind, Saint. When I first met him in The Hamptons, he sent chills down my spine that I have never been able to shake. But that monster, that beautifully flawed, dark and demonic monster *loves* you. In his own fucked-up way he does. And if anyone is an expert on fucked-up love, it's me." She rolls her eyes. "You should fight for him." Even though I already knew what she had said, it still pains me to hold back the tears that threaten. I already love him. I think I loved him the very first day he took my hand and led me into his hell. He didn't lead me into hell to suffer; he brought me in to sit beside his throne.

"I will fight for him, Madison." I place the egg muffin back onto the tray, my appetite suppressed. "I will *always* fight for him."

"Good," Tillie adds, placing her now empty mug on the platter and stretching her arms over her head. "Because if there's anyone that can tolerate Bran Bran, it's you."

We continue eating as Madison shares the story of when she first met Bailey. She said she was a fighter from the beginning, and when she found out that she was a Vitiosis, she wasn't at all surprised.

"I'm scared, though," she mutters, placing the breakfast platter on the floor. "She and Abel were a force. They were what love should look like, you know? That young teen love. The kind you find when you're not like us and choose psychopaths."

I chuckle.

Tillie chokes on her grape, banging on her chest.

Madison sighs. "But they were very co-dependent. Bishop is going to pull him in when we get back tonight. Do all of the things he should have done instead of chasing after me."

"What happened when he came to get you?" I ask, tilting my head.

Madison winces. "It wasn't pretty. It was the foundation being laid of a ruined castle, but we're here. We still have a long way to go, but that's who we are as people, as a couple. I think that's something I need to come to terms with." I lean back in the bed and draw my legs up to my chest. It has been almost two hours since I woke up and Brantley still hasn't made an appearance. I'm thankful that the girls don't ask about why he isn't in here. I know he needs space, but how much does he need?

"All right! I have a meeting with The Lost Boys before we leave." Tillie rolls off the bed and moves toward my door. "Honestly, I just want to be home again so we can send off our friends."

I smile up at her. "Me too."

CHAPTER THIRTY-TWO

Brantley

The first time I figured out that my parents weren't like other parents, I was probably around five years old. I don't remember much from that age, but their toxicity was something that poisoned my view on things like *marriage* and *starting a family*. I knew from a young age that I didn't want any of that. Then I grew to be who I am and knew without a shadow of a doubt that I did not want to carry on the Vitiosis last name. It was to end with me.

Now I'm met with the reality of not getting something I firmly wanted.

"Hey." Madison sits on the empty chair beside mine. I'm glad we got the fuck off that island ASAP. I'm desperate to put Cash and Bailey to rest, and we have the issue of pulling Abel out of a dark fucking tailspin. Since leaving Saint in bed this morning, I've made it a point not to have anyone approach me right now. I can't. I know I should talk with Saint about why I'm feeling so apprehensive about things, but will she really understand? Has she ever really understood me? No. Because I've made damn sure that darkness didn't touch her. That's on me, not her.

"Mad, I don't want to talk right now." I clench my jaw and sip on the whiskey as the jet jolts when we hit turbulence. "Well, I don't fucking care."

Her words shock me, but I'm impressed. Madison and I didn't have a surface friendship. Ours went deeper than that, but it wasn't by choice, it was by the unfortunate events we went through together as children.

"Man, if I knew swearing at you would be all I needed to do to get a smile out of you all those years ago, I would have had a field day." She crosses her legs at her ankles.

I glare at her. "Would you have?"

She sighs. "No. No, I wouldn't have."

I chuckle, my lip curling.

"You're going to be a great father, Brantley."

I shift in my chair, turning to face her. "How do you know that, Madison? Did you find a time machine while you were in New Zealand that could show me my future?"

She fake laughs, her eyes dead. "So funny. No, I know this because you know exactly how not to be a parent. They make some of the best, you know. The ones who didn't come from a good home."

"Well, I don't have a choice now, do I?" I snap, resting my head back on the headrest.

"Well, you do, technically speaking. Saint could have an abortion."

My fists clench on top of my knees. "The only thing that would anger me more than having a kid is killing it." I run my fingers through my hair, covering my mouth. I bring my eyes up to hers.

Madison leans forward. "Brantley. We are all in this together forever. You having a child is probably a good thing because it's in the window for this generation."

I divert my eyes to Saint, where she's sleeping with her head resting on Bishop's shoulder. She has an earbud in one ear and him with the other. "Why the fuck are they like this?"

Madison turns over her shoulder to follow my sight. Her shoulders relax and her mouth breaks into a smile. "She brings out a side to him that I've not seen." She turns back to face me. "Has that happened before?"

"Are you fucking talking about Khales? Still?"

"No!" Her eyes are wide in shock.

I glare at her.

She winces. "Okay, sort of."

I shake my head in disbelief, pulling my gaze off her and back out the window. "Madison, shut the fuck up."

"Always nice chatting with you, Bran." She stands but rests her hand on my shoulder. "I mean it. You're going to be a staunch father and uncle. We need that. We all need you." Then she leaves, and I'm left with the faint echo of her words for the remainder of the flight. I can't think about it right now. I just need to bury Bailey and Cash.

The jet lands and I stretch my arms over my head, yawning. Saint and Bishop are laughing together, and an unreasonable side of jealousy rears its ugly head.

"So, did she tell you the good news? Hmmm?" I say to Bishop.

Bishop looks between her and me.

Saint shakes her head. "No, I haven't yet."

I choke on a laugh. "That's a fucking first." I make my way to the door. "Congratulations, Uncle Bishop. You're having another baby." I take the steps down onto the tarmac and smirk when I see the Bugatti parked up beside Bishop's Maserati, Nate's Lambo, and Spyder's Porsche. I make my way for the Bug but pause when my hand is on the door handle, staring up at the jet. Matte black with the letters TEKC in cursive writing on the side. So fucking extra.

I point to it when Bishop steps off the stairs and onto the tarmac. "We need to upgrade to a 747 if we wanna fit all these fucking kids on our future flights."

Bishop cracks out a laugh, dragging his aviators down over his nose. "Actually not a bad idea."

Saint is walking down the stairs, hoodie on, loose ripped jeans, and Converse. I don't know if she means to do it, but everything looks like a fashion show with her. Saint looks between the Bug and the Mas.

I flex my jaw. "Try me, Saint. See what happens."

She turns toward the passenger seat of my car and opens the door. I nudge my head at Bishop. "We're going to stay at the hotel until I figure shit out with the house."

"Which one?" Bishop raises his eyebrows at me. "I mean, the manor or The Coven?" My face falls. I forgot about that fucking house. Every parent in The Elite Kings leaves their houses to their kids when they pass, as well as all businesses. It's why I'm stuck with Vitiosis Hotel in New York, passed down from generation to generation. Remodeling the hotel after Lucan passed was one of the first decisions I made. The hotel was child's play. It's the casinos we all own where the real money is, and it makes it easy for us to funnel cash. Most business are all under The Elite Kings, and we split it equally once our generation takes the gavel. So now, not only do we have decisions to make when it comes to the underbelly of crime, we've also got our legitimate businesses that we have to continue to oil. Needless to say, I'm not ready for a kid.

I slip into the driver's seat and hit the window down. "I'll go there after the burial. Benny has a lead on the other two as well."

Bishop disappears into his car beside me. He revs his engine. "To VH?"

Nate's car roars loudly, and then Spyder's. "All in!"

I slide into first gear and floor it forward. We shoot back in our seats as I direct us toward the exit gates where men are holding the tarmac lights. Saint is on her phone, unbothered with the speed before she turns the radio on. I look into my rearview mirror, ripping up the emergency brake to drift sideways onto the street that leads to the freeway. She starts humming to the song in the background, and I instantly want to know what the song is called just because of how it sounds coming out of her mouth. Ray-Bans are covering her eyes, her hair wild and sprawled around her shoulders, and I fucking swear to God my heart skips a beat as the setting sun hits her skin. "JOYRIDE" by Sonia reads across the computer screen built into the dash. Damn. She sings the shit out of this. Once we hit the freeway, I settle down to a more respectful speed, letting Nate and Bishop have at it. We all know Nate won't give it to anyone else, and I don't give enough of a fuck about winning a race like I used to a couple years ago.

I wait until she's finished the song before I turn to face her. "What if the baby is a girl?"

She pushes her glasses down her nose to look at me, her feet up on the dashboard. "Then she's one lucky girl."

"How the fuck can you even say that? Do you have proof that I'm going to be good at this?"

She removes the glasses completely and places them in the pocket between us. Her eyes burn through mine, but every so often, I have to check the road. "Brantley, I *am* your proof." I pale when I realize what direction she's going. "You raised me when you were still growing yourself. Why do you think I'm not the least bit worried about that? Why do you think *no one* is worried about that?" She has a point. Saint is, though different, painfully perfect.

"But you aren't a Vitiosis. We're not good people." I drop it down a gear with a flick of my finger.

"Well, good thing this child will be a product of both you and me. Heaven and hell no longer walking side by side. Heaven and Hell combined as one."

I feel the tightness in my chest ease slightly, but not enough to feel excitement. "Hate to break it to you, baby, but your other half isn't looking very fucking compelling either. A Hayes and a Stuprum." I run my palm down the side of my face. "Fuck, we haven't even been *together* for very long."

"You're not worried about that either," she says matter-of-factly. "Stop deflecting. You're mad because you're greedy and you wanted more time with me."

I chuckle, turning off the freeway and onto the connecting street that takes us to Vitiosis Hotel.

"Wow." Saint shuffles farther up in her seat. She watches buildings pass, her lips parting. I'd forgotten that she hasn't seen New York yet. She hasn't seen many places. I need to fix that before she has the baby.

Fuck.

I swallow down the buildup of saliva. *I'm going to be a fucking dad.*

I pull us into the circular entry, where a valet worker stands, his eyes sparking up when he sees the Bug. The license plate is VITIOSIS. Everyone who works here has either seen or heard of this car. And the owner.

Saint climbs out as I toss the keys at the valet's chest.

"Boss." He nods his head, his blond hair falling over his forehead. He looks no older than twenty-five. Still older than me.

Saint's hand dives into mine and I still slightly, before

relaxing. Human interactions with her come naturally, but there are always times when I need reminding. I direct her into the lobby, over the black marble floor and dark glittering chandelier that hangs above our heads. Vitiosis Hotel is the only six-star hotel in New York, and it fucking shows. From the dining to the rooms to the workers. You walk into it and you know you're going to be looked after—if you have enough money. I'd thought about branching out and building another one somewhere in the Southern Hemisphere, but with my work with The Kings, I've lost my appetite to do that. Maybe when the gavel drops…

The elevator doors part, and I step inside, pulling her under my arm while swiping my keyring and pushing TL.

Saint sinks into my chest. "I could sleep for days."

I kiss the top of her head. "Then you do that. I've just got a few things to sort out, one being checking on Benny since he's babysitting Ophelia and Ivy and the animals."

"Where are they?" she says through a yawn, and I feel her body go limp beside me. I scoop her up into my arms when the doors part, opening directly onto the top level, also known as my apartment. She wriggles into my neck, her lips pressed to my skin and I squeeze her into my chest farther. In this moment, carrying her to the master bedroom, I know I would do anything and everything for her. Including be a father.

I pass the open-style kitchen that overlooks the city behind floor-to-ceiling windows and step down into the sitting room, before hitting the hallway. "They're in one of the penthouses a level below us."

"Oh," she murmurs, "I figured you would take care of them."

I ignore her sleep talk and place her body on top of the covers of the California king. Everything in this apartment is black. I designed it that way when Lucan died. The blinds, the bath, the bathrooms, the furnishings. If it's not black, it's mahogany wood.

I pull a blanket over Saint's body and step backward slightly, my eyes on her. Her bright white hair beams off the bedding like a fucking snowflake lost in a storm. My phone vibrates in my pocket, pulling me out of my daze, and I turn, swiping to answer while shutting the door behind me. I unzip my hoodie and toss it onto one of the barstools that hide beneath the counter.

"Yeah?"

"Madison is tired, so I'm going to take her back to HH."

"Yeah, Saint is already crashed."

"What does she think of VH?"

I chuckle, pulling open the fridge, thankful to see that the front desk sorted someone to restock the fridge. "She hasn't seen it yet."

"Are you sure you want her body in Perdita?" I know who he's talking about, and it ain't Bailey.

"Yes."

"Okay. Cash's body will be back later tonight, but it's going straight to the mortuary where it'll remain with Bailey's until the burial." It's too convenient for EKC to also own a mortuary and funeral home, but it has always made things like *making bodies disappear* easy for our cleanup crew.

I squeeze my eyes closed, leaning my shoulders on the counter. "Have you spoken with Abel?"

"He's not answering his phone. I'll drive to his house in the morning."

"I'll come with you. Where's Spyder staying?"

"The only six-star hotel in fucking New York…"

I laugh, tipping my head back and sipping on my water. "Ah, victory." There has been an underlying battle between Bishop and me about hotels since taking over.

Bishop hangs up on me and I snicker, tossing my phone across the kitchen counter while running my hands over my face. I know tomorrow is going to be filled with organizing the funerals and dealing with the events that happened around both of them. Bailey's parents are pieces of shit. They don't deserve to know their daughter, much less make an appearance at her funeral, but I pick up my phone and send off a text to her father anyway. I hope it fucking pains them, but I know it won't. I move into the sitting room and look out at the bright lights beaming off the city. Bringing a kid into this world isn't something I wanted to do. Yeah, we're feared, but we're not untouchable. With power comes enemies. Mostly, they stay in their lane, but every few years, we'll get someone with balls too big for his conscience who will try to be the person or group to bring down the most powerful organization in global history. The problem with that is there will always be casualties. Our enemies always fall, but that never stops them from trying. And what happened with Cash and Bailey, can happen to any of us at any given time. There's no price to power; there's just blood.

I turn the treadmill up another speed when I find myself not running out of breath. The burn in my chest needs to match the one in my mind. Sweat drips off me and falls onto the conveyer belt as I beat it out to D12. Fatigue throbs at the crux of my bones, but I can't find the will to stop, because when I stop, I know I've got one hundred things to do to organize burying a King and my cousin.

My phone goes off, cutting through Eminem rapping about having a screw loose.

"What!" I snap, jumping off the treadmill. The timer reads 1:43:89 minutes. Damn. It's not until my feet hit the ground that my legs wobble like jelly.

"What happened?" Gordon Vitiosis, aka my piece of shit uncle and only branch of family I ever had, though he's a fucking disappointment to not just our name, but the entire existence of humans in general, asks.

"There was an explosion at the manor and she was inside." I flip open my bottled water and take a sip. "Not that I owe you a fucking apology, since you left her out to die."

He doesn't answer.

I grit my teeth. "Just so you know, Bailey grew to be a feisty, opinionated, and above all, passionate girl who would do about anything for those she loved most. It's your loss that you missed out on that." I hang up my phone and shove it into my pocket, making my way out of the gym. I pause when I find Saint in the dining room, biting into a bagel.

"Have you slept?" she asks, her head tilting to the side.

"No," I answer truthfully, ignoring her interrogating gaze. When I turn back to face her after pouring coffee, she's still watching me. "Say it, Saint."

"I didn't say anything." She moves a spoon through whatever it is inside her glass. "This place is beautiful. Do you stay here often?"

My eyes narrow. "Are you asking me if I bring girls here because I never have to the manor?"

She puckers her lips and I know that's all she's been thinking about since waking up. Saint isn't insecure, so her bringing this up means it must be bothering her. "This isn't the right time to have this conversation, so we'll leave it for later."

"Yeah," I answer, boring my eyes into her. "Not right now." I don't put her out of her misery by telling her no way in hell did any girl or woman *ever* fuck me in my space, but I'm too pissed at her for bringing it up. The elevator door dings and I know it's one of The Kings or Benny, since they're the only ones who have access to my elevator without my permission.

Ophelia and Ivy walk in first, with Benny not far behind them.

"Girls wanted to see her," Benny says, gesturing to the both of them as they pull Saint into a hug. Benny leans against the counter, his focus solely on me. "So double funeral?"

"Yeah, just separate plots." I empty my coffee down the sink. "How were these two?"

Benny smirks, a little too fucking wide. "Ivy is a dream. Ophelia, on the other hand."

"What? She's immune to your charm?" I roll my eyes. "Who would have thought."

He stares at me with wide eyes. "Nothing works on her. At all."

"Good. Leave her alone." We both watch them as they talk between each other—with the exception of Ivy. "What'd you find on the other two?"

Benny leans forward to rest his elbows on the kitchen island. "We couldn't find anything on Frankie. Looked everywhere, but Frankie came from a rough home life. Poor as piss with parents who didn't give a fuck about her. Alessi, we found tucked back up in her family home in Detroit. Not sure what happened there but didn't want to disturb the dust. As far as she knows, it ain't nothin' to do with us."

I nod. "Thanks, Benny." I squeeze his shoulder before moving through the sitting room and down the hallway that leads to the master bedroom. Once I'm out of the shower and dressed, my phone starts blaring again. I fall onto my bed, swiping it unlocked.

"Yeah?"

"They're both at the funeral home. We've all agreed that the sooner they're buried the better, for all of us."

My knee jiggles. "I agree."

"So Bailey will be buried in the Vitiosis plot, and Cash in The Kings' crypt."

"Yeah, how are we going to work that?"

"We'll have the wake at my house."

"What, your actual house? It's ready?" Bishop and Madison started the build of their home in Riverside before she went running to New Zealand. I didn't realize that Bishop hadn't stopped the building process. My lips crack in a smirk. Because the fucker knew he would get her back eventually.

"It was ready last week, but we were out. It gave Madison enough time to do all that girl shit and furnish it. If I knew the furnishings were going to be in the digits they're in, I would have done it myself. I think she's punishing me by spending money."

I slip on my boots after putting him on speaker. "Would you rather her just shoot you again?"

He pauses, and I know he's giving me a dirty look. Him dragging her back from New Zealand wasn't easy this time around. He has a scar on his chest to vouch for that. "Fuck off."

I laugh, shaking my head. "She's going to be fucked-up over Cash. Make sure you're doing all the right things and not being a complete fucking bastard to her."

"What, you're better?" He scoffs through the phone.

"Motherfucker, I'm cold, not a bastard. There's a difference."

"Mmhmm, and I suppose only Saint sees that difference."

"Are you done?" I ask blandly, about ready to end our conversation because it's going nowhere fast.

"No." He silences, and I know he must be second-guessing the next words that come out. "We need to talk about Reaper shit." My blood turns cold.

"—I'm not giving it up, Bishop. Not until the next King, being my own, takes my place."

"Even if it bothers Saint?"

"Even if it bothers her, which she hasn't told me it has. She knew what I did before she crawled her way onto my dick. Non-negotiable."

"Because you still need it?" Bishop asks quietly.

I pause, my lashes sprawling out over my cheeks every time I blink. "Yeah, I can't imagine a time I won't."

"All right. I'll see you a little later tonight. The girls have planned a wake."

"Of course they have." I end the call and toss my phone onto the bed.

"Was that Bishop?" Saint asks from the doorway. She has obviously showered, wearing fresh clothes, but her face is free of makeup.

"So you girls planned a wake without us knowing?"

She moves farther into the room, before spreading her sexy as fuck legs wide and sinking herself down on top of me. Both knees are buried into the mattress, her fingers around the back of my neck. I rest my hands over her ass, looking up at her. "While we were on the flight home last night…"

"Hmmm," I say, leaning up and swiping my tongue across her bottom lip. She has six seconds to say what she needs to say before I'm about to fuck her until she breaks.

"That's what happens when you go quiet on me." I pick her up and fling her onto her back, spreading each leg wide while resting between her thighs.

I grind my hips into her. "Wanna see what happens when you come sit your sexy ass on my lap without any warning?"

She smiles up at me, and it looks so fucking cute. "Actually, yeah." She leans up and sucks my bottom lip into her mouth. I groan, fighting my eyes from rolling to the back of my head. "Do your worst." The final word barely escapes as a whisper before my teeth sink into the side of her neck.

CHAPTER THIRTY-THREE

Saint

DEATH IS THE ENEMY THAT NO ONE CAN CONQUER. It doesn't matter how skilled you are, or how many weapons you own. Death takes who it wants, and there's absolutely nothing you can do about it. I didn't know Bailey long. I haven't known any of these people long, except for Brantley, but how easily they've all pushed through my soul and set up there is terrifying. I couldn't bear losing anyone this close. Not now, not ever. I'm hoping now that Veronica is dead, things can settle. We can move on and try to rebuild everything that we've lost. Brantley asked me if I wanted to know the details about her death, but I said no. I don't need to. But that was only after he had told me that Valentina used her death to make a statement to the people of Perdita. She killed Veronica with an audience, and now people are falling into line for Valentina. I was partially surprised that Brantley gave her the option, considering how much damage she had done to him and The Kings, but he said he needed to stay adamant on the already few rules he had. No women, no old people, and no children. I respected him a lot for that, and I think in the back of my mind, it made me feel a little more at ease about what he does. He had every right to kill Veronica, but he didn't. He allowed something that was more important to come from all of the carnage she left behind and agreed to allow Valentina to kill her in front of The Lost Boys. And now, I can start thinking about this baby and how Brantley and I are going to move forward, instead of being caught in an endless whirlpool of uncertainty and danger.

I wander around Bishop and Madison's newly built castle. I would say house, but it's literally a castle. Even the driveway is an obvious show of opulence. Sculpted hedges line the road, and stone sculptures are placed neatly in strange places. With sharp-pointed rooftops reaching for the sky, the endless glass windows, and the swarm of workers moving around the property, you definitely feel as though you're about to meet royalty. It's a palace fit for a king and queen.

Literally.

Well-played, Bishop. Well-played.

Most of the people who are here are on the main level that sprawls out onto the back yard which then overlooks endless greenery, but I find myself lost in the castle itself. Finding room after room, a massive library that has shelves built into walls that reach the ceiling, an underground bar and poker room, and finally, the pool. I did wonder why the pool wasn't outside, but it turns out, they put it inside on the bottom level.

"Jesus, Bishop." I shake my head, moving around the evergreen of plants and vines that wrap around the colosseum-style pillars. This house had to be close to a billion-dollar build. This kind of money should not exist.

"Mmmm, right? It's over the top and totally a Hayes' move."

Abel's voice interrupts me from behind and I spin to find him in the darkest corner, a hoodie over his head and two empty bottles of vodka around him. I move closer, noting the powdered substance dusted out over a small mirror table, a one-hundred-dollar bill rolled up beside the lines of, what I know, are coke. I know this because I've watched *Scarface*. Many times.

"We are both Hayes, so…" I take a tentative step closer to him, before slowly lowering myself to the edge of the pool. I kick off my heels and slide my feet into the hot tub side, sighing when the hot water relaxes all of my muscles.

"I'm no Hayes any more than you are," Abel says from behind me, and for all the alcohol he has clearly drunk, his speech is impeccable. Must be the cocaine offsetting the effects of it.

I smile, but it doesn't reach my eyes, and I know he can't see me since my back is to him. "Maybe, but we're still family, Abel, and I am here for you."

"I'm not Bishop," Abel sneers, with almost too much bite in his tone. "I don't need to have family or people around me. I'm aware of that even more so—" He pauses, and I can almost hear the pain in his throat. It hits me all at once. His sorrow. The cracks in his heart that suddenly spread to my own. "—now that she's gone." I don't know much about Abel. I did plan to get to know him more in the future, but how naïve was that? To assume I would always have that chance. Death is anything but predictable.

"I'm sorry for your loss, Abel."

There's silence, and then I hear glass clatter to the ground and scuffling behind me before he appears at my side, kicking off his shoes and sliding his feet into the water while falling beside me. "You're the first person to say that to me. You know that?"

"No," I whisper, trying to block all of the emotions that are throbbing against the side of my head from him. *Pain. Sorrow. Regret.* "I didn't." Abel's energy is much different than Bishop's.

When Bishop and I met, it was as though we had been looking for each other all of our lives. We became magnets that could never be parted. Abel is different. Not uncomfortable, just— uneasy. I overheard Bishop casually talking about his troubles one day, and how he came from a very different life than the rest of them.

Abel leans against his hands, and I finally turn to face him. Now that I'm looking right at him, I see the alcoholism over his features. The way his gaze is distant and disconnected from reality. "I won't survive without her."

"Yes, you will."

"Would you?" he asks, and I search his high cheekbones that are even more sunken in than I remember, and the dark circles that taint the rims of his eyes. "Would you survive without Brantley?"

"I, uh—" Words struggle to get past my tight throat. Just the thought of losing Brantley kills everything inside of me. I already know my answer, but I also know encouraging Abel isn't what he needs right now.

"You don't have to say anything," he mutters, looking back to the water. "Your face said it all."

"No," I answer truthfully. He shuffles beside me. "I probably wouldn't survive without him. I would walk around barely the shell of the girl I am right now. I'd be barely recognizable. I'd either eat myself into a coma or I wouldn't eat at all. I might pick up an unhealthy addiction like alcohol or whatever you have scattered on the table over there." I take a deep breath. "When Brantley dies, he'll be taking my soul with him. My body would wither away eventually, but my soul? My soul would be buried right beside him in that scary graveyard."

"So you understand?"

I shake my head, resting my hand on the lower part of my belly. It wasn't obvious if you didn't know I was pregnant. "I wasn't finished. But I have something that anchors me to this world. Something that reminds me of him. So strongly that I need to be here, whether my soul is not."

"I don't have anything," Abel whispers, and it's almost too painful to swallow his words as a second wave of his emotions thrash into me so fiercely my knees buckle together. I squeeze the concrete.

"Yes, you do, Abel. You have all of the memories you had with her. You have to hold on to those. Memories anchor your feet to the earth."

He stands and moves to where he was sitting, collecting his things but casting one final look at me before leaving. "Bailey was the kind of girl that not even her own memories could replace." He smiles weakly, but the purple ring around his lips and the look of sadness in his eyes are too much. Too much darkness and sorrow. "It was nice meeting you, Saint." His eyes drop down to where my hand rests. "My niece or nephew is lucky to have you as their mother." Then he leaves, taking all of his energy with him. Upon his departure, it's like a black cloud up and shifts from the room. The oxygen becomes lighter, the sadness drawn out.

I sit for a few more minutes quietly, before standing and buckling my wedges back onto my feet. I squeeze my black leather jacket around my torso as I move back through the way I came. Even though Abel left physically, I still feel the chill he left down my spine. I reach the large cathedral-style living room that opens out onto the back end of the house when Brantley finds me. He's standing off to the other side of the room, sipping whatever it is in his glass. Whiskey, no doubt. He's talking with someone I don't recognize, but his eyes are solely focused on me. Just when I think he's not going to disconnect, he slowly drops them down, inhaling my body. Usually when he does this, it's to check if I have any injuries. This time, not so much. Heat rises to my cheeks and sweat rolls down the curve of my spine. Not enough to get rid of that chill in my bones, but enough.

"Hey." Ophelia hands me a glass of what looks like chilled orange juice. "A lot of people here, right?"

I nod around taking a sip. Perfect. Just what I need. Something to only intensify that chill. "Cash was a Divitae. His family managed a lot of the finances and social aspects, I think."

"Ah," Ophelia says, looking around the room. "That's so sad." I'm glad I have O here. She brings me a kind of comfort I can't find in anyone else. "So Benny is really goddamn annoying."

I snort into my glass, smiling politely at someone who's passing by. He's wearing a suit and looks important. Although most people here do. "Have you slept with him?" I ask casually, people-watching discreetly.

"Yes," she huffs, crossing her arms in front of herself. It looks cute on her because Ophelia is anything but. She's powerful and loyal, and strong as all hell. But she also has a softness to her that I've connected to from day one. "And it was annoyingly good."

"Well," I say, running my hand up and down my arm. "The bad ones usually are."

"Hey, are you cold?" she asks, turning to face me while carefully taking my orange juice.

"Yeah." I shiver, tightening my grip around my belly. "I can't shake it."

"Well," Ophelia says. "As long as it's not in your bones, girl. Then we good." Her words stop my shivering briefly.

"What do you mean in my bones?" I start noticing how people are dressed. Without jackets and big fluffy coats. My skin is warm, but the inside is cold, and I can't get rid of the goose bumps that have risen over my flesh.

Ophelia drinks the rest of my OJ, waving her hand. "When you feel a coldness that rushes through your veins, that's Death's energy, but don't worry. You're clearly cold on the outside, too."

She raises her hand to my forehead as her skin turns an unnatural shade of gray. "Oh."

"Yes," I growl under my breath. "Oh." I gasp, just as my body turns rigid. "Abel."

"Shit." She places the empty glass on top of the food station beside us. "We need to get you out of here."

"Why?" I snap, my eyes flying around the place in a panic. "It's Abel. Ophelia!" I yell as she moves me through the sea of people. Sweat falls down my temples and my vision goes hazy. "Ophelia, the baby. What's happening to me?" I can't seem to grasp reality as I hear doors closing in the background.

"Hey! Hey!" Ophelia lays me down onto something soft, but it's hot there, too. I don't know where I am. *Where am I?* "Shit." There's silence, but then I hear the swirling of trees. Like leaves brushing in an angry, violent storm that's threatening to close in.

"What's happening?" I manage to whisper incoherently.

"Brantley, we're in a room. Third door down. Get in here now!"

Darkness. An endless room filled with darkness. No light in sight. I reach forward but touch nothing. I move sideways and bang into nothing. I run forward and I'm met with nothing. There's absolute silence as I stand still, catching my breath from running.

Nothing. I've dissolved into nothing.

My hands come to my belly, and a soft cry leaves my lips. *No. I don't want to die. Please.* My legs give way and I collapse onto the ground, curling my knees up to my chest.

"Killing me only gave me a direct line into your head. Isn't that beautiful? Bishop, Brantley, and Nate—not getting everything they want for once. See—" I feel her now. Her presence. Even though I don't see her, I feel my heart pound against my chest and a slight breeze blow over my cheek. I think I hold my breath. *"The road will always lead back to them."*

"Get out of my head," I whisper, closing my eyes and deciding to keep them that way. "Get out of my head."

"Tsk, tsk," Veronica whispers, and I feel an ice cube slide over the nape of my neck. *"How sad, that they can kill me, but I can still exist in the deepest and darkest part of your brain."*

"You're not real—" I shake my head. "You are *not* real."

"But I am—where it matters, at least." She must move closer because her voice is almost close enough to taste. *"And better yet? I'm going to be here until the day you die. To twist you. Torment you. Play with you. I can't promise it'll be over quickly, you see, now I'm pissed."*

My stomach rolls. "No."

"Oh, yes." Veronica laughs, and food almost rises in my throat. *"Or maybe I'll never kill you. Maybe I'll leave you like this, stuck. Though, I really do need to destroy that baby in your gut."*

"No!" I scream so loud my throat bleeds.

She laughs, ignoring me. *"They thought they won the fight between us the second they killed me, but all they did was start it."*

"What did I ever do to you?" I whisper through the burning flames in my throat. "Why?"

"Simple, really. I'm going to strip Brantley of any and all happiness that he could ever have."

"You started his wrath, you stupid bitch. You did this to yourself! Don't you dare blame him!"

"Aw, how sweet that you're sticking up for your boyfriend. This was always the plan, Saint. Do you think a twelve-year-old girl wants to give birth, hmm? Do you think I wanted to be fucked and raped and prodded as soon as I hit puberty?"

I pause.

Footsteps echo from somewhere, but the room is still dark. *"I'll give you a hint, I didn't."* I suddenly feel the weight of her hands on my thighs. *"I'm never letting you out."*

CHAPTER THIRTY-FOUR

Brantley

I shove the door open, not knowing what I'm about to walk into. When I find Ophelia kneeling near the sofa and Saint spread over the top, her jacket undone and her face pale and gray, I know something's wrong. A brick drops in my gut as my knees buckle and I fall down beside Ophelia. Ivy moves around us, placing a cool cloth on Saint's forehead.

"What the fuck is happening?" I look to Ophelia for answers, but her mouth doesn't open. Her eyes are swollen closed from the tears that are clogged around the edges.

"She's stuck," a foreign voice says, and I follow it up to where Ivy stands over the sofa, patting Saint's hair. I have to fight the urge to whack her hand away and remind myself that she is her friend.

"What the fuck do you mean *stuck*?"

Ivy takes a deep breath. "When you killed Veronica, you didn't win."

I pale. "What the fuck?"

Ivy ignores my outburst. Doors open in the background and I know everyone else is here. "When you killed Veronica, you only gave her easier access to Saint."

"But Ophelia taught her how to keep Lucan out. She can do that again."

Ivy shakes her head, and I kind of want to cut it off. "Yes, against someone who isn't experienced in what we are. Veronica is a different being entirely. If she wants" —Ivy gives me a sad smile— "she could keep her there forever."

I push Ophelia out of the way and sit next to Saint on the sofa. Bishop comes in behind me. "She's strong. She can do it."

My head dips and I squeeze my eyes closed to stop the pain from turning into anger. My usual coping mechanism. "She fucking better or I'll kill her myself."

Ophelia shakes her head, swiping tears off her cheeks before her shoulders square and a flash of determination displays over her face. "Okay. First thing, when this happened, she felt death in her bones. That is what would have made her emotions vulnerable to Veronica's entity."

"I still don't believe this shit—just sayin'," Eli grunts from the other side of the room. We all ignore him.

"Which means the death that she felt was not her own."

"How do you know that?" Madison asks, leaning against the edge of the sofa.

"No, she's right." I lift my eyes to Bishop. "Because if there's one thing my father would always love, it's the torment and the chase. We know he and Veronica are working together, so they won't kill her straight away."

Ophelia stands, her shoulders back and her mouth turning into a straight line. Her eyes move across the floor as if she's trying to figure something out. A missing piece. "The feeling she had, it could be from the already dead. I mean, it's just death. It's not that there's going to *be* death necessarily; it could just be because we're at a wake. A wake equals death." She makes sense. I let her continue as both Tillie and Madison tense beside me.

Ophelia lets out a soft cry, falling down onto the sofa opposite us, her hands buried in her hair and her shoulders limp. They tremble as cries escape her. "I can't help her. All I know is what Veronica chose to teach me. It's like she planned this from the start, even her very own death."

"You think she knew I was going to kill her?" I ask, watching as Ophelia slowly lifts her head up and her eyes connect with mine.

"I'm saying she was probably counting on it." Her answer isn't what any of us want to hear.

"I don't buy it," Bishop growls, picking up Saint's head and sitting where she lies, her head now on his lap. "Vitiosises have a notorious will to live."

"Not this one—" My eyes connect with his. I know he catches my meaning. "—Not this one if she doesn't come back."

Bishop's jaw flexes, and amongst the chaos, I've not noticed how many people are in the room. Bishop, Nate, Tillie, Madison, Ophelia, Ivy, Eli, and Hector and Scarlet.

Hector's eyes narrow on Saint. "This is the cost of holding that curse. Every day for the rest of her life she's going to bear this, Brantley. When everyone else is closing their eyes to get sleep, she will be closing hers to meet people on the other side that she may not want to. It's why it's called a curse. You can't escape it or break it. Fucking gift, my ass." Minutes turn into hours. I go from drinking whiskey to water, to switching positions with Bishop as he helps escort people out of his house so no one suspects what's happening in here or why most of us have disappeared. Tillie is asleep on the floor, spooning Madison, and Ophelia and Ivy are asleep on the other side of the room. Hector is asleep, resting his head on the back of a single sofa with Scarlet curled on his lap, his tie pulled and jacket unbuttoned. I still don't know how I feel about him running for president. I think it's a shit idea, but it will work for TEKC. We've never had one in the White House before so it will be a game changer for us. Though we're looking at years and years from now when he would be going. He wants to build, run for governor, do all that fake shit before running for the presidency. I moan inwardly at my poor attempts of distraction.

Bishop is the only other one who is awake. He's back at the top of Saint's body with her head on his lap and I'm at the end, her legs draped over mine.

My eyes are locked on the flames from the fireplace. I only just figured out that we're in the library. It's interesting how if you have so much background going on, you can miss other important details. "You know what's going to make this that much more unlivable?" I ask, unable to move.

"What?" Bishop breathes out in a sleepy voice.

"The fact I never once told her that I love her." I hiss, curling my lips over my teeth. I need a fucking drink to calm my nerves, but for once, I don't want them calm. I want them wild enough to catch her when she wakes.

"She knows you love her, Brantley." Bishop shuffles farther down the sofa until Saint's head is on his stomach and his head is resting against the top. "In your own way, she knows."

"It doesn't matter, B. I never told her." I turn to look at him and his eyes flash glossy as they land on mine. "Bishop, this fucking girl makes me weak in *all* sense of the word. I don't know how to be when she's around, yet I somehow know that whatever I do, she will accept." I shake my head. "You know she told me that she loved me weeks ago, and I never said it back. Now what if I will never get that chance?"

Bishop keeps his eyes on mine. "You will get that chance, Brantley. She's a Hayes, a Vitiosis, and a fucking Stuprum." He turns back to the fire. "There's no way she's going down without a fight."

"Do you know how fucking useless I feel right now?" I squeeze my eyes closed. "I've always had control over her. What she did. Now, from my own fucking parents, I have nothing. Zero. She could die right now, and there's not a fucking thing I could do about it."

"Aye." Bishop taps my thigh with his. "Stop talking like that and sleep."

Angry flames, heat brushing against my cheek, and my ears ringing so loud they feel as though they're bleeding.

I throw myself up from the sofa, dropping Saint's legs in the process to cover my ears with the palms of my hand.

"Fuck!"

Saint is sitting upright, her face pale and her eyes dilated, wide and fixed on the wall in front of her.

Bishop has his hands up, his face clean from the sleep he was probably in and his mouth agape. I see shuffling from everyone at the corner of my eye, but I can't see anything past Saint.

Because she's awake.

CHAPTER THIRTY-FIVE

Saint

There's a pounding in my head that won't let up. *Thud. Thud. Thud.* My eyes are fixed on a single spine from a book on the shelf. It beams at me like headlights guiding a stray car on a stormy night.

Tears pour down my cheeks as my heart cracks in my chest. No matter how hard I try, I know I'll never stop the tears, so I let them run rampant. Run wild and free. My mouth slams closed and the silence that interferes is almost deafening, considering how loud my screams were.

"Hey!" Bishop pushes my hair back off my face and I turn to see him. Brantley must move closer, too, because his fingers wrap around my hand.

"Hi," I whisper, but my throat throbs and my eyes sting. "What happened?" My mind is blank. I try to think over the last thing I remember but come up short. It's not until I look down at what I'm wearing that I remember.

The wake.

The pool.

The castle.

The feeling of death.

People surround me, but I can't see them clearly yet, not until I crawl onto Brantley's lap. He stiffens before his heavy, long arms wrap around my body, pulling me into his chest. He spreads his legs out to cradle me comfortably. "What happened, Dea?"

I close my eyes. If it wasn't for the fact my t-shirt was drenched, I wouldn't have known I was still crying. "I—" It all comes back at once.

I whimper, moving into Brantley's chest. "It doesn't matter. It's over."

"No, it does matter."

"Saint," Hector says, leaning forward while resting his elbows on his knees. Scarlet is quiet beside him. "Please. It will be good to know you are not going to be haunted every time you close your eyes."

"I won't be," I say, swallowing past the emotion that's sticky in my throat.

"How so?" Bishop asks carefully, his thumb circling my arm.

I turn to face Tillie. My beautiful sister who is filled with so much strength and resilience that it bled down to her daughter. "Because my niece made sure of it."

There are gasps.

I roll off both of the men who hold me and fall down in front of Tillie, whose eyes are filled with a pain I have not seen before. Either she conceals it well or I've unleashed something I maybe shouldn't have.

I bring my hands to hers and watch as the first few tears fall down her cheeks. "She has your eyes now."

Tillie chokes on her tears, her hand coming to her mouth.

I continue, because everything I experienced, she and Nate need to know. To understand. To just *know*. "She has Nate's mouth and face shape, but she has your eyes. She has a strength I didn't know existed."

"Is she? Is she—" Tillie shakes her head, unable to get the words out. Madison's hand finds hers.

"She came to me as a young girl, not a baby. I'm not sure if that was intentional, but it's what she chose. She has blonde hair and eyes the color of teal. She didn't speak. She guided me through a pitch-black tunnel and to a spot of light—" I shake my head, unable to muster up the memory all at once. I stand from the floor and move toward the bookshelf. I curl my finger into the crack of the spine and pull it out, bringing it to my chest. I carry it back to Tillie, where Nate is now sitting behind her.

I slowly hand her the book. "I don't know what this means, but I think it's of significance to her."

Tillie bursts into tears and Nate crushes her face into his neck, holding her tightly.

"It was quick. I'm sorry. Veronica wasn't going to let me go. But Micaela—" I turn to Madison, "And Daemon, and—" I suck in a breath, knowing this next part is going to push them all over, "—Lucan."

"I'm never letting you go, Saint." Veronica's words were harsh as she finally clicked her fingers and light came spilling in. We were at the cemetery now, and it wasn't until she began twisting and turning, her eyes flying around the place that I realized she didn't mean to take us here.

"Watching you continue to be a spiteful bitch was entertaining, Veronica." Lucan. I paled, and everything deep inside my gut

told me to run. That fight-or-flight instinct kicking in. I didn't want to fight him. Not ever. He would win every time.

"No!" Veronica turned over her shoulder, and I finally looked up to see Lucan sauntering closer to where we sat. He leaned against the unmarked headstone, tapping his fingers on it. "Since I died, Saint, I've been trying to keep this bitch away from you."

"Shut up!" Veronica spat, glaring at him.

Lucan ignored her, moving forward. "I appeared as Brantley for one reason, and one reason only: to gain your trust. I thought if I came as him, you might trust the words I was going to tell you. Only that fell to shit because one, you knew it wasn't him, and two, well..." he shrugged, "...because of who I am. I'm no saint—" He snickers. "And I'm everything bad they say I am, but if there's one thing that I will always fight for, that's for my heritage. Brantley had every intention of stopping the King Vitiosis lineage, and I simply could not let that happen." He turned to Veronica. "You're so hell-bent on your hatred for me that you became desperate and obsessed with destroying our son."

"Our son," she seethed, "killed you and ordered the kill on me. Our son is nothing but evil."

"Maybe," Lucan answered. "But look at his parents. You thought I thought you were dead all this time, but I knew you weren't. I knew of your hatred for him and it ran too deep for that to happen."

"You took me when I was twelve years old!" she screamed, and I winced. For a moment, I saw her as a young child, hopeless and at Lucan's mercy. I felt sick with the image in my head.

His head tilted. "Veronica, you were homeless, being tossed around from man to man for The Vatican. I took you, yes, but I gave you everything you wanted. I didn't treat you the way that all the other men did. I didn't even fuck you the way they did."

Her face turned blank, as if being triggered by her past. In this moment, I felt for her. She was a woman in pain, who directed it at the wrong person.

I cleared my throat. "Veronica, you directed your hatred at the wrong person. It was never Brantley's fault for what you went through."

Lucan smiled at me, and I couldn't help but curl my lip in disgust.

"Helping me doesn't make what you did to all those people right, Lucan. What you did to your son. He still lives with those demons, he and Madison both."

"I'm not trying to right my wrongs, Saint. I'm just making sure you live to have that baby."

I don't realize that I'm holding my breath until I notice everyone watching me with eager eyes. "He helped them push her out. I'm not making excuses for him, and I'm not making excuses for her." I bring my eyes up to Brantley. His jaw is hard, his eyes cold. "They were both bad people. You are not, Brantley. You are not going to be like them. You were the product of their war. It's why you could never find peace." I sigh, closing my eyes to stop from watching pain flash over his. "Micaela and Daemon were there to get me through. They said I wouldn't have to worry about anyone again. Not from The Kings' world anyway, unless they get through the two of them. Something tells me, no one will be able to do that." I stifle a laugh, snuffing my runny nose.

"All of the chaos she enticed." Hector rolls his cigar between his fingers. I turn to face him and Scarlet. Two people I never had an interest in knowing, yet I've woken with the will to do it anyway. "Lucan was fighting to keep me alive so that I could" —I flick my hand up and down my stomach "—and Veronica wanted to kill me, but in a way that would destroy Brantley, so she became close to him, knowing he would never allow anyone near me if he didn't trust them completely. She was smart. Planned her destruction when he was a child, but she was angry.

I don't think it was from Lucan either, though getting someone pregnant at twelve is nauseating, but even before her life with Lucan, who apparently gave her everything, she had a rough life. She rolled all of her events into one task, and that was to destroy. She knew if she used the curse, she would have an excuse to take me when the time came. It was *all* a cover-up." I take in a deep breath. "As soon as Brantley and I finally started getting closer, Lucan knew Veronica would begin the first phase of her attack, so he started sending 'texts' to me. To entice Brantley to get jealous and push us together faster, I'm assuming. It didn't work because I never told Brantley about the texts, not until recently. Then when he started coming to me in my sleep, he came as Brantley in hopes that it would draw some unspoken trust out of me, but he didn't realize I would catch on that it wasn't him. He still enjoyed tormenting something that belonged to his son—" I wince, suddenly exhausted. "I think they were both severely unstable, but I think above all—" I look around to all of the people sitting in this room. All wide awake and listening. Tillie is still sobbing into Nate, as is Madison with Bishop. "I think they just really liked the game and being the instigator of it all. Both of them were working against each other, but they enjoyed it. I don't know what kind of mind games and riddles you all played in the past, but I get the feeling it's a generational thing that skipped me—until Lucan and Veronica."

Brantley rests his hand on mine. His thumb glides over the rock on my finger as his other is on my lip. "I don't think I've told you this—" The corner of his mouth turns up slightly. Not enough to call it a smirk. "But I love you."

My heart flatlines.

CHAPTER THIRTY-SIX

Saint

Burying both Cash and Bailey was emotional. We had one ceremony at a local church in Riverside before we drove to the EKC plot and buried Cash, before driving to the manor to bury Bailey. Being back there was hard, to put it lightly. It took me thirty-four minutes to exit the car, and even when I did, my knees buckled. The house is a danger zone right now while it's under construction, as well as a crime scene, but they managed to clear a path, leading to the cemetery in the back.

I told Brantley to knock the house down, as I never wanted to come back here again, but he refused. He said he wanted to rebuild the areas that were damaged and use it for the next generation as they see fit, since he sure as *fuck*—his words, not mine—does not want any teenagers around his house.

It made sense.

But it also terrified me because amongst the funeral chaos and only now just settling into the penthouse in Vitiosis Hotel, I had somehow managed to forget that I was *pregnant*. When the background noise becomes too loud, it drowns out important areas.

"What are you thinking about?" Brantley asks from the doorway of the master bedroom. I look between him and the dogs curled up on the bed, with Medusa's enclosure in the corner. I have everything I love in this room right now, only that's not true. I've come to love a lot of people since Brantley finally opened the doors into my life.

"I wasn't entirely honest with you all when I told you who helped me through the dark vortex that Veronica kept me in."

"Oh?" Brantley says, his brows raised. "You don't say…" He makes his way to the edge of the bed and falls on top, facing me.

"What, you knew?"

"Saint, you may be able to read everyone else because of your gift, but I can read you because of your soul."

I smile at him. "Okay, fair point."

"Carry on," he says, gesturing for me to continue.

"Bailey was there, too," I whisper through the pain in my throat. "I didn't want to say anything in front of everyone because this is more personal." I reach forward, squeezing his hands. I don't ignore the way his body turns rigid at the mention of her name.

Brantley nods, his eyes on mine. Dark and beautiful. The kind of peace that washes over someone right before a disturbance.

"She said we need to be there for Abel, Brantley. That he won't survive otherwise."

His eyes search mine. "What is that crazy girl asking for from her grave?"

My mouth opens then closes. I wipe my clammy hands

down the covers. "She wants him to work closely within The Kings. With you three."

"No." Brantley shakes his head, looking away from me. I bring my hand up to his cheek and force his eyes on mine. "Brantley, he needs you all. He needs to feel like he belongs somewhere. He needs a close family. Please. He's—he's my brother. Please."

His jaw tightens and I see the exact moment I win. His shoulders sag in defeat. "I'll run it past Bishop and Nate, but no promises."

"Thank you." I sink my knees into the mattress on either side of him, sucking his bottom lip into my mouth. "It's been too long since I've tasted your blood in my mouth." I roll my hips over his erection. "Rectify that, please."

His mouth curves beneath mine.

I wake up the next morning, stretching my arms over my head while twisting over to see the time. 9:09 a.m. My eyes pop open. I slept in. A lot. I swing my legs over the bed so fast that both Kore and Hades jump slightly.

Brantley walks out of the bathroom, his hair messy in that way I love and his eyes barely open from sleep. His chest is bare, exposing all of my bite marks on his chest.

I pause, and then take the steps needed to reach him. I run the tip of my finger over one mark on his neck, smiling. "I want a tattoo here."

"Really?" His arm is hooked around my waist, and he turns his head, studying my body. His eyes zero in on something in the same area where my finger is on his neck, right on the other side of my Vitiosis tattoo and below my ear. "Then you're getting a matching one."

"Deal." I hook my arms behind his neck. "Can you come back to bed?"

He kisses me gently, the swell of my lips still fresh from the night before. "I need to run something past you."

I lower myself back to the soles of my feet. "Okay…"

He gestures to the bed and I slide on top of it, curling my legs beneath my butt. "The Daughters of the Night, we can't cut the coven off, so I was thinking about granting Ivy and Ophelia the deed to the mansion."

I pause. "You would do that?" Truth be told, I thought a lot about that coven and what would happen to it now. I wanted someone different to take over, but I knew that was a long shot, since I didn't actually know anyone who would. Brantley had told me that the likelihood of Frankie being dead was high, but that Alessi was back with her family. Even when so much was going on, Brantley still made sure to check on them because he knew I would want to know.

He glares at me. "You wound me. Truly. Of course I fucking would. For you, I would do just about anything, which is exactly why I never wanted this" —he gestures between our bodies— "to start in the first place, by the way."

I ignore his whining. "Yes. I think that's a beautiful idea, and Ophelia and Ivy would truly take care of the people."

"You forgot you can visit them anytime you want because they'll be in Riverside."

"But will we be in Riverside?" I ask. Since VH is in New York, I wasn't sure what the plan was from here.

He reaches forward and catches my bottom lip with his finger and thumb. "Do you want a house there? We can build one."

Images flash through my head. Black modernism architecture, a personalized garden that lives throughout the house and leads to an indoor greenhouse. Our house would be everything I'd ever wanted.

"Yes," I say, pressing my lips to his. "Yes, I want a house there."

The fact is, I don't know what happens when you die. Not even for someone who has come painfully close too many times to count. I think death can come in all forms. It can come in a person, like Brantley, or it can come in losing someone you love. Death is the experience you feel when you lose someone you love; pain is just the aftershock.

I never did think too much about the day I would die, and there was a reason for that. Because I didn't have to think it, I would experience it. But over tiresome months of being with Brantley and going through our troubles and the hurdles we needed to jump, I've learned that it doesn't matter. Because not even death could separate us.

It had tried.

Many times.

The only thing stronger than the pursuit of death is being loved by it.

One Year Later
SAINT

"This house has to be on the same level as Hayes Castle. I swear." Tillie moves fluidly around the executive-style dining table in the kitchen. She tilts her head up to the glass ceiling. "I get why you did that. So no matter where you were in the house, you always had a clear view of the sky, good for plants and all that jazz, but you and Madison are some serious money splashers." Brantley hated the idea of the ceiling because it gave too much light, but I fought for it because of my plants.

I point at her with my wine glass. "You cannot judge!" The living and kitchen area are clean black slate with stone marble countertops and plush leather seating, but as soon as you find yourself going deeper and deeper into the house, you'll see secret doors that lead to other rooms. Plants line every crack, skirting, and line that they can, in a way that is also aesthetically appealing. Since it took so long to build and we had the baby while in New York, it had made the whole process complicated. Brantley ended up dropping more cash down to recruit two construction companies to get it done faster.

"I'm sorry I'm late!" Madison says, rushing into the kitchen while placing a tray of cupcakes on the counter. "Halen didn't want to wear what I chose for her, and then Priest went wandering and I couldn't find him!" She sighs, rubbing her eyes with the back of her hand. "Why did they have to be early walkers?"

"It has started," I say, pouring a full glass of Pinot and sliding it over to her. "I'm glad Vaden isn't at that level yet, but I'm sure he's not far behind." Just as the words leave my mouth, Brantley comes in with Vaden on his hip. I can't fight the smile that spreads over my mouth. I don't even try to hide it either. Vaden Bai Vitiosis, my one and only chance at having a child. The birth was bad. I was in the hospital for the final two months of my pregnancy because I couldn't hold anything down. Doctors told me that it would be in my best interest not to conceive again. When I brushed them off, they pulled Brantley out of the room and told him that the hemorrhaging during birth made me a high risk, and that every pregnancy after Vaden would be like playing Russian roulette with my life.

That was all Brantley needed to get a vasectomy, much to my sadness.

"The grill is hot. Pretty sure Nate is going to hurt himself on it. I'm sure you don't want his pretty face to get ruined." He smirks at Tillie.

"Aw, Bran Bran." Tillie pats his shoulder and moves around him. "When are you going to see that your face is just as pretty."

She moves out of the kitchen and Brantley turns over his shoulder, snarling at her. "Fuck off, it is."

I step forward and take Vaden in my arms, kissing his head. He has black hair like his dad and the same contrast of skin as the both of us, but his eyes. It's his eyes that are extraterrestrial. One dark brown eye and one ice blue. Two halves of both our souls.

"Motherhood is going to rob us," Madison mumbles around her cupcake. "We're going to be like *The Real Housewives of Riverside—Mafia Edition*." I keep placing small kisses on top of Vaden's head. "Do you see how terrifying that is?"

I burst out laughing and gesture to the sliding doors that lead out to the full wraparound patio. The scenery is one straight out of *Architectural Digest*. Surrounded by forestry and peace, I knew instantly I wanted to build here. Of course Brantley had to buy the whole ass mountain and name it Mount Dea, because the thought of so much as having *any*one else living near us terrified him. Vampires… huh?

The infinity pool spills over the edge in smooth black movements. We had to import the specific black mosaic tiles from France, because nowhere else had them as dark as Brantley wanted. I've got to admit, the pool is scary. I strap Vaden into his chair, right beside Halen and Priest and next to War. I pause, and all of the laughter and talking that was happening before I came out stops. It's as though everyone is seeing what I'm seeing.

"Look at them," Nate says proudly from behind me. "We all made those. I can almost hear P.O.D.'s 'Youth of the Nation' blaring through my ears."

War with his full head of blond hair and green eyes, Vaden with his unique yet perfect face, and Halen and Priest, both with dark brown hair, but where Priest's eyes are blue, Halen's are green.

"Nope," Madison says, sipping on her wine while pulling up a chair beside me. "That terrifies me. Are we not all terrified?"

Bishop's arm is around Madison's waist, pulling her down on top of him. "Nah."

"How?" Madison says, turning to face him.

"Because Daddy is a psycho and Mommy owns guns."

I think over the next generation as we all eat. We do this every Sunday at a different house. I think it centers us. There's not to be any business talk at the table, and even if one or two of us are fighting with each other, the rule is absolute. We still come together on a Sunday as a family. Abel sits beside me, a smile on his face as he goes back and forth with Bishop on why it's a good idea to build a racetrack in Riverside. Abel smiles with his mouth, but not his eyes. I think that's the cost of losing someone you love. They say the eyes are the window to the soul, after all.

Brantley's hand is on my knee, squeezing. "You okay?"

"Yeah." I smile up at him, reaching for my phone and sending Ophelia and Ivy a quick text then place it back on the table. "I'm so much more than okay."

EPILOGUE

Brantley

I had thought about whether I wanted to do this a lot over the past year, but I knew eventually it needed to be done. I was a father, a husband, an uncle, a brother, a fucking killer. But I didn't need to carry their shit anymore. I was sure that whatever bullshit the Vitiosis name carried, I knew it would fall down to Vaden as well. It was inevitable. But I wanted to be better for him. For her, too.

I run my finger over his name. "I didn't do this for you because I still hate you. I hate what you did to me as a kid. Now that I have Vaden, I can't fucking imagine *ever* allowing such vile shit to happen to him. In fact, it makes me fucking murderous to think it." I lean down, eyes narrowed on his brand new headstone. "I did this for Vaden and the next generation that will be coming. I know what you're thinking. You think I put your name here so they'll know where to piss, but that's not it either. I did it because you saved her. It's really as simple and as tragic as that." I stand, pushing my hands into my suit pockets. "So thank you for trying to help her, even if it was for your gain. We're even now." I step away from his stone and begin walking away when I stop. Turning, I look over my shoulder and find Bailey's. My heart cracks in my chest as I make my way to hers.

I clench my jaw and fight the emotion that's stuck in my throat. Emotion I never knew I could feel until I felt it for Saint. Loving her will kill me one day.

"I'm sorry, Bais. I'm sorry I took your time on this earth for granted and didn't spend enough of it with you." I chuckle, shaking my head and looking to the ground. "You'll be happy to know that Abel cracked into our circle. He's better now, off the drugs, though we know he misses you daily. Every second. We see it in his eyes when he thinks no one is watching." I press a gentle kiss to my fingers and press them against her headstone. "See you in Valhalla."

PREVIEW OF RUINED CASTLES
(The Elite Kings Club: Finale)

PROLOGUE

Madison

Nothing is going to make sense once you flip open this first chapter. You're going to wonder why the fuck I made the decisions I did. Why he did what he did. I'm not going to make this easy for you. I'm going to guide you through loops that you're going to wish I had just skipped, but I'm not going to do that either. You're going to feel my pain, my loss, and my heart breaking in my chest. You're going to watch me trip and fall, and get back up again. You're going to wish you could slap the shit out of Bishop and me, but amongst all…I'm going to take you back to when I left the love of my life and ran.

This is an open letter to you.

Good luck.

Mads

Xo

ACKNOWLEDGEMENTS

Thank you to the good people in my life. Friends, family, friends that turned into family. To my team of editors, I applaud you. To my readers, I can't thank you enough for being a part of my journey. I hope you're enjoying the ride. To the bloggers who read and review, thank you for taking time out of your busy lives to do so. I appreciate all of you. To my PR team for making sure everything runs smoothly, thank you. To my wolves… you all show true compassion and strength. Thank you for being there for not only me, but your fellow pack members, too. My blogger and bookstagram teams, thank you for going above and beyond. To all the other authors who I chat with occasionally and have built some sort of foundation of a friendship with, thank you for reminding me that *shiiiet*. This shit is hard sometimes.

Grateful for you all.
—A xox

OTHER BOOKS BY AMO JONES

Sicko

Midnight Mayhem
In Peace Lies Havoc
In Fury Lies Mischief

The Elite King's Club
The Silver Swan
The Broken Puppet
Tacet a Mortuis
Malum: Part 1
Malum: Part 2
Sancte Dioboli: Part 1

Razing Grace: Part 1
Razing Grace: Part 2

Perilous Love (Sinful Souls MC, #1)
Intricate Love (Sinful Souls MC, Volume 2)
Tainted Love (Sinful Souls MC, Volume 3)

Crowned by Hate (Crowned, #1)

One Hundred & Thirty-Six Scars (The Devil's Own, #1)
Hellraiser (The Devil's Own, #2)
The Devil's Match (The Devil's Own, #5)

*F*ucker*

Losing Traction (Westbeach, #1)

Flip Trick

Manik

Printed in Great Britain
by Amazon